THE THREE MARKS OF EXISTENCE
(Mujo, Ku, Muga)

CASSANDRA PASSARELLI

Sea Crow Press

THE THREE MARKS OF EXISTENCE

Contents

Foreword   vii

Part One
Impermanence

Family Trees   3
The Toad and the Diputado   11
Writing the Vessels   17
Bone Metre   27
Tinderbox   33
Whitechapel Boys   39
Sky-goer   47
Narrow Neck of the Land   55
Dorf and the Daisies   67

Part Two
Suffering

How to Preserve a Butterfly   81
Erosion   89
Whorls   93
Gait of a Barrow Boy   101
His Father's Land   107
Absent Women   117
Shortcut to Heaven   125
The Upturned Bowl   129
Empty Pockets   135
Cane Stalks   141

Part Three
No-self

Mu!   147
Footprints   153
Us and Them   159

Conversion   167
Fifty-one Rolls   175
The Great Hush   183
Chalco Millonarios   191
El Jebha   199
Mercedes and the Pigeon Man   205

A Note on Sources   211
Acknowledgments   213
About the Author   215
About the Artist   217
About the Press   219

FOREWORD

Here's the thing about impermanence, or *mujo*, one of the three marks of existence. We all know, instinctively, that everything changes. Nothing lasts, not even our own lives. Everything around us is temporary – except perhaps stories.

A tricksy get-out clause? Maybe. The truth, as the tales in this book remind us, isn't always easy to face. Nonetheless, it seems to me that stories are something different. They perform the same act as a child clutching a butterfly net to catch a moment of beauty, a memory, a sudden realisation, before it flits away. Stories like these are glimpses into other lives, windows into moments in time, snapshots of people in the process of changing, as everything does. Reading and travelling have that in common: both are ways of experiencing worlds beyond our own.

Of course, stories are not only windows, they are vessels too. The stories you are about to read span the globe, with journeys across continents and time zones, between cultures and backgrounds, through generations and memories. All human life is here: lost souls, thinkers, drifters, kleptomaniacs, gringos and emigrants, dreamers, stoners, loners, erratic uncles, and plenty more besides. Many of them are busy chasing something elusive and impermanent: endangered languages, half-forgotten histories, and evasive happy endings. Perhaps this is another, more ironic truth: that despite the fact that everything changes, some things in human nature never do. The permanent fight against impermanence is branded into our DNA, written in our nature.

The world we live in may be impermanent, but what a startling and captivating world it is. Passarelli takes us through forests and abandoned rural towns, through cities caught between past and present, into kitchens and bedrooms that store memories like treasures. These various settings are vivid and rich in detail, showing us some of the ties that keep us bound to the world despite its impermanence, those bonds and connections that both sustain us and hold us back – often at the very same time.

Uncle Charles, a character who inspires the narrator's fascination with the Pigeon Man in the final story, is shown fastidiously collecting local information to keep something of the past alive despite the rapid pace of change. Devoted to his research, 'He burrowed till he struck cores of common truth.' The same is true for Passarelli's stories, which weave their way through the intimate details of diverse individual lives towards the essence of what it means to be human. If stories are a means of exploration, an act of investigation, reading them is a journey of discovery. Nothing lasts, but the sparks of deep truth uncovered in this book will linger long in your mind after turning the final page.

Sam Meekings is a British poet and novelist. He is the author of *Under Fishbone Clouds*, *The Book of Crows*, and *The Afterlives of Doctor Gachet*. He currently works as an Associate Professor of Creative Writing at Northwestern University in Qatar, where he researches the intersections of narrative and trauma.

The Three Marks of Existence

All existence is characterised by impermanence, suffering, and no-self.

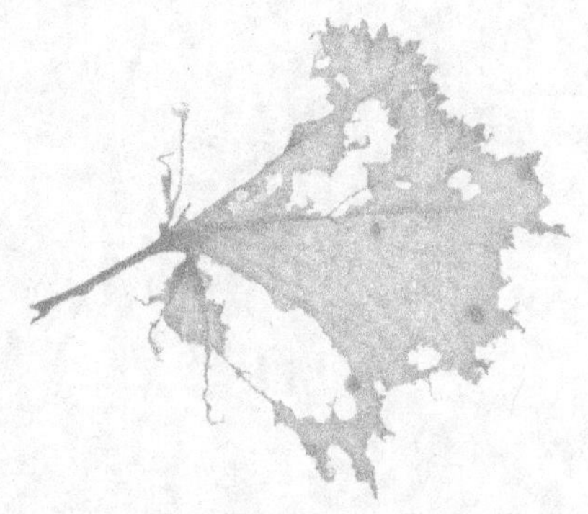

PART ONE
IMPERMANENCE
MUJO

All things arise, change and pass away.
Accepting impermanence means seeing reality.

FAMILY TREES

'Here are the roots of trees, here are the empty places.'
– *Saṃyutta Nikāya*

One of my earliest memories is of Uncle Luke pulling up outside JFK in his pick-up. My parents in the cab up front. Me crouching in the wagon; hair wind-whisked, soul soaring beyond the cedars, chestnuts, and elms. Raised in a Georgian house, with an oblong of cement for a back yard, I revered the one plane tree that grew there. In summer, its foliage filtered the sunlight into my bedroom window and I fell asleep to the sound of the wind raking through its leaves. In winter, its branches formed a lattice between me and the Pimlico mews to which grey skies clung. As I floundered through adolescence, I observed it reaching the middle pane and overshoot the lintel. We buried my dog between its roots.

'These trees are less than a century old; the pilgrims chopped their antecedents down as they moved west,' Uncle Luke told me.

This was my parents' homeland. They left not as refugees, nor economic migrants, but as deserters of fifties' consumption, saccharin family ideals, and intellectual insularity. But in vacation morsels, it wasn't so bad. Much of its flavour was attributable to my uncle, a handsome leviathan with his outcrop of Peloponnese curls, olive skin, garlic-bulb nose, and ample beard. Lifted in one of his bear hugs, he enveloped me in resinous scent. In suede work boots, chinos, white t-shirt, and checked wool shirt, he strode like Hercules, axe in hand, chopping down the firs he sold in New York City's Christmas streets. Humour and kindliness ran through his speech, characterised by its distinctive New Hampshire drawl.

Train 54, the Vermonter, leaves New York on an overcast midday. The skyscrapers are a receding clump, fading from sight. Beyond the glass, baseball-courts cut yellow discs of sand into clean-cut lawns. The train glides over a bridge, passing stray swans and a barge's skeleton, and chugs into the forest. My daughter and I gaze through the leaf patchwork that fills the window panes.

At New Haven there's an announcement that we're about to change to diesel and the cafeteria will close. The stewardess serves me a coffee, warning those queuing behind me that the electricity will cut out; she slams the till shut decisively. A bell clangs as the cab approaches, followed by the rising sound of the locomotive reversing and the hiss of latching on.

A little later: 'Ladies and gentlemen, we're coming into Claremont, New Hampshire. The doors open on just one side.'

Uncle Luke is waiting for us, exactly at the spot we get down, in his ex-wife's silver Ford. He opens his arms like boughs to give us Sampson hugs.

We pull into the crescent drive to his brick house, a ramshackle A-frame colonial, with a sloping porch, wood-fire, gables, dark parlour, and creaking stairs up to several bedrooms. And behind it, his cherished woods. The wives and the biological, foster, and step-kids came. And went. The trees remain.

The next morning I rise from profound sleep. From the front gable I watch cars race past the clapboard house. When Uncle Luke moved here in the fifties they chugged along, then accelerated over the decades as Uncle Luke wound down. Their swish shrouds the house the way cobwebs swathe an antique. Uncle Luke is already up. He makes his ritual thermos of diluted, sweet coffee, toasts home-made bread and slathers it with peanut butter and jelly. The kitchen, designed for the last wife and four foster children, is super-sized. Two double sinks with waste disposals, a hefty electric oven matched by a gas twin, two L-shaped counters piled up with string, green Velcro ties, empty plastic bags, and rigid clamshell boxes. The godforsaken fridge has declined into riotous wilderness; a fallen potato has sprouted anaemic leaves that cling to the middle shelf. Uncle Luke baits mice-traps with smears of peanut butter then puts the victims outside on the steps for the ants to devour. He calls this arrangement the Tower of Silence.

Two sofas, both with a rocking-chair feature, frame the wood stove. A yellow chainsaw sits on the floor. A door leads to the old house's vacated rooms and its oak floors, open brick fireplaces, mercury light switches, and peeling paint. Once generous for its half dozen occupants, his home is swallowed up by its own emptiness. From the porch I overlook the mowed front lawn, as neat as a pin; just five tomato plants grow there and several sapling walnuts planted by squirrels. Crickets chirrup, the occasional groundhog chomps timidly. Beyond, the forest of spruce, aspen, hornbeam, maple, oak, pine, walnut, and cherry trees sweeps the sky from a spongy bed of needles. A brook froths into the culvert that runs beneath Unity Road.

Once we appear, Uncle Luke switches off public radio and holds forth in his maple-syrup cadence. My daughter is transfixed by his tales that bubble from a wellspring of nine decades, many spent in solitude. He walks us around the house, each tree prompting an anecdote: one was struck in a storm, another recovered from a disease, a third has grown sixty feet in half as many years. He bakes bread every morning. Walks to the library in town twice a week. His days are like backwoods trees, a blur of forest, or infinitude of discrete trunks, depending on how carefully you look.

He agrees to call on Martie, his first wife, as if it never crossed his mind. My mother had Martie down as a bad egg ever since an impromptu pregnancy forced Luke to drop philosophy at Harvard. The visit begins innocuously enough with us rattling the door. A red Lab (Loomis, after a fly rod) barks the house down. Just when we're sure no one's home, Martie appears at the screen door. A small, rugged woman, her Irish ease saw her through two divorces, four children, and small-town life. She puts the kettle on the burner and offers us tea, chewing her words like the granite girl she is. They chat with choreographed composure. Afterwards, each tells me they haven't spoken to the other in years. She telephones Luke Junior even though he's just upstairs 'coz she can't be shoutin all over the place'. He comes down and gives me a mighty hug. The same age as me, he has his father's build and his mother's fair looks.

Martie invites us to stay for a dinner of traditional Irish stew and a tablet of stringy brisket. Uncle Luke throws me a glance and I nod. Sitting back from the table, legs too long, he relates a story or two in considerable detail, with Martie chomping at the bit to throw in her dime's worth. Giving up, she disappears into a back room and rummages, returning with some black and white photos of Cousin Lukie and me circa 1968. The two of us in a steel-rimmed, hooded pram; me in a bonnet, he a bobble hat. Another of me, sitting on my uncle's living-room floor, pumpkin face grinning fit to bust. Another shot from the seventies frames the three cousins on a Cycladic ferry. Me, flat-chested in a rainbow bikini, my puppy, Spike, in my lap. Lukie bare-chested in jeans and a leather belt. His older sister, Becca, pouting.

It surprises the three of them how simple conversation is when a visitor is there.

'Loomis got caught in one of them traps, didn't he?' Lukie says. 'I rang Fish n Game and had an agument with the guy. He passed me onto his soopavisa, and we had another frickin agument. He darn hung up on me. So, I took things into my own hands, took a walk along the banks, found half a dozen and threw them into the river.'

My cousin drives us home. On his father's front porch, he asks, 'Watchyoodoing?'

'Hanging out.'

'Wanna go for a drive?'

'When?'

'Now.'

He shoos Loomis off the front seat and we head for the wild. Lukie works for New Hampshire; in winter, he builds snow paths with diggers and in summer he repairs covered wooden bridges. He knows the state like his own Ford. We cruise along the highway, slip onto smaller roads and deeper into tracks until we're off-road, in wooded depths. Lukie's breakneck idiom burbles as the clapboard farmhouses thin and disappear. From his burnt freckled brow down to his L.L.Bean sandals, he's solid hick. I drink in towering trees, the shadows, mud so fresh I can smell it, down to the biting skeeters and deer-flies. He points out loons, wild turkeys, and the ducks he'll be shooting in a couple of weeks. He references bald eagles and peregrines like Londoners talk about lattes and apps. Here, he saw a bobcat. There, he found a stag's shed horns. Yonder, deer are hunted.

He pulls into a clearing, by a huge log pile.

'Still smoke?'

'Did I ever?'

'You sho did last time you were here!' He jogs a slip of memory.

As he fills a colourful glass pipe he tells me, 'Sour Cream's an indigenous crossbreed between Chem and Mass Superskunk. Five seeds cost me two hundred and fifty bucks.'

'You kidding?'

'No, I frickin ain't.'

Refusing it'd be like turning down Martie's Irish stew, so I take a few tokes.

'Wanna drive?'

'Nah.'

'C'mon, what's the worse you can do, hit a few trees?' Suddenly we're kids again and he's daring me to dive from the highest rock.

He starts a rambling stoner's tale about parachuting, going up 10,000 feet in a helicopter with an instructor. Jumping out in tandem, the fear and wonder of it, dropping, dropping, seeing mountains and rivers just like a bird, till they deployed a ram-air parachute and sank down to the earth. I sense my own rush, a calming sweep of air, lifting and disconcerting. His dope-loosened tongue non-sequiturs to a family fall-out.

'My sista shows up two frickin hours late at the library, like she always does. I lose it, shouting six-mile and stormin out. Never seen either since. Till tonight when my father sits down at the same table as Martie. Mom's unstable, you know it. Had a box with my pipe, credit cards and four thousand bucks insurance money to buy a new bike. One mornin, bucks were gone.

'She ain't that friendly face she puts on. Been a restrainin order on her before. Can't help herself, frickin klepto. I got a padlock; no other way to keep her out. My sister Sandy ain't right neither. Can't keep a job down. Had one at Sturm Ruger but pulled sick leave. After two months Martie told her: Either you get out of bed or I'm buryin you in the back yad myself.

'As for the old man, forever lecturin us as kids about saving. Where'd all his bones go? Into that bitch's pocket, I warrant. Don't blame her for leavin; he weren't no piece of cake to live with. It was lonely up there, I remember. Sometimes no food in the house and he'd be doin headstands and all that shit. He's a thinker. Bout all he does is think.'

Lukie pulls into a gas station, picks up an eight-pack of Harpoon and a bottle of water for me. He drives us to the other side of town. I follow him through the open front door of a tumble-down house to a campfire out back. A silver German shepherd does disconcerting killer-dog circles around me. Randy, a goofy, blond guy, tells me about mint he's growing that tastes of chocolate. Jo, short and plump, delivers a story about the Hell's Angel, ohmygod, that zoomed straight into her headlights that morning. Jo says she hates Starbucks because they don't support the US military.

When they run out of things to say, Randy suggests going upstairs. My eyes adjust slowly to their bedroom's white lights. Behind black plastic sheeting are some DIY Formica shelves with marijuana plants in pots. On the carpet are jars filled with furry dried buds. Randy throws Lukie a Harpoon from the mini-fridge. They talk state taxes, drug legislation, guns, and their 'nigger' president. Jo describes a barbeque ohmygod, and clams with sweet sauce. Randy had a plate of chicken, spare ribs, pork chops, and sausages with hand-cut, hand-cut ohmygod, French fries.

Apropos of nothing, Randy pulls a gun from under the bed, with a cylinder the size of a salad bowl, and asks me if I know what it is.

'A gun,' I say, stupidly.

'Sixty rounds.' He squints his red-rimmed, bug-eyes. He hands me a heavy, copper-tipped silver bullet, which I roll in my palm.

'See them ridges? They break up inside someone's body and cause maximum damage, lodging bits in their ribcage. Take it,' he offers.

I shake my head.

'Go on,' in that dare tone of Lukie's, only harder. There's a silence in the room; I can feel Jo and Lukie willing me. I take the moulded metal hunk, a thing out of a sci-fi movie, turn it around and hand it back.

In the lull that follows, Jo asks softly, 'Do you have kids?'

'Yes.'

'So do I. Two boys. My eldest is in the US navy in Eye-rack.' She finds a photo on her phone, a soldier with a broad expressionless face, and her eyes water up.

'See that pin on his chest? That was ohmygod hammered into him to draw blood,' she says, beaming.

'What about your other son?' I ask, hopeful.

'Skateboard crazy,' Randy says.

The third time I mention I'm jet-lagged, Lukie gets the hint. I thank Randy and Jo for their hospitality. Outside, Lukie hangs a U-ey. Lit by Lukie's headlights, we watch as a mouse runs from one cat into the jaws of another. Prompted, Lukie recalls the barn cats that got run over on Unity Road.

'Dad can't look after anything,' he says as he pulls into his drive, 'not even a lousy cat. Thinks I'm a libertarian. At least I work; eighteen years for the state. Never a day's vacation, not a day sick. From seven dollars an hour I've upped it to fourteen.'

When I get in, Uncle Luke is waiting up. He asks how the evening went. I tell him fine. It was the wrong thing to say.

'Why is he still living with his mother?' he asks. 'Why doesn't he use his faculties of reason? Lukie has all these notions based on thin air. When we talk he gets all wound up and we get into deep water. He thinks poor folk on welfare are just milking the government. Doesn't he realise the only thing between him and welfare is the union, which he doesn't support?'

'Uncle Luke, why did you study Sanskrit?' I ask, to steer him onto another topic.

'I started with philosophy then I got interested in Eastern thought. Lived in Pune for three years, working in a translation house.' I picture a younger Uncle Luke in a white *dhoti*, fan whirring, *ashok* rustling at the open window, hunched over his typewriter translating Hindu texts. Outside, against a *margosa*, leans the dusty bicycle that took him halfway across the continent.

A few hours later we stop talking about the past. But the future is meagre to a man of his years.

'When I'm ready to burn my bridge, I don't want to go to hospital.' He looks out of the kitchen window to the yard outside. 'See that cherry tree and that maple there? They'd make a beautiful little house. My kids aren't interested in this place. I'd like to find a struggling family with young kids who want to take it on. They could make maple sugar or turn the place into a bed and breakfast. And when they're ready to move, they could pass it on.' He hesitates, then adds, 'You could live here. Think it over. Lakes, rivers, forests. In Hanover, Cambridge, or Boston there are concerts, plays, and good bookshops. Interesting people from different places... with ideas.'

I love him so much the suggestion sounds plausible. But the fustiness of weed on my clothes, the Ruger's cold metal funk, and the sinister image of Jo's deadpan son in navy crackerjacks and white Dixie cup are too fresh.

Uncle Luke changes into his boots. I follow him onto the porch. He takes me around the back. Shows me blackberry bushes and the walnut trees he planted thirty years ago. Walking into the woods, he points to an ash that pinned him to the ground last year. Flourishing oak saplings. Further up, a larch that survived lightning. A sycamore that keeled over and died. The towering overgrown firs, remnants of his years selling Christmas trees, span upward like spires.

THE TOAD AND THE DIPUTADO

The *diputado* shows up with a bottle of Don Julio's Mexican tequila (a hundred per cent agave), English Worcester sauce, and a six-pack of tomato juice. This morning my guys shifted armchairs, bed, and the crucifix; filled an entire corner of the Beneficio with furniture. They'll finish before the *gringos* move in. So we lie on our backs on the grassy riverbank, under the shade of the avocado tree, drinking from plastic cups.

The *diputado* talks. My mind wanders. Selling the weekend house will solve my little problem. But I'm getting sentimental, recalling light-filled mornings like this, staring through chains of blue eucalyptus, stars of jade *chiflera* and *liquidámbar* at blue heavens. Two-litre bottles of Pepsi, flasks of rum, and icy bottles of Gallo. Dripping kids combing the river for crabs. And heavy afternoons, Ranchera or Norteño booming on the speakers. On torrential evenings, Damaska in the dark, dusty salon, light filtering through cobalt panes, armchairs throwing dark shadows on grey walls. Her uniform crumpled on the cement floor. My palms filled with her firm flesh and my nostrils with her sour scent. Her frizzed yellow hair loose, lime eyes laughing, long honeyed limbs twisting beneath mine. Complaining the huge black crucifix over the fireplace gives her the creeps. Raised in a shack, on beans and *tortillas*, she's my earth angel. A grandchild of the German *finca*-owner who fathered the litter of blond, freckled, green-eyed bastards whose half-bloods inhabit Chi'o today. Her mother lives with the last of her young in a tumble-down hut, her father with his own brood in the hut beyond.

After too many sleepless nights, I convinced Liset we should sell the house. I had one of my boys peg up a wooden sign on a pine next to it: 'FOR SALE, 15 *cuerdas*, ring 7834 3892'. That afternoon a *gringo* called to see it. We met fifteen minutes later. I walked him and his dreamy wife around, named a price. We shook hands under the *níspero*.

A few tequilas later, the sun drops behind the tile roof into a rose-petal sky. The *diputado* is still talking:

'... things between Edelmira and me are tricky. In the dream I'm in a dark cell, surrounded by men with desperate eyes and *machetes*, my throat's dry. It's a warning to get out of politics, business. I could turn that mountain I own into an eco-park: throw up a few bungalows, sell some, rent the rest. I came to see if you want in.'

Life starts to wear thin after fifty; the more you darn, the quicker it frays. I hear what he's saying. And what he really means. The *diputado* is no eco-park type. He's in some mess, probably political.

'Mynor, it's not the right time for me,' I say. 'I'm selling the Chi'o house. I imagined my grand-kids playing here and their grand-kids. But with the price of cardamom so low it's hardly worth picking and...'

'How about we take a drive up there, check it out? Let me paint the picture for you.'

I'm a diplomat, so I fumble the gate shut and climb into the *diputado*'s four-by-four. He starts down the road, bouncing into potholes, over rocks and ridges. We pass Damaska's shack. Her little brothers, throwing balls of mud at each other, fall silent and stare. Bedraggled mongrels bark and bare their teeth. Damaska's eldest brother Bernardo comes out to quiet them. When he sees me he comes to the road, smiling. The *diputado* slows, I lower my window. Bernardo leans in to shake my hand:

'*¿Como está, joven?*' I ask.

'*Bien, bien, gracias, Don Francisco.*'

Bernardo's gaze pulls away from mine toward the sound of

advancing motors. A shadow falls across his face. I glance into the side mirror. Two gleaming black *picops* pull up, either side of us. Their doors open simultaneously. Bernardo steps away and retreats up the path, whistling to the dogs. The children turn tail and follow wordlessly. Their hut swallows them. I glance at Mynor's whey face. Eight heavy-set men swing themselves out onto the road. Shotguns dangle off their shoulders, pistols hug their hips. They push a wave of fear before them like an earthmover. We freeze, *tepescuintles* caught in a hunter's torch.

My mind throws a silent tantrum: this is nothing to do with me. I'm a family man, cardamom grower, mayoral candidate of the left-wing UNE party. I've never done a shady thing in my life. Never been involved with *maras*, *narcos*, or dirty politics. But as the men walk slowly toward our four-by-four the time for excuses is past. I wonder if they'll shoot Bernardo to tie his tongue, but he bothers them less than the fat drops of rain that have started falling, *splotch, splotch,* on their shades. My door opens and one of them puts his hand on my shoulder. I take in his gleaming brogues and his features locked in indifference. He's done this before. I'm no more to him than his shoe-shine boy.

He pulls me from the car like a rag doll. The dull pain in my groin rises to my head and my face is in the mud. I can still trounce my grandsons, but I don't struggle as they bundle me into their vehicle. Nor as they blindfold, gag, and tie my hands. I hear five doors slam and three motors start up.

After an hour, perhaps two, I try to speak. When they get fed up with my grunts they pull off the gag. I'm a smooth talker, that's how I got into politics.

'*Chavos,* I don't know who you are, who your boss is. But this is a mistake. Perhaps you're after my friend, the *diputado*. He just happened to stop at my place to share tequila. If you just let me down here I'll thank the Lord you saw the light, go home quietly, and leave it at that.'

They let me talk for a spate. When they get bored they gag me. The driver flicks on an evangelical station. One lights a cigarette.

Psst. Another opens an *agua*. I groan. Someone takes the gag out, tilts my head back, and pours some Lift into my open mouth, sweet and warm. It runs down my chin onto my shirt and dries in a stiff patch. Someone rolls the radio dial, a presenter says '… here, in the Alta Verapaz.' So, we're still in the mountains. Perhaps Tactic or La Tinta. As we slow, I hear the sounds of a market, possibly Telemán. I could throw myself against the window to attract attention but it would be a short-cut to whatever's next. If they were after a ransom, they'd have made the call by now. It's not money they want, it's revenge. I run through my list of enemies. Unfinished business comes to mind.

The first call came two weeks ago. The gruff voice perfunctory:

'Don Francisco? Good. Listen carefully. We've *plata* that needs cleaning. We're gonna be generous and give you three per cent. We need account details. You'll give them to my guy who'll meet you next Thursday at Boquitos. Ten p.m.'

And the second call:

'Are you crazy, Toad? Don't you value your life? Or your wife's? If you're not there tomorrow…'

And the third:

'OK, you whore's mother. If you don't get your ugly Toad ass down to Boquitos tonight, you're as good as toad-leg soup by Friday.'

But the Toad doesn't compromise. Everyone knows that.

Bernardo will have told his neighbours. They'll have decided to call someone. Not the police, nobody ever calls the police. The *guardián*, Carlos, with his hard-luck face, will have phoned my lop-sided foreman. Jorge, blessed with tremendous sense despite village-idiot looks, will have limped over to La Montaña and spoken with my first-born, Andrés. He'll tell Liset. She'll call the rest of our kids. Our youngest, Cisco, will hop on the next *Monja Blanca*. Andrés, good lawyer that he is, will instruct Jorge, who'll ring Carlos, who'll send for Bernardo to come to the Beneficio. Dominga will put her arm about Liset. Lucila will cradle her baby. Andrés will perch himself on the edge of my desk and Cisco will fold his arms. Bernardo will blurt out what he saw.

Did I ever tell my family I'd do anything for them? That for them, I did everything. Things I shouldn't have. I wish I'd held Liset more gently. Or smiled at poor old Adolfo, hunched over the Bene's figures. Perhaps nodded at the scrawny *campesinos* toiling to bring in the crop. Or hugged my mother tighter, may she rest in peace. I'm abandoning my kids to a host of uncertainties: bankruptcy, bereavement, worse. Since the *picops* closed in on us, I've been kidding myself this fiasco will be over soon. That it's the *diputado* they're after. That I'll be home for turtle soup on Holy Friday... or at the latest Glorious Saturday. I start to splutter.

'He's having a fit,' says the driver, 'he's gonna kick the bucket.'

'*Puta madre*,' says the other, 'save us the job.'

Everything stills. I repeat prayers I've mumbled my entire life, attending to each word as though my soul depends on it. I feel the weight of His cross, grating across blistered hands, splinters embedding into sinewy shoulders. Sharp stones slicing bare feet. His parched throat is mine, our sweat mingles; His crown of thorns presses at my temples.

I see the procession of immediate and extended family clustered around my coffin; pickers, dealers, neighbours, and friends marching behind. Dry-cleaned suits, slicked-down hair, pungent aftershave. Cars double-parked along Zone Four's usually empty streets. Flowers and condolences. Damaska in black, her angular beauty heightened by grief. The word of the community. The police will chase their tails then close the case. The silence of the law. The ambiguity of obituaries. And all of this meaningless from where I'll be. On the cusp of judgment, my mother's Hail Marys or Liset's votive candles won't mitigate my transgressions. What will His pronouncement be?

Am I the father my family believes in? The God-fearing Catholic my fellow Cobaneros assume I am? The indulgent benefactor Damaska takes me for? Or the silent powerful head of a *narco*-trafficking mafia my assassins know me as? Perhaps it's these eight men, who never set eyes on me till a few hours ago, who understand me best. They alone know what I must account for: the tally of addicts' deaths and dealers' homicides.

It's why they're so at ease with hauling me out of the *picop* and onto my knees. The others are already there, the *diputado*'s erratic breath is near; the shot shudders through my eardrums and I smell his pooling blood. One of the assassins sharpens his *machete* and presses its steel against my wrist. The blade works its way up my forearm, hacking chunks higher and higher. Though I squeeze my blindfolded eyes shut, I see. My mother's countenance, Liset's brow, and Damaska's soft-eyes blur into a smiling Madonna, framed by iridescent feathers. Beyond the angel... sunlight, the whispering Chi'o, fallen *níspero* leaves, the taste of grass.

I'm at the weekend house, beneath the trees. There's light in the kitchen, Liset is at the stove. Her hair is twisted up, the way she wore it when we were courting. The smell of *kak'ik* fills the air. At our kitchen table sits Don Garcia, the man who gave my killers their orders, BlackBerry glinting in his fist. He smiles, cheeks broadening beneath Versace shades, and raises an icy Gallo to my wife. She laughs, hand on hip, gaze lingering.

My hitman pulls the trigger to finish the job. He'll rub his hands on a handkerchief, twist it and throw it into the undergrowth. Strolling back with his accomplices to the *picops*, he'll drive in the direction of the sunset, hymns playing on the radio. Back to San Lucas his wife preparing black beans, *tortillas*, and eggs *revueltos* the way he likes them. Back to his kids still up, watching MTV, waiting for Papi to come home.

'The Toad, Notorious Drug Lord, Butchered,' will be *Siglo XXI*'s headline tomorrow.

The final verdict.

Writing the Vessels

There are no beginnings nor endings, she thinks. No cardinal primordial pulse of a new-born's heart. Or its mother's or grandmother's. But to make narrative sense a start is needed.

To impose your ABC is a natural thing, hence deplorable.

She begins like a toddler with what she can roll around in her mouth. Really understand. Here. Now. The weight of her thighs on the office chair. The dust on the wooden table littered with papers where her laptop sits. The wan warmth of the single orange electrical bar that hangs in the air like a promise. The darkened window reflecting the room like an antique oil. The stencilled lampshade above her head, ochre tiles underfoot, a staircase to where the tilted, dissected, bed lies all day till they fill it with their words, sweat, coitus, sleep.

Sedentary hours in front of their computers have brought them past midnight. Innumerable Israeli coffees, neither filtered nor dissolved, keep them on edge. The Winston Blues he smokes furiously are the hallmark of her headache. Biting cold creeps doggedly under the door, licks at the window frames. Drunken cries, alarms and trance music, punctuated by bottles smashing, conspire toward insomnia.

… people can perform contrary actions together while taking one fresh gulp of air.

Beyond is a high Jerusalem stone hallway. Through one door and down two steps is a bathroom. Through another, a sitting room of dusty bookcases, a large divan, some coffee tables. The third is ajar to a kitchen that opens out to the balcony. Downstairs, the fortress-like unswept entrance hall, too remote for her to consider. She would be unsurprised if the door of the study opened to clouds, or a sheer drop. The last time she walked in Ben Sira (yesterday, or the day before) she noticed it was in the throes of change; few buildings like number eight still stand on its narrow pavement. Most have been levelled and are awaiting development, many already replaced by deluxe hotels or malls.

The balcony, part of the known world, overlooks the crumbling Mamilla graveyard with its flocks of bickering crows, bitter almond trees, mangled clothes, and smeared dog ordure. In the branches of the pink pepper and dusty loquat trees, turquoise hummingbirds shimmer. Caramel-coloured doves copulate on the wing. Between the Sufi shrines and Mamluk headstones, home to sleek blue-grey and ginger tabbies, stroll Orthodox Jews in fur or black hats, women clad in knee-length skirts, shapeless sweaters, hair tucked into knitted caps or bound in scarves. Poorly dressed Ukrainian Jews, affluently attired American Jews, well-heeled Spanish and Hungarian Jews. Demurely clothed Ethiopians, colourful Moroccan Jews, and badly dressed Arab Christians. Israeli Muslims stop at the path's bend to sit on the wall and lunch out of a plastic bag, washing their faces, hands, and shoes before returning to work. Visitors stop and pose for companions to take pictures with their phones, from Senegal or Sudan, Milan or Madrid, the New York, London, and Paris diasporas.

The couple reside in different continents; resisting the cities they inhabit. Tired of urban demands, the noxious hostilities, and placid indifference, she flavours her dream worlds with flight. Engaged in interminable feuds, his dreams are laced with fight. Desire paints an alluring alternative each is in denial of. Their habitual communication is through framed, disembodied faces, the Babylonian art of haruspicy refashioned into a Skype-stream physiognomy. An affair built on the interpretation of expressions. A cleaving to this smile, that gaze, or some curl of smoke, channelling what began as a visceral love affair into a visual one.

The people outside have purpose in their step. They are inside societies, members of families and congregations, knowledge-holders of rituals and traditions. But their steps, his and hers, are stopped. In their self-constructed miasma of introspection, outside references are static. The refuge of gentle kisses and thoughtful words has disintegrated. Tensions, specified and vague, are the pillars of this madness.

I am against action; for continuous contradiction, for affirmation too...

His legal entanglements play their part: dragged-out court cases with the People's Bank; prior employers; the Ministry of Justice; a Jerusalem landlord; a Paros neighbour; a misunderstanding with a phone company; another over a parking violation. All contributing to a chronic cash crisis: debts to friends and family, no telephone, only half the house supplied with electricity, no fuel.

A rare genetic condition suffered since his birth creates ongoing suffering, compromised joints and organs. An issue with a clavicle, fractured in a bike accident. A sleep disorder sporadically addressed with Provigil. Nicotine and caffeine addictions. Irregular eating patterns.

A halite pebble buried in Dead Sea bitumen, his heart glimmers with pellucid kindness. But debts weigh, the dearth of occupation stifles, a lack of solidarity crushes. Mood-altering medication and chronic pain exacerbate. From man of promise to man of disillusion. Yet still the nacre shimmers.

At the other end of the spectrum is her almost obsessively ordered personality that ruptures on a cyclical basis. She looks to open up her space while clinging to a tiny tightrope of existence. A self-contradictory girl in the body of a grown-up, unwilling to give up on free will. A drifter who is, by turns, a militant maker, shifter, and weaver of dreams. Old age lies not too far on the road ahead; the splinters of two broken marriages and, further back in the rear-view mirror, a chronically dysfunctional family. With a learnt distrust of men, she appreciates their energy, but swerves from collisions. In this man now, there is much to trouble her. But also, a rare cadence that resonates, vibrating her spirit into ecstasy. A truth, or at least a dedication to truth that is rare.

How can one expect to put order into the chaos that constitutes that
infinite and shapeless variation man?

The web of Nachlaot alleys spidering between Ben Sira and Jaffa Street are lined with cafés, pastry shops, galleries, and specialists in religious artefacts. Brimming with strident revellers whose hollers and alarms climax in a frenzied peak in Thursday's early hours, screaming Jerusalem's deep schism. A historical, inherited, conditioned neurosis. A pathology that is touching and vicious. Easy to over-simplify, harder to comprehend.

It's a city reconstructed from unforgotten ashes with the phoenix-like pride of Zionists. Where burgeoning conservative orthodoxy dominates a fading reformism. Where women assume the hippy-chic of flower children till they marry and are recast in suburban retro. Where the booming bass of a low-ceilinged snooker bar spills its rap into the synagogue opposite, where Hasidim hunch over Torahs, rocking their prayers. Where grimy, stoned Arabs saunter past wide-eyed Sudanese kids with corn-crakes. Where a dread-locked boy in the Mahane Yehuda souk rubs shoulders with a Haredi in a *shtreimel*, blowing a brass trumpet while his sidekick chides fruit-sellers, shovelling cheap strawberries into bags at breakneck speed, for not packing away in time for Shabbat.

The couple relinquish their screens and begin to talk. They dance and dive. The sophisticates' waltz morphs to deranged tango and dizzying Sufi spins, supplicant arms reaching. The discussion moves from the concrete to abstract and back in a few breaths. From what it means to be the leftovers of the leftovers of the ashes to conceiving a child with a gentile. Perceptions of reality and deep listening to the value of visualisation and chanting. Dreams of having a family to visions of forming a community. From the faith of one in medicine to the experience of the other in self-healing. Of his mother's feelings for his father: 'She loved him so much but she couldn't stand him.' The whispered prescience of an augury.

With the blue eyeglasses of an angel they have excavated the inner life
for a dime's worth of unanimous gratitude.

And mostly, what it means to be with another. Not in one's own sphere. Not having conversations with oneself. Nor an interminable relationship with a character on the tarnished screen. She withdraws from his insistence. She opposes his coercion. Sabotages his mind-training. Checkmates to save that measly relic she calls her identity. Reminds herself he's overbearing. Repulsively dismissive. Aggressively insistent. That he interrupts. His smoke makes her lungs ache for fresh air. He accuses her of generalising and proves her memory is deficient. She resists him at every level. And he identifies her dissent, scrupulous psychologist that he is, like a Lagotto rooting for truffles.

And then they are in Hadassah Hospital arriving on the light rail to a bus that takes them past a ghetto for children with disabilities, the so-called Swedish village, and into the Forest of Jerusalem. A monument to the seventies, funded by the Women of Hadassah, the walls a mosaic of donors from Chicago to Boca de Raton in Florida. In the redundantly high-ceilinged admissions room they sit, fingering the numbered ticket. Then shoot up to the seventh in one of the huge lifts.

In Neurology's grubby and chill corridor, doctors come and go, filling vial after vial of blood. Women with lined faces mouth prayers, books pressed against their foreheads, while from the wards cries for help are punctuated by the wheezes of a dying man. Plump Argentine doctors work alongside Russian, Arab, and Orthodox nurses. The couple sit, talk, fill in papers, and wander, trying to locate the doctor who suggested the angiography. In one corridor they bump into the neurosurgeon, José Cohen, who shakes the patient's hand but has no recollection of the case. Androgynous and ageless, he still sleeps in the student dormitories, eschewing a private life, living to work.

Seven hours after admission the bed is wheeled to theatre. The plump anaesthetist asks for a signature. Doctor Gomori, a Harvard-trained neuro-radiologist with small bright eyes, olive skin, and a beard discusses arteries: the vertical that rises from subclavians to form the basilar, entering the seat of the skull and feeding the circle of Willis with blood. The patient explains his symptoms. The doctor listens and recaps: he has had an 'event', he was brought to hospital, where the 'event' was repeated. The angiography will write the vessels' flow.

Entering the arteries through the groin, passing through the heart and into the base of the brain; a journey to ascertain vital information. His genetic condition significantly augments the risks. 'Would you do it?' he asks the doctor. The doctor smiles: 'Difficult to say. From the outside it seems a good idea.' He doesn't ask her the same question; she has already voiced her nescience. Instead he asks her, 'May I have your permission?' She would prefer not to, but she leans down to him, kissing away the suggestion that it might be her last. As she stumbles out, corridor walls palpitate in sync with her heart.

Science disgusts me as soon as it becomes a speculative system.

In the theatre, they screen his head from the rest of his body, shave a triangle of pubic hair and place a blue sheet over him. The anaesthetist plunges a large syringe above his groin. But nothing prepares him for the second incursion of a longer needle, a barrel through which they fire a broader projectile. Cohen takes the driver's seat, conducting the catheters toward the brain, while Gomori revolves huge lenses over his body, the scanners virtually subtracting organs or bones so only veins are represented on the bank of screens. Orders fly back and forth, everything contracted into the space around the bed by the concentration of the medics; compressed by time, honed by the criticality of life and death. Contrast media is shot into the lumens. The iodinated material threads itself like sugar syrup in cold water. It unfurls in smoky tentacles, seeps from coarser shafts into finer threads; its spectral translucency tunnelling a wraithlike progress, a naked tree pulsing branches into existence.

Half an hour later a technician calls her. She finds him in a wheelie bed, weak and tired. As they return to the ward, he tells her of the artery spurting warm blood on his thigh, of the sundry languages spoken and the quickening of monitors' bleeps with each intrusion. He sleeps as she sits in that timeless, grey room with its Star of David sheets, blueish curtains, and green plastic chairs. After two hours, the nurse removes the weight below the bandages and dinner is delivered onto the empty bed beside him. He shares the dark bread, yoghurt, tahini, Satsuma, and tomato, leaving only tired chopped cucumber. They steep the Wotsovsky tea bag in two plastic cups. Later they go downstairs to fetch Kallil long espressos with milk and brownies. He smokes a cigarette.

Art is not as important as we, mercenaries of the spirit, have been proclaiming for centuries.

She sleeps on two chairs pushed together; under a lumpy quilt, his fleece as a pillow. Waking, she finds the dawn transcendent and the buzz of nurses comforting. The day is expected to be a drawn-out affair. That morning in a slow shuffle down to the garden at the back they visit the squat synagogue with its astonishing Chagall stained-glass. Twelve panes, facing the four directions; Jacob blessing his sons and the twelve tribes of Israel. Implicitly complex in childish symbolism, they throb with Mediterranean vibrancy. His father finds them there. A small, rosy-cheeked Holocaust survivor who emanates a defiant energy even at eighty. He has brought a box of biscuits and good French chocolate, which they share in the crisp air of the garden outside.

Two days later it's his best friend's birthday. The Loft is in an empty industrial site in Talpiot, full of fifty-year-olds getting down to sixties music, the DJ half their age. On the walls are projections of slinky girls pouting in *haute couture*. There are plastic plates of crudités and crisps and a corner bar. They throw their coats into a seedy room with an en-suite shower. It's impossible to speak except for on the balcony where smokers huddle under a patio heater. There is nothing to do but dance.

Art is a private affair, the artist produces it for himself; an intelligible work is the product of a journalist...

Friday night is spent with his mother, Malka, a petite French-Moroccan. His nephew, Yair, arrives, followed by his twin, Noam. Malka breaks a plate and picks out shards from beaten eggs she's dipping schnitzel into for the son who won't eat lamb. The rest of the food is wrapped in a big blanket on a hotplate which has been stewing for hours in advance of Shabbat. The nephews fight their uncle with pillows. When his brother arrives it's obvious the twins are angelic miniatures of the brothers; one smooth and flexible as rubber, the other dark and emphatic. Immediately Malka calls them to sit at the table, where a huge plate of osso buco, lamb, truffles, and brown eggs fill a platter. Yair, hopping from one foot and back again as they eat, tells them, 'This week we were a doing a test and a book fell from my desk, open at exactly the page with the answer. This girl in my class saw it and she said she wouldn't tell but she's blackmailed me. My punishment is to stand up for two whole weeks even when I eat.'

Married to logic, art would live in incest, swallowing, engulfing its own tail, still part of its own body, fornicating within itself... a heap of ponderous grey entrails.

After, he washes the dishes. And goes downstairs with his mother to smoke. She makes coffee and serves biscuits. His brother goes for a run. The boys loll on the sofa, Noam translates a super chef programme to her, word for word. Yair nestles up to his uncle under a duvet and soon they all fall asleep. When she awakes Malka complains her back aches and she offers her a massage. In the bedroom Malka asks what their plans are.

'Marry,' she orders. 'Marry! Where will you live? Can he get work in London?' she persists. 'Does he know what he wants?'

When they get home, they discuss truth, empathy, faith, and honesty. Around two in the morning, when there is no possibility to form the words anymore, they fall into bed. When morning light creeps through the window, the iPhone screams and they crawl downstairs. To drink coffee. He smokes. She cooks oats with sesame and figs.

Freedom: Dada Dada Dada, a roaring of tense colours, and interlacing of opposites and of all contradictions, grotesques, inconsistencies: LIFE.

His face today is tired and lined. Hers is puffy and tight. But she adores the cut of his cheek, the hook of his nose, smooth scalp, and haunted eyes. The marked skin and sleek chest. Even in his presence she longs for him. His strumming fingernails digging into her haunches. His moan as she goes down on him or her in-breath as he shoves his hips against her. If the price is sanity, it's too high.

At times it seems they are constructing the relationship. At others as though they are dismantling it. Love may be hijacked by more practical considerations. They will reach a compromise. Or keep this distance between them. Or they will part.

Bone Metre

Tigone dreams blind, submerged in a deep-blue ocean. She hears something. A slow patter, perhaps the first droplets of rain on a tin roof. Or the measured groan of hinges. No. Wait. Listen carefully; her life may depend on it. The clip hastens to canter and gallop, a stallion's hooves answered by another and several more, crescendoing to a neck-and-neck derby. She's rider, ridden, and trampled. The speeding Morse code catapults her into bolt-upright wakefulness: heart pummelling, temples thudding. She has no idea what woke her.

She found the first bone at dawn. Stared at it some time before squatting among the coal, olive, and liver pebbles. Let her fingertips play across its surface. Bleached white by the sun, face pockmarked; a disc with wings, an angel's skeleton, so weightless it might take flight. She squirreled it beneath her sweater, back to her cave. Standing it flat upon her patio, she rolled a cigarette and sat cross-legged on the cement, moulding her palms to its contours.

The hunchback fisherman shouted a hello from the quay below as he scrambled out of his boat. A lone seagull traced an alpha overhead, gliding, wings static. The sea's surface ruffled in random swirls. She closed her eyes and listened. Thought of water begetting post-Diluvian beasts. And carrying ships to other continents. Of it cradling the land. She let her fingertips explore the bone to decipher its Braille-like relief, wondering whose it was. If it was fish or mammal; content or dissatisfied; if it had spawned young or fought battles.

Tigone rented the cave from Spiros, the dwarf fisherman, who lived with his daughter. Anargiya was known for a neck goitre and litter of unruly children, fathered by donkey-men, rubbish collectors, and, some said, their own grandfather. The dwelling was a single vault with two shuttered windows and an outhouse, up some steps. Anargiya had done her best to decorate. But Tigone packed the doilies, plastic knick-knacks and fly-ribbons into a cardboard box and handed them back. She appreciated absence; of lovers, of things. I don't want a cleaner, she protested, when Anargiya showed up with bucket and mop one morning. But her landlady was deaf to objection. So Tigone left her keys behind the geranium pot and took a walk when she was due.

Tigone spent afternoons in the *taverna*, making mandalas, a knack picked up in Tibet. Bending wire and threading tiny beads, she wove spiders' webs of golden strands and gems that, in her hands, blossomed into constellations, yin and yang or lotus flowers. The months between travelling and the selling season were her favourite. By summer, when tourists arrived in search of novelty, they'd find her seated on the whitewashed *plateia* wall before the church, a character escaped from a Jean Renoir movie, straw hat over silver Medusa curls and sunglasses. Italians, Japanese, and Americans snapped her photo or bought a mandala. She made enough for *retsina*, smoke, rent, and her winter airfare. But as the crisis bit, money and her desire to travel thinned and she stayed entire windswept winters.

This year she avoided the paved road to the village and various errands that once drew her there. Instead, she chose precarious rocks that connected the port of Amoudi with Katharos and its sculpted pumice cliffs and pebble beach, studded with sea-drenched boulders. After the howling *Meltemi* whipped the sea into several storms, the shore was sown with chalky squid beaks, lengths of velvet driftwood, a cow's skull picked clean. And man-made jetsam: creased plastic bags, crumpled PET bottles, chunks of yellowed polystyrene. She harvested rubbish, winnowing and depositing it into the municipal wheelie bins on the pier. Farther from the port she threw her clothes down and stepped into the water. The iciness between her legs spread over her skin till it burned. Then she lay naked, on the stones, letting sun and wind lick her dry.

She came across the second bone some days later; a fraction smaller. Cradling it in her arms, she brought it home and positioned it next to the first. Sitting before them, a hand on each, she fell into meditation. And so she sought more bones. Some days she found none; others, two or three. The ambles grew longer, the miles stretching into afternoons. On her return, she fell into deep sleep on the hard wooden *kanape*. In the early hours, roused by the thunder of hooves in her head, she stepped out into crystalline nights.

The lights of the island opposite, Thirasia, glimmered reassuringly. Wide-awake, she rolled a cigarette, poured a glass of *retsina*, put together a plate of fried cheese or some chickpeas. Laughter and *rebetiko* drifted over from Katina's: the last customers lingering. But she wasn't tempted. She was done with congeniality. Solitude taught her the art of paring down. The landscape was her solace. Over men and women, she chose rocks, sea, sky.

And bones.

Spring brought rain and sunshine. The fields above the shore brimmed with poppies, lupines, lavender, and daisies. Fishwife's gossip brought Alexandros to her gate; a soft-spoken sunburnt man with a bald pate and porpoise features. Anargiya had told him Tigone was filling the cave with a monster's carcass. Tigone stood in her doorway wishing he'd go, but he didn't. So she made Greek coffee while he examined the bones. Nearly two hundred crowded sills, tables, and chairs, the largest on the patio outside.

'An incredible collection,' he murmured when she brought the cups, voice full of admiration. He sat on the low stone wall and she on the toilet steps. 'You're interested in whales?'

'Whales? No, not specially.'

'You aren't a zoologist?'

'No, an artisan. I make mandalas.'

'When did you start gathering bones?'

'Since things went quiet... four, maybe five months ago.'

He frowned, impressed.

'Are you sure they're whale bones?' she asked.

'Absolutely… of one particular whale.'

'How d'you know?'

'There's no duplication: if you put them together they'd make a complete skeleton. I work for the Palagos Institute: I've spent most of my life photographing whales and gathering stats along the Ionian trench that stretches from the mainland towards Crete.'

'There are whales in the Mediterranean?'

'Until the fifties there were many. Now, perhaps a hundred and thirty. They're very special; enclosed in the Aegean bowl they don't migrate. They speak a different language from the Atlantic variety.'

'Language?'

'They echo-locate, like bats. But they use clicks to communicate in codas.'

When he left, Tigone tentatively placed some bones close to one another below the window. She shifted them this way and that and, confused, started again. By moonlight she arranged and rearranged, spreading smaller bones across the *doulapa*. At first light, a colossus was taking shape. Blowing out the candles, she rolled up in a blanket and fell asleep. The next morning, she cycled up to the hardware shop and bought a reel of galvanised 3/8 thread, some hooks, rawl-plugs, a drill, and masonry bits.

When she passed Katina's on the way home, Alexandros was sitting beneath an umbrella, collar turned up against the freak wind, clutching papers. He invited her for a Mythos.

'You might find this interesting,' he said, passing her some printed papers.

She knit her brow. '"Coda Diversity in Mediterranean Sperm Whales". Why sperm whales? On account of their sex drive?'

'No, on account of their noses,' he smiled. 'A third of their body is nose. Inside is the spermaceti organ. Whalers thought the gloopy stuff was sperm… familiar, I guess.'

'What's it for?'

'The whales cool it with seawater till it solidifies, adding forty kilos, like a diver putting on weights. They can stay underwater up to two hours. It's handy for escaping predators.'

'And they're hunted?'

'They were, by whalers after oil, baleen, and ambergris – the gunk that forms in their intestines around indigestible squid beaks, like pearls around grains of sand in an oyster. It has this musky smell and was used as an aphrodisiac.'

'But hunting's not allowed anymore?'

'There's been a moratorium for twenty years. Still, they get entangled in swordfish drift-nets, or swallow plastic bags, or get sliced by speeding boats.'

'I think you love them?'

'Once we measured civilisations by what they destroyed. One day, we'll measure them by what they preserve.'

'How old is my whale?'

'Judging by its teeth, my guess is it's an immature bull. Probably around eleven or twelve metres.'

'How do you think he died?'

'Since you've found so many bones together I suspect he was beached and then the carcass broke up. You have a rare find. A museum piece, even.'

After he'd gone, Tigone dropped off her materials and biked back up to town. In the internet café, she Googled whales and read Wikipedia. She watched footage of shapeless parallel backs breaking the water's skin; of blowholes spurting; of soundless dives of unexpected grace and thrusting tail flukes heralding huge downward-chuting bulks. She found a recording of sperm-whale codas. Her throat went dry as the familiar clacks of her dreams reverberated in her eardrums. She sat replaying the wordless mantra through her headphones over and over till her hour was up. Then she cycled down to Amoudi, printouts of skeletons flapping in one hand. Pouring herself a *tsipouro* and knocking it back in one gulp, she stuck the blueprints to the wall with duct tape.

One diagram was a perfect pterodactyl profile; long unwieldy beaked jaw, high cranium, small rib-cage, elongated spinal column and thalidomide arm of scapula, humerus, and metacarpals. Somewhere, towards the tail, a few vestigial hind leg-bones floated. The other was an elaborate lace of white bones mapped onto a stumpy silhouette.

An under-slung jaw lay at the base of an enormous shovelled snout, while shoulder blade and phalanges fit snugly inside the flipper. The skeleton gave shape to all but nose cavity and tail. But not support. She'd read that gravity was not a problem underwater, but beached whales were crushed to death by their own weight.

She bore holes and hung several hooks from the ceiling. Carefully, she began to scaffold. Ordering the fifty vertebrae along the cave floor, she placed thirteen chevrons on her bed and twenty-two ribs beyond the arch. The cranium she positioned near her front door with five hyoids at one side. She rested mandibles, maxillae, and vomer up against the window niches. She was guided by diagrams; the bones taught her the rest. She spent the remains of her savings at the hardware store on bolts, nuts and washers, rods, connectors, and epoxy resin. She began assembling, drilling holes and sanding their edges smooth. Passing wire through the channels, she mixed bone dust with adhesive to fill in any gaps and cemented the smaller fin, pelvic and ear-bone complexes. For six nights and days she didn't leave the house. She ate leftovers, cornflakes with condensed milk and dry *paximadia* drenched in olive oil. Half-made mandalas gathered dust on her work board. But she didn't stop till the whale filled the cave; from the beak resting on the window-sill to the last vertebrae curled in the rear alcove.

That night she pulled a pillow and blanket from her bed and nestled them in the ribcage. She sat inside the structure, rolled a cigarette and finished her glass of *retsina*. Gurgling noises, interrupted by the sound of jetting water, filled her dreams. The familiar rhythm began, quickening, faster and faster. The clicks grew thunderous till her ribs vibrated. Three massive rumbles followed by a single one. She lept upright. Her skin was wet, brine seared her nostrils. She peered through the darkness for something familiar – stars or Thirasia's lights. But only the deepest darkest blue pressed against her, sluiced into her throat. Viscous creatures brushed lightly against bare arms and slapped her cheek. She struggled to stand, fought to find her balance. As she made it onto her feet, a vast wave gushed over her and everything was water.

TINDERBOX

A tall, scratched fridge-freezer stood outside one of those terraced columned homes in Blenheim Crescent. Jorge hefted it away before dawn, in the hope of making Rosario smile. My lifts were out of order, but Mohammed from the sixth helped Jorge lug it to his place on the fourth. Mo watched as Jorge plugged it in. There was a silent moment till it whirred into action, then they cheered.

This lower edge of Ladbroke, once known for its piggeries and brickyard trenches of stagnant water, was one of London's more surly Victorian slums. Life expectancy hovered at around eleven. Irish immigrants lived in potteries whose floors dipped into swamp. At the drier end of buildings, families slept on straw mattresses. These morphed into rooming houses, let to Windrush arrivals. Slum clearance in the sixties made way for the low-cost, socialist utopian Brutalist generation: the likes of me and my cousins Trellick, Brunswick, and South Bank. Inside my slabs, the low-rise units of Lancaster West Estate were imagined into existence, my citadel torso towering over these rigor-mortised limbs; a misanthropic, unsociable colossus embodying hostility. In Old French '*guarin*' is guard and '*ville*' settlement; my name sidled its way into English: Grenfell.

When Rosario came home from vacuuming office floors a couple of hours later she laughed and opened her mouth to Jorge's kiss. That was three long years ago. Before the cough crept into her lungs and the

St Mary's diagnosis. Before the complications. Before Jorge lost her. Everything else kept going as before; the sun rose, the daytime guard stubbed out his last cigarette before leaving Jorge to the monitors of The Portobello Hotel. In Ciudad Bolívar, Mamá answered the cell phone each Sunday. The FF175BP Hotpoint chilled Jorge's beers and take-away leftovers.

Our pared-back structures were championed as honest, the government's answer to the housing problem. We gave a dehumanised workforce termite-cartons, with views onto the city they served and were disregarded by. For forty-three years in my hundred and twenty-nine compartments, people came into the world and left it. Loneliness, anger, joy and desolation blossomed and withered in my fuselage. Kith of all ages, ethnicities, sexual and religious inclinations came here. They made love and fought. They hung mezuzahs on their doorframes, placed prayer mats toward Mecca, genuflected to Coptic statues of the Virgin and offered malt liquor to the dead. Syrians extricating themselves from civil war, Afghanis fleeing persecution, Ethiopians running from collectivisation, Somalis escaping starvation, West Africans taking flight from political unrest. Around forty Jewish and Muslim Berber families sought sanctuary within my walls. Neighbours observed various Sabbaths, celebrated Chanukah or Ramadan, shared food from their homelands with one another. Circumcisions, baptisms, bar mitzvahs and aqeeqahs were marked by kin. People dozed on my sofas, cooked meals in my kitchens or slept, dreamless, on my floors. Friendships were formed and marriages brokered. Allied in privation, my tenants didn't turn from one another. They lived hand-to-mouth, shoulder-to-shoulder.

Oppressive stairwells, juddering lifts, stinking rubbish chutes and strip lights are implausible constituents for home, yet these people made me theirs. No warm welcomes awaited them. Unaided, they trawled the gridlocked avenues of the National Health Service. They decoded the obstacle course of social services, unravelled Jobseekers Allowance or Universal Credit. Made sense of Housing Benefit, Citizens Advice, and Mental Health Services. Without language or funds, some found unregulated and illegal work. Others studied or started small enterprises. They persevered because they had no choice.

Daughters skipped out to the Aldridge Academy in grey blazers and plaid skirts, backpacks heavy with books. Toddlers dawdled in St Clement and St James forest-green sweaters. Mothers stumbled back from early-morning cleaning jobs. Fathers stalked the early hours after their shifts. Teenage hoodies groped in my stairwells or smoked weed in my recesses. Old-school Londoners with drinkers' noses snuck in late from the Sun in Splendour or the Elgin. Their blotched and weary wives, laden with Westfield carrier bags or pushing prams, returned like ants on pheromone trails. Agile North African boys, bathed in sweat, were buzzed in after lifting weights in the Leisure Centre. Against my silhouette, drill gangs shot videos and wielded machetes or dealt drugs in my urine-soaked corners. Kids in QPR strips strode out to watch games on Loftus Road with their old men. Families walked out at the weekend, to Kensal Rise Cemetery or Wormwood Scrubs.

Until Jorge's night off in mid June. Around midnight he smelled smoke from behind the fridge. He called the fire brigade. Flames were licking at the ceiling by the time they showed up. They hosed my walls and left. A little before one Jorge fell asleep on the sofa. He was awakened by the fire's flaring-back slurp. Jorge dialled 999, threw Rosario's wedding ring and his passport into a carryall and rang his neighbours' bells. Signs in my hallways told them to stay put if the fire was not in their flat. Jorge took a lift down and waited for the fire engines to arrive. His neighbours stayed. But slowly, my dwellers abandoned me; by two in the morning half were on the street, bundled in duvets or bedspreads. The contagion spread up my eastern side, across my northern face, and engulfed my cladding from the second to the twenty-fourth storey.

Shortly before three, the fire brigade told my remaining occupants to leave. For many it was too late, my stairwells flush with fumes, smog seeping under doorsills, smoke pluming from windows. Like crabs, those who remained scuttled upstairs to the firetrap of the twenty-third. Outside, the conflagration drew sirens, flashing lights, choppers, neighbours, camera crews, journalists. It gushed viscid soot, tar and ash, sobbing men and women, knotted sheets lowering bodies, falling people, a swaddled baby miraculously caught. Jorge ran to bring bottles of water and flasks of tea from nearby houses. He hugged people he knew and took the hands of those he didn't. During that relentless night, Jorge saw those that wouldn't make it and the already dead. He worked alongside Mo, caught sight of Amira nursing the baby, and their three daughters. He glimpsed his first love at a window, silhouetted against flames, heedless. He hugged his own Mamá, carrying a baby he didn't recognise. Rosario, looking up from an old man she was tending, mouthed '*Te amo.*' Even Papi's ghost was there.

Around him, people were shouting into their mobiles:

'Try the stairs.'

'I love you.'

'Wrap your face in a wet towel.'

'Breathe out the window.'

There were no fire escapes. No alarms. No sprinklers. No drills. No fire-engine access. No instructions to leave. No shelter. No information about missing loved ones. No food or clothing. No counselling. No apologies. No register of residents, or whom they sublet to. No consolation for those who stumbled down stairwells, tripping over dead bodies. No words of comfort for those from whom a hand had slipped, swallowed by the clag. No school for the children that survived.

How does Jorge live with this story? Does he blame the fridge or the family that dumped it in the street? Not Mo, surely, who helped lug the fridge to the flat. The government in power the year I was built? The Borough of Kensington and Chelsea that saved £293,368 fitting aluminium rather than zinc cladding? Should he curse the Lady of Chiquinquirá Mamá prays to? Or his neighbours' Allah? Maybe Jorge bears a staggering weight of agony, like the old Hotpoint he hoisted on his shoulders. How do we live with this story? The paving stones, our clothes, food, bus, packages, music and home... all laid, stitched, cooked, driven, delivered, played, built, and cleaned by those just like the seventy-two. Or seventy-seven. Or eighty, perhaps. Who will ever know?

And me? A lanky, blackened and scorched skeleton; a macabre

monument shrouded in a white *kaffan*. I'm no longer a Brutalist wet-dream nor a newly clad version of it. No genius solution to anything. No sanctuary for anyone. Without synapses or soul, severed limbs prone in my shadow, my carcass is a charred *memento mori*, dark warning to the scattered skyscrapers across this city.

Whitechapel Boys

Harold, more than eighty years ago

Harry slips from Mam's hug, a smoke in her hand as she tucks his shirt into his shorts with the other. He bites at the mole below his lip as his father's bronchial cough drowns his brothers' laughter. They're tussling in the bedroom again. He runs down wooden stairs, reaches up to unlatch the door and escapes into the yard. Alfie is knuckling down marbles, the Schuster sisters are chanting rhymes and the Brower twins from along the hall are making a chip pass over the washing line. Out in the street, he almost knocks down a full-bearded old man in a long dark coat, a felt hat settled on the wings of his black-framed glasses.

It's one of those smoggy chill November mornings, smoke rising from Alie Street's chimneys. The street smells of yeast, wet leaves, hair spray. A bicycle squeaks past, and the rear basket catches his fist, knocking the ha'penny from his grasp. It careens across the road and rolls under a shiny grey Wolseley. Dismayed, Harry ducks beneath its undercarriage on his hands and knees. He sees it, less than three inches from the drain. Snatching it up, he rubs its sail boat clean and puts it firmly in the pocket of his shorts. He skips past bent-over grannies in curlers and pinnies; plump mothers in full skirts and cardies, young girls in heels and make-up. Lawrence Lord is laying pillows 'of every description' out on a fold-up table; he notices a stray dog peeing on his shopfront and throws it a kick. A fellow in a faded homburg sits on his suitcase, the gramophone in front of him whirring out a Bo Diddley number.

Avi Goldberg's boy is hanging liverwurst from hooks inside the butcher and poulters. Birds hang in the window from their rigid reptilian feet, stiff goose-pimpled necks stuccoed with dank feathers. Through the back door Harry sees a kid no older than himself hauling squawking hens from a crate. Under the bare bulb's glare, he passes them to a man chewing on a cigarette who cuts their throats. Then he hands them to an accomplice who sticks them upside down into metal cones to drain. Harry checks out the Lyons shop window, but it's too early for bread pudding. Mrs Wolfe is hoisting dresses up on a pole onto the bar that stretches across her shopfront. Under upside-down pineapples hanging from hooks, Mike the Pike is polishing Orange Pippins on his jacket and stacking them in pyramids.

From a balcony of the new flats, Mam's second cousin clocks Harry as she hangs laundry.

'Oi, Trouble! Who let you out?'

He waves and runs on, bumping into two women, who call on the Lord to strike him dead; their little girl, a red bow in her hair, pulls a face at him. His schoolmistress in a lama coat and cloche calls out, 'Morning Harold!' He grins shyly. Two handsome Sikhs amble past as if they have all the time in the world. He stops a moment outside the hardware store to pat the rocking horse he's dreamed about for ages but remembers his mission.

He can smell the sugar from across the road. He joins the queue of heavyset scarfed ladies. Although he's already made his mind up, he runs through the options one more time; mallows, liquorice, rock, ices, boiled sweets, wine gums and toffees. Mrs Aldridge shovels his ha'penny worth of pear drops into a paper bag. Retracing his steps, he sees the old man from upstairs being shaved in the barbers. The wet fish shop is thick with women, gossiping, arms folded. A little further on, a lad in overalls has shown up with a crate of five piebald puppies. Harry joins the throng gathered around him. When two kids peel off, he tails them. They saunter down the street and clamber over a broken wall.

Amongst the rubble is a page torn from a magazine covered in footprints. It's a cartoon of a huge rock with a cockroach sneaking from underneath, lifted by a young woman and man. The caption reads, 'Look what's crawling out again.' Beneath it: 'What is Mosely's Union Movement? It is the British Union of Fascists revived. If you value democracy, FIGHT IT NOW!'

He hears the boys yelling and follows.

They're creeping into a derelict church. Harry takes a deep breath. He's never been in church before. He breathes in the dank smell of abandonment. His eyes adjust to the dark and he makes out the boys high above him. One is hopping up and down on a tipped-over pew while the other is careening through the air on a rope like a trapeze artist.

'Push us, then!' shouts one. 'Go on, Billy-boy!' Billy complies, but a minute later he's calling out:

'My turn now, Pauly!' Billy tugs at Pauly's shirt and clambers on himself.

Harry sneaks closer. 'Can I have a go?'

They stare at him.

'Depends,' says Pauly. 'Wot you got there?'

'Ha'penny's worth of pear drops. You can't have em, though.'

The boys laugh nastily. 'You got nuffin else?' says Pauly.

Harry produces a small pebble and a cracked marble from his pocket.

'Gis yer mib!' cries Pauly.

Harry reluctantly hands over his cat's eye. Pauly spits on it and rubs it on the leg of his shorts.

'That'll do nicely, won't it, Billy? But keep yer trap shut, mind you, not a dicky-bird bout our hide-out.'

Harry nods solemnly and clambers onto the wardrobe, grasping the rough rope in his hands. He jumps off, and air rushes past his ears. Through the broken Gothic windows, motes of dust dance in the sunlight and Whitechapel market appears and disappears. Below are the empty pews, worn kneelers, several torn hymn books swept into a corner, a cracked vase of chrysanthemums and a bare mattress, straw spilling.

'Time's up, my go, time's up!' yells Billy and, though he never wants to let go, Harry slows, the circles getting smaller. He slips down to the ground. The rope burns his palms and he lets go too early, falling to his knees. Leaping up, he swings the rope-end back to Billy.

'Tara!' he shouts with a wave and turns, skipping back to the street. He legs it back to his yard, through his front door and up the steps to the parlour. Mam is peeling spuds at the kitchen table; the old man is coughing into his hankie and his brothers are hunched around the wireless listening to a BBC report on Hitler's appointment as Chancellor in Germany.

'Did you get your sweets, Harry?' Mam asks.

'Yes, Mam,' he says. 'Pear drops,' and he offers her the paper bag.

'Nah, give one each to David and Michael, and then hurry up with homework. What on earth have you done to your knees, you little tyke? They're all bloody.'

'Must have fell. Mam, who's Mosely?'

'Homework, Harry! Hurry up, now. Or Miss Wainwright'll be bending my ear first thing of a Monday morning.'

Abu, today

The lift doors open on Abu, smiling at his own reflection, a gap between his middle teeth, a raised mole on the bridge of his nose. A plump boy in pyjamas printed with fork-lifts, one hand on his hip, the other fist to the sky.

He addresses the empty lift: 'I don't think so, Hawkgirl.'

He skips through a marble hallway, scans the fob that releases the door into Meranti House's large vacant underground parking lot. Winding his way between Mercedes, BMWs and Porsches he bleeps himself into another basement and onto another lift that delivers him into a reception. He waves at the Thai caretaker and descends in a third lift to another basement and through swing doors into a large, new and well-equipped gym supervised by a muscle-bound Barbadian and slips through another set of doors to another reception.

He signs the visitor book, asking the Colombian concierge the date, and saunters into the vestibule of a deserted changing room. The sensor lights switch on over a wide mirror with a marble table stocked with cotton buds and pads, tissues and body lotion. He goes through to a spotless, locker-lined changing room of wooden benches, wriggles out of his pyjamas and slips into his trunks. He glances at his pudgy chest and fleshy hips in the glass, flexes his biceps, and throws himself a punch.

'We don't believe in fate!' he growls at his reflection.

His bare feet turn on a beige mosaic floor and he traipses through swing doors to a pool of softly lit glycerine water against a white marbled bulwark. He pads past the steam room and the sauna that he's not allowed to use and presses on the shower controls; he selects mint-julep lights over violet, and a spray over pulse or downpour. Adjusting the temperature, he steps in. The water mists over his chunky form and he jiggles from one foot to the other, making the neon slip across his feet. Dropping to his elbows and knees, he snakes across the floor. He opens the sauna door and inhales the woody smell. Then he wriggles to the steam room and creeps his hand around the glass wall into the gilt-tessellated mausoleum and rubs a clear patch. He squirms across to the pool steps, wide enough for a dozen kids and, lying on his left side, rolls into the mercurial water. It's warmer than the pool he goes to with English Martyrs Catholic Primary School. He splashes a while. And paddles to one end. Then back. He turns a somersault. And tries a few handstands. Sitting on the wall dividing the pool from the jacuzzi, he lowers his feet into the warm water and kicks. He jumps back into the pool and paddles back and forth, singing, 'Baby girl, what ha'nin? You n yorass invited...'

An hour or so passes. No one comes. Abu sighs loudly and pulls himself out of the pool, takes a shower. He dresses and heads back through basements and lifts, tracing the letters of the sign that states the lift carries 14 people and 1,050 kilos. He jumps as high as he can, smearing his fingerprints onto the smoked-glass mirror. 'I'm handling this.'

He lets himself into apartment 407. Umi is scrambling eggs; she puts cucumbers, tomatoes, olive oil, and za'atar on the table while he plays Injustice on the iPad. He flops down at the table. Between mouthfuls of flat bread, Abu chooses to side with Batman to defend Brainiac.

Suddenly, Umi is shouting: 'For God's sake, can you put that thing away?'

Her face is blotchy and her dusky silver eye-shadow is smudged with mascara. He rubs his eyes with his fists and makes a face. Umi is beautiful, but she thinks she's fat and won't come to the pool. She changes into her pyjamas behind the closed door of her bathroom. Her large brown eyes under purple-kohled brows are sad and full, painted lips cut straight across her jaw. Thick dark locks fall below her shoulders. He loves his mother more than anyone, but since they moved to London, she's been like Gorilla Grodd seeking world domination. She talks at him, without expecting a reply.

'This city never quiet. Not even when I wake to pray. I get fed up before always cooking, always home. I want to use my mind. So, I go back to my old profession. Too many years in England, volunteering, this aid agency or that, raising you and your brother, no time to make English better. Now Fawzi is at Lancaster, costs big money. And this. Too much money for flat! Stupid Ukrainian want to sell it me for one and a quarter million. For this, I could buy three flats! Two here and one in the Med with sunshine and balcony. And legal partner... fifteen years I think he is good man. But he's just legal adviser. So sneaky, doing deals behind my back like old husband having affairs. Telling me, no this client is mine, no cut for you, even though I set up meeting. For this I studied hard, prayed, respected my mother, bless her, my father's second wife when first produce no children. And now you sit across from me with your Injustices. Where is your homework?'

'Here... somewhere,' Abu says, shuffling through a pile of books on the dinner table. He scans the sitting room. He finds it in his schoolbag and waves it triumphantly. 'Don't underestimate me!'

But Umi is stabbing her iPhone with a furrowed brow and doesn't look up. He goes to her, puts his arms around her and kisses her soft cheek. After a minute, she pushes him away.

'Homework!' she cries. 'Do it.'

He climbs into the chair opposite her. 'But Umi, I don't want to go back to school. They bully me.' Umi's expression is slack. 'And they make me pray. Not just put my hands together but say Amen out loud even though they know I'm Muslim. I don't want to go anymore.' This is Abu's last card; if he can persuade her his soul is in danger of infidel conversion she will surely take him out of English Martyrs. Umi claims she's not religious but she prays every day since they moved to London.

'I don't know, Abu, about the bullying. Is it true? I will speak with your teacher next week if I can get off work early. And as for praying, just be a good boy, it's all the same god we pray to.'

Umi has lost it. If Allah is the same as God, why are Daesh on suicide missions? She might as well be saying, 'Do you not know me, stripling? I am Grodd.'

SKY-GOER

dakini: *The female embodiment of enlightened energy*

There were two telephones in my childhood home. One was post-box red and sat on my father's desk downstairs; the other was ivory and lived on the wind-up gramophone in the living room. One was pleasingly heavy, and its long electrical cord extended easily to my bedroom next door. Our phone number, '3791', was typed on the central plaque. 'Pimlico' above implied the '828' code. In the grey area to the left was 'DIAL 999'; 'FIRE, POLICE, AMBULANCE' on the white half to the right. Below was '100 OPERATOR'. The stolid handset had a shower-head earpiece and cupped mouthpiece with an elastic coil, perfect for slipping fingers into. One of my brothers had replaced the card with a black-and-white, waist-up photo of a naked woman, plump arms raised above her head. Each time you dialled, she spun, a little for low numbers, a three-quarter circle for 9. The hours talking to my best friend were spent staring at those breasts.

There weren't many public images of naked women around then. Just the odd photo of shirtless, long-haired, flared trousered, children-of-the-earth, their conical breasts loose. Or the framed posters of porn stars, nipples hidden by stickers, outside Wilton Road's art-deco Biograph, the adult cinema that stank of urine.

Mother never objected to the whirling mammaries; a head teacher, she had little time for domestic issues. Our unclad icon spoke volumes about our family. About society at large. Half-century-old phrases drift back now: 'built like a brick shit-house', with the accompanying gesture. My father's advice to my teenage self to find a boyfriend with big hands.

She sits down with determination at the refectory table. Olive-green eyes, alive with harvest lights, a strong Ashkenazi nose over defined crushed-raspberry lips. Her lucent neck pulses warmth. Two fine gold rings with tiny knots pierce her right ear. One in the left, another through her left nostril.

'Where are you from?' I ask.

'Nataf, a village near Jerusalem. Eighty families. I believed it was huge as a child. You've been to Israel?'

'Three times,' I say.

'Why?'

'An Israeli boyfriend.'

'Where else have you travelled?'

'Latin America. Africa. The Middle East.'

She grows attentive: forbidden lands. I trace the journey for her: Egypt, Sudan, Ethiopia, Djibouti, Yemen, Oman, Dubai, Iran.

'I've been trekking the last nine weeks with my father and his two friends.'

'Two months in the Himalayas, just the four of you?' No wonder she floats like a sky-going dakini.

As a child I was an adventurer and a coquette, climbing trees and turning pirouettes. As a teenager, shy and precocious. The first of my friends to have a boyfriend. The first to leave home. The first to marry. The first to divorce. And remarry. And divorce again. With my family history, I was destined to have problems with love.

Passing each other on the stairwell the next morning, we lift our heads but don't meet the other's gaze. In the meditation hall, I feel her presence behind me so fiercely I can't turn around. After the last breakfast I approach her table to exchange emails. An hour later, as I'm leaving, pack on my back, she's in the hall.

'Would you like to meet for coffee?' she asks. 'I'd like to talk more with you.'

'Tonight?'

'Where?'

'Boudhanath? The gate with the burning butter lamps. At six.'

Later, she will ask me what I thought about that day. My mind skitters. Something significant passed between us, but perhaps I'd imagined it. Which thoughts are projections, which reality? Delusion is central to my thoughts after a week of teachings.

The dakini Jadzima built Boudhanath Stupa after having four sons by four different fathers. From hours before dawn to hours after dusk, monks from various schools, elders and novices, circle the stupa. Reciting mantras, nuns from the northern border of Mongolia to the southern tip of Sumatra join its sweep. Dreadlocked trekkers, earnest seekers, and Tibetan women in *pangdens* rub shoulders and are drawn into its swirl. Maimed beggars crawl over sleeping strays. Nepalis prostrate themselves, worming forward, or turn prayer wheels. It's impossible to counteract the clockwise Diakon flow of pilgrims around the hemisphere. I walk, as I have each day.

And then she is beside me. Everything contracts to the lilting swagger of her small frame. The bright, clear eyes and that smile. The undone coconut shell buttons of her rust-orange cotton shirt; the pilled thighs of her walking trousers. We walk with the flow till she suggests coffee. Then noodles. Then more coffee. Everything is closing, but our conversation has just begun. I invite her back to my room. The last door on the balcony, next to the monastery. We sit, me on the sagging bed and she on the old armchair, under yellow bulbs, the leaves twisted about the window bars.

Around midnight she gets up to check her phone.

'It's late, I should go.' She sits back down heavily.

We look into each other's eyes.

In silence.
Beyond what's acceptable.
As if this will give us an answer.
I pat the bed beside me.
'Sit down,' I whisper.

She crosses the room and thuds onto my mattress, crossing an ankle beneath her.

My numb fingers reach up and cup her chin. Her small hands caress my face. We stay a long time, leaning into one another. And our lips touch. Softly, gently, like kittens licking. Till the feeling comes back into our fingers. And we begin to touch. Everything a jigsaw. Our clothes come off. I have no idea what to do. But she does and it's okay for me to have lost all bearings. She leads me in a dance I was never taught the steps to, perhaps never even heard the music for. Gracefully, she chaperones. Clumsily, I improvise.

It takes time before I can look at her. Really look. Indigo tattoos; a mandala on her right shoulder and a paper windmill on her upper left arm. Her breasts are ample with peachy nipples, her alabaster skin lies taut across her back, her underarms are full of copper-coloured hair. A lissom waist and round belly flare to solid hips, marble thighs, strong calves and small feet. I have no memory of the rest of that night. When the monks begin to chant and drum, around five or so, we're so wired we only manage a fitful nap, and then, in a hypnagogic buzz, we shower and head out. We sit cross-legged on Sunshine Bakery's floor, knees touching. As we finish our pancakes, she gives me directions to her end of town.

I take refuge from the rain's deluge outside Boudhanath's walls. When it lets up, I head upstream, knee-deep in water through streets turned to rivers, shoes in hand, past a drain splashing into the sky like a fountain. I shower, dress, and take a cab to a travellers' ghetto and find a hotel she half-spelled. I wait on the steps of a Thamel coffee bar, seedy guys asking if I need company or dope. Dacia takes me to a café. Then back to her ochre rooftop room, with its blue satiny curtain and windows open onto high-rises. I'm surprised by how natural it already feels in each other's arms. We fall asleep wrapped around each other.

After a breakfast of *shakshuka* and French toast we lie on the ground of the sub-tropical Botanical Gardens as squatting women replant the grass and palm-squirrels zigzag. She expresses fluent thoughts in imperfect English; her dreams of studying gender, travelling, and having children. She tells me about her childhood in India, her brothers, friends, and her lovers. Of two years in the army, a summer as a sous-chef. Her studies, what cooking means to her, coming out and the year of travel she is two-thirds through.

That afternoon, in Boudhanath, Dorje puts us in a better room at the other end of the balcony, furthest from the chanting. The next day we head to Bhaktapur in a rattling bus, ram-packed with students, workers, mothers and babies. Our breath synchronised, we manoeuvre our thighs against the other's, our gaze fixed on the view as Lauryn Hill oozes through her headphones: 'You can't hide, gonna find you... and take it slowly.' Lush undergrowth replaces Kathmandu's sprawl. A student offers to hold my backpack; he and his friends eye us, who have eyes only for each other.

Arm in arm in the streets of Dhulikel we pass a couple frying rice. Their kohl-eyed baby gurgles as we eat *pulao* on the street. We climb to a huge Buddha monument, descend into fields and later reach a guesthouse. We fall asleep in an unclean room with a leaky sink, mosquitoes, and the sour landlady's dark stories. Waking early, we descend to a thoroughly washed restaurant where cheerful men bring us hot chapatis, honey, eggs, and decent coffee.

We start in the direction an old man points toward, over maize-fields and into a glade of tree stumps. Four hours later we come in sight of the Thrangu Tashi Yangtse Monastery perched on a mountainside; rust and cream temples with golden roofs. Water dragons, peacocks, Buddhas, lotus petals, victory banners, and malas encircle the temple. We eat noodles on a balcony; a thick dark mass of cloud closes in and we dash inside as the rain pelts down. In the village below, we sit on a step, waiting for the bus.

Six days later, Dac silently walks me to the gate early in the morning. When the taxi door closes, darkness falls. At the airport, I move dumbly through passport control, no longer sharing the same language as my fellow human beings. Intimacy has made everything else slight. Back home, I tell everyone I meet I am in love. I have good friends who are kind and happy for me. Now you're a lesbian, one says. I'm in love with one woman, this particular one, I say. At a David Harrower play I watch a miller seducing the plough-woman. He stands over her, sifting a scoop of white flour onto her raised pelvis as she grinds against the plume.

Several weeks later, she flies nine or so thousand miles to visit me. On the train platform, my face burns, looking for her small frame and blonde curls. And then we're in each other's arms, hugging, kissing, laughing.

I wake before her and make breakfast. We walk along country lanes. Cycle to the sea. Skinny-dip at Jacob's Ladder. Sunbathe naked on Rousdon beach. Visit friends in East London, go to a club; sitting on my lap to kiss me, she causes a small stir. The next morning, my friend places her baby on our bed to keep an eye on; Dac cries.

We make dinner together; she sous to my chef or vice-versa, depending on the dish. She cooks unhurriedly, intent on getting the best from each ingredient, knowing when to follow, when to lead. She is the same in bed. We listen, fathoming the subtle differences and similarities between us. She is responsive and conscious in her ascent to desire; her quest becomes a journey into my own. To start I'd been confused by soft skin and tumescent curves, daunted by her voluptuous body. Now, it is as if I've found my way back. Back to this slip of a girl. This dreamy, half-person half-spirit, wise beyond her years. With rapt whimpers and sighs, she yearns deeply but holds her own. She listens with her stubby fingertips, urgent tongue, filmy nipples, wide thighs, deeply buried clitoris. She tastes of lemons, sweet and bitter; smells sour, like fresh-cut grass. She swells, slippery on my fingers. Each morning she kisses me; she tells me I might be the love of her life. We make love in the shower late in the morning. On the sitting-room floor in the middle of the day. On the beach, after swimming. At night, the blankets thrown to one side. Sometimes we take our time, pouring into one another till we come slowly. Other times we play, throwing our weight back and forth. Dac's desire comes from a place of joy. Mostly she initiates, but I'm seduced completely, falling into her world.

Her inquisitiveness galvanises mine. What was it like in the army? *They played pop all the time, it drove me crazy, so I learned to like it.* How did you end up living with your father? *My mother moved out with her boyfriend, I stayed.* What was your boyfriend like? *When I finally slept with him, he just dropped me; my mother blames him for 'turning' me.* Who was your first girlfriend? *This girl in the orphanage started on me. I fell in love with her... but she married someone else.* What was it like, walking in Ladakh? *So much time to think.* Where does your arachnophobia come from? *If I don't think of the spider, he will disappear, but... how not to think of him?* Did you enjoy what happened last night? *You are the sexiest woman in the world. I can't be this way with anyone else.*

And her blue-bolted questions.

What do Buddhists think about death? Tibetans believe it's the stopping place, *bardo*, before reincarnation. *Aren't you scared of living with me?* No. *Haven't you thought of being with a woman before?* Never. *Aren't they more interesting than men?* I never thought so. *Will you have children with me?* With you anything is possible. *Could you live in Israel?* Anywhere with you, my darling. *When I first met you, I would look at your hands, that are so beautiful, and dream that you would touch me. I never imagined... I was so nervous to speak to you.*

Intense. Precocious. Exhausting. Light-hearted yet profound. Her generosity leaks through her eyes, her smile, into her laugh. Her affection is spliced with sudden chills, her moods dark chocolate in intensity. More frequently, as time passes, she is troubled. Her imaginary spider appears only once when we are together; she wakes sobbing and I hold her tight. Swinging from self-deprecatory to giddy. 'How do you put up with me?' she cries.

'Two of one of a kind' is Dac's phrase in the last days. She's become fiercer in her love and more gentle. Our future features again; she names our hypothetical kids Kea and Tairn and calls me *lovie.*

Sometimes she makes plans to study in England. Sometimes, she considers fraught futures in Israel. Her kisses are rose-scented *malabi*, her mannerisms hard like kohlrabi. She strides like a boy, laughs like a girl, dances like a rapper. Makes love like a dakini.

'Sorry,' she will say not long after. 'I'm almost ready, but not quite.'

Narrow Neck of the Land

Camaris considers her reflection in the mirror; she brushes mascara onto her lashes, crayons kohl onto the waterline of her glassy teal eyes, deftly applies lipstick and fluffs up her dark hair. Her made-up Pierrot face gives away nothing. From the bedroom next door come stifled cries, wild laughter and racking sobs. They're berserk. In the kitchen she pulls vegetables from the fridge. Half-heartedly, she chops lantern-shaped zucchini into segments.

Children run past and out the front door, arms flailing. Ginger Augusta leads, amber-haired Clarissa a fraction behind, russet-headed Joseph, toting a tabby cat; Thomas, a wide-eyed toddler with a large henna thatch, brings up the rear. They are fleeing the pallid, myopic Olive, melon head topped with saffron candy-floss.

'Dracula, Dracula, Dracula!'

Olive trails them disconsolately, echoing their shouts, exposing a gappy grimace of incisors. She doesn't realize they are running from her – the ugly smile and something else they can't name.

Blood! The word flares in Camaris's mind before she can quell it. Camaris throws Freedom a dark look. He's been at the kitchen table, sharpening a piece of wood with his penknife all morning. His face is as pretty as hers, except for the ragged scar that runs from the bridge of his nose across his forehead. He'd stormed home from school three months ago, blood dripping down his cheek onto his school shirt.

'I almost killed them! I swear I almost did,' Freedom stuttered as

Camaris ran to fetch the first-aid box. Schoolmates had ambushed him with stones. He hasn't been back to school since. She still hasn't figured out what to do with him.

'Settle them!' she implores.

Freedom puts down his knife and stick with a sigh and lopes outside after the yowling kids. Camaris scrapes zucchini into her slow cooker and starts on the onions, naked and white, without the bronze parchment they're wrapped in at home. Everything is different here. Water that comes or doesn't. Buses that roar past, choking them with exhaust. Rain that starts without warning and falls for days, hammering so hard on the tin roof she has to speak her thoughts. She's given up home-schooling altogether. Last week, in his make-shift office, the local head teacher conceded Camaris could register Olive.

And her three youngest?

Sin papeles, imposible.

But what about the law that all kids should be in school? she ventured.

Fíjese, el problema es... He's short six classrooms. Government hand-outs have tempted parents to put their kids in school. When eight hundred arrived on the first day of term, clinging to their mother's skirts, he had nowhere to put them.

When locals ask about her kids she parrots parochial Spanish.

Fíjese, el problema es... She tries out different excuses in a reedy voice that makes them sound like lies. Sometimes she blames references, lost in the post. Then there's the longer version about the Guatemalan Embassy refusing photocopies. Occasionally she tells the one about no paper trail. These are all met with a blank stare.

Olive is too young for paperwork. They're making her do pre-school, on account of her not having Spanish. Whatever, there's no school today. Days without school are as common as the *chipi-chipi* that mists the air when the rains abate.

Freedom saunters back, dragging Olive by her ear. Camaris doesn't look up from her carrots.

'Outta control this one,' he complains.

'Sit. At the end of the table,' Camaris mutters, sweeping peelings into the bucket, 'Not a peep out of you.'

There's no will in her voice, her face feels like it's pressed against a wall, that familiar hardness of exhaustion. By the time she's unwrapping the meat, Olive has wriggled off her chair and slipped outside.

'Run, run, she's back,' the other children call. 'Dracula!'

Blood! She startles herself: did she say it out loud? She cubes the pork, hacked from the bone by a woman with arms thick as hams and hips wider than a sow's.

Bits of the foetus were still left inside, the doctor explained. He was young and good-looking. She asked him to tie her tubes while he was at it. Brent was back in Utah for a few weeks, none the wiser.

Naomi walks into the kitchen, opens her fist, and drops fresh rosemary on the table. 'Good with mutton, don't you think?'

'Mutton! How old-fashioned.'

Naomi unpacks a string bag. She puts a melon, a pineapple, a bag of flour and Mayan chocolate wrapped in brown paper on the kitchen table. 'What about brownies? Too old-school for you?'

Naomi ties her apron, washes her hands and starts sifting things into a plastic bowl. She's just a few years older; bobby-pinned curls give her that little-house-on-the-prairie look.

'And what in the world d'you s'pose...?' says Naomi as she unwraps the package. 'They said chocolate. Chocolate, shmocolate!'

Camaris glances at the disc, rough with sugar crystals, and shrugs. She doesn't try to replicate Colorado City life out here. There's a bakery in Carcha that makes sponge that the kids eat. She doesn't waste time baking, growing herbs or home-schooling like Naomi does.

'Hello, hello? Anybody home?'

The women stiffen at the man's voice.

Naomi continues to stir chocolate on the gas, so Camaris rinses her hands in the *pila* and, wiping them on her slim hips, walks to the door. Standing at the porch is a tall black man with a shaved skull. He's wearing John Lennon tea shades. Camaris's mouth smiles, but her eyes don't.

'Hello... you must be Camaris? Jerome, Eton's director.' His accent is flat, crisp and foreign. So this is who runs the Spanish school she spends three evenings a week at. Her rag-doll eyes are expressionless, her full mouth with faint lines at the corners, slack. He holds out his hand, she raises hers. A waft of aftershave hits her.

'We've not met... but I've heard good things about you from your classmates. Could we talk a minute?'

'Sure... come in.'

With the toe of her red pump, she kicks the hosepipe that snakes its way across the sludge covering the patio. The kitchen seems more dismal than when she left it, and she fixes her gaze on the jumble of vegetable tops and tails, strung with pork fat, in a pile on the plastic tablecloth. Freedom, slouched over his stake, stares at the newcomer. From outside comes the caterwaul of feral children. Naomi flickers a smile.

'Excuse me, I didn't realize you had guests,' says Jerome.

'No trouble at all.' Camaris echoes his mannered tone.

Jerome fills the doorway, arms folded behind his back. Nobody invites him to sit. Camaris picks up the knife and takes a proper look at him; she's surprised by how handsome he is. She's never had a black man in her house before.

'We're in a tight spot. The teacher we had lined up for the Montessori school had a crisis back home and left yesterday. We're looking for a full-time teacher.'

Camaris says nothing.

'It's a little different to teaching English but... the director recommended you.'

Children rush in through the front door, sucking bedlam after them. The screeching girls come first, snivelling toddlers hard-at-heel waving sticks in the air. Camaris shouts into the vacuum they leave: 'Sticks at the door. Kids?'

'They're yours?'

'Freedom, Augusta, Olive, and Thomas are. Clarissa and Joseph belong to Naomi. My twins are out some place.' It's Jerome's turn to be astonished.

'How old are you?'

'Thirty-three.' Camaris stifles a smile.

'Hard to believe! And all ginger...?'

Camaris flashes a look at Naomi. 'They're cousins.'

'You two are sisters?'

'Sort of.'

'Seems your hands are full.'

'And I have no qualifications,' Camaris admits.

'Who does, in Guatemala?'

'Well, in that case if you're serious, I'd love to.'

Jerome feels Naomi frown.

'It's short notice – we'd need you to start a week today. Of course you'll get training.'

'Sure.' Camaris's tone is reckless.

'Perfect. Which part of the States do you come from?' Jerome asks.

'From the Arizona–Utah border. You?'

'I'm British.'

'You live in Coban?' Camaris doesn't hide her curiosity.

'In the City. I have another school there and a project in the dump.'

'What sort of project?' Naomi's voice is tight.

'A school.'

'In the dump?'

'With *guajero* kids that sort rubbish and resell it. The *relleno* is a city in itself.' Jerome glances at his watch: 'Gosh! Come into the office this afternoon, Camaris, to run over everything.'

Camaris nods and sees him to the door.

The staffroom is a converted dining room in what was one of the prettiest colonial homes in Coban. Set around a courtyard with a stone fountain, the sun streams in through the open windows onto the tiled floor. When Jerome walks in, the following Monday, Camaris looks up from her desk, cheeks streaked with mascara and tears.

'Gosh! Sorry. Would you like to talk?'

'I'm not sure there's anything to say.'

'That bad, eh?' Jerome sits on the desk, beside her.

'Yes. No. It's a great school. I like the Montessori thing and the kids are different from village kids. It's just me.'

'I doubt that.' His hand rests gently between her shoulder blades. It surprises her how good it feels. 'You seem quite serene to me.'

'Or sedated?' It slips out.

'These kids are spoiled. Their maids pamper them; their parents never say no. Montessori is diametrically opposed to their culture. But never mind who you're teaching, it's always tough to start. I gave notice on my first day.'

She smiles. His hand is back in his pocket now, but his palm's igneous imprint remains.

'No, really, I did. Swore I'd do anything else. Wash floors, wait tables, shine shoes. Anything. Then I remembered my mother had done all that to send me to university. And my boss told me I had to finish the term. So I stuck it out...'

'I never went to university.'

'Not such a bad thing.'

'I was raised on a settlement.'

'What kind?'

She hesitates, waiting to see which version will occur to her. 'Mormon Fundamentalist; Church of Latter-Day Saints.'

The silence is dense.

'How do you feel about having a boss with the mark of Cain on his brow?'

'We don't believe in that anymore,' she answers, deadpan. 'You know about us?'

'Know thyself, know thy enemy.'

'That's in the Bible?'

'Sun Tzu. So that's why you've so many kids. Your sister has a bunch too?'

'Naomi? Seven.'

She doesn't take her eyes off the knot of wood in the desk.

Camaris grows into her job. The stuff she does with her own children is taken for granted: here, she's appreciated. Jerome rarely visits Coban, but she thinks about him. Then, there's a staff party. She visits the *temazcal* in San Cristobal and sweats her skin bright and shiny.

She washes her hair and puts on a light cotton blouse that slips up over her belly-button.

She's told Brent it's a work thing. A religious historian, Brent pays little attention to the present, nor much, she feels, to the past. He devotes himself to proving Guatemala is the promised land of The Book. Once, she overheard Freedom murmuring, under his breath, 'Like elephants,' while Brent was discussing his evidence with a colleague. When Camaris threw him a look, Freedom mumbled, 'Things in The Book, like elephants, ain't in Carcha.'

Crammed onto and around the sofa, the kids are an eight-headed pyjamaed beast watching a bootleg of *The Princess and the Frog*. Camaris's eldest kids, the twins, sit at the kitchen table feigning boredom. Fear of their father keeps them here, along with a conviction that their call to serve will come any day now. Camaris says a quick goodbye then revs into the night and onto an empty road. Since she got married, she's never gone out like this before, alone after dark.

The bar is perched like a tree-house, in an attic, up spiral stairs. The rest of the teachers are already there. She sits at the bar by herself. The wall poster of a curvy, bikinied girl covered in glistening drops of water prompts her to order a Gallo. A middle-aged Ladino starts making conversation. After an hour he doesn't know she's a Mormon, has six kids and that she isn't enjoying talking to him. He buys her a second and third beer. He's just admitting he's a notary public rather than a real lawyer when Jerome arrives. Jerome stops to speak to the rest of his staff before he makes it over, saving her from a fourth bottle.

'Just in time,' she sighs. The notary is already sidling up to another woman further down the bar.

'So how's the family?' His hand comes to rest on her shoulder and stays there. She thinks of her brothers holding down a steer as her uncle applied the firebrand.

'Fine, I guess.'

'You got a babysitter tonight?'

'Naomi.'

'Your sister?' When his hand falls to the bar, she wishes it hadn't.

'She's not... she's my husband's first wife.'

Camaris searches his face for a reaction, but there's none.

'Are you his only wives?'

'He has three.'

'Like an African chief,' he smiles.

'We're best friends. It's not how you think. If it weren't for Naomi, I'd have gone crazy years ago. We've known each other since we were kids. What about you, Jerome? Are you married?'

'No, I almost was. But no. Past my sell-by date for that. I like my freedom too much: women sniff it a mile off.'

'But you seem so settled with Eton and the dump project.'

'Married to my work. I can stay at my computer till midnight, sleep in all day Sunday, party on Friday. Whatever. And I have the illusion of being able to choose. Whereas you, what happens if you want out?'

'Out?'

'Of the brotherhood?'

'I don't know... blood atonement.'

'Sounds bad.'

'Better than hell-fire.'

'Does the blood thing... that still happens?'

'Officially, no. But...'

'Do you want to leave?'

'Everyone I know is Mormon. Well, except you guys from Eton and the folk in my village.'

'How are you finding Eton?'

'Better than at the start. I need to get out of the house. I love my kids, don't get me wrong, but I'm doing them more harm than good. The twins are beyond me. The youngest are suffering from a disorder; Olive has fits... outsiders call it Polygamist's Downs.'

Another splash of air hits Jerome's blurred image: achondroplastic skulls and wide-set eyes. Camaris finds comfort in the stillness of his face. 'Our community has its problems,' she sighs.

'Why did you leave Utah?'

'Arizona. Brent's convinced Guatemala is the narrow neck of land promised in The Book. And... our community broke up when they put our prophet behind bars.'

'Wasn't it Warren something or other? For rape?'

'Warren Jeffs; for arranging illegal marriages with minors. The lost boys made some other charges.'

'And the lost boys are – friends of Peter Pan?'

'Young guys the elders kick out. My cousin was one. They drove him a few hours out of town and dumped him with nothing but the shirt on his back.'

'Why?'

'Because he hung out with a girl earmarked for an elder. Every man has three wives, but there aren't enough to go around. They have to fix the math.'

'Gosh, that's frightening,' Jerome murmurs.

'Must be the Gallos talking. You know what I discovered lately? People out there, I mean out here, in the rest of the world, are okay.'

When school breaks up in October, Camaris tells Jerome there's a good chance she'll be moving to Utah. Her husband's getting tenure at Brigham Young University, she says. She'll know more in a few weeks. But Jerome hears nothing further from her.

In early January, before school opens, a private investigator from the City shows up at the administrator's office. He tells her Brent hired him: Camaris has gone missing. He asks questions: 'When did you last see her? Did she seem depressed? Do you think she was having an affair?'

The administrator knows very little about Camaris. She figures Jerome might know more, but doesn't mention that. When the PI leaves, she phones Jerome. He cancels the rest of his meetings and drives to Carcha. On the drive, he reflects. Five years in Guate and he's only just beginning to plumb its depths. What began as exotic or passed unnoticed has grown menacing. Last week, one of Eton's teachers was accused of abusing a student. She'd made the mistake of dating the student's brother. The family belonged to one of Coban's foremost cartels. Despite her innocence, Jerome had to ask her to leave. For her own safety. And the school's survival.

He hears the children's screams as he pulls into the drive. There's a pick-up on the patio filled with crates. He calls from the yard. The hose still lies snaked across the patio, the mud dry and cracked. Naomi appears, mouth drawn, from the gloom. She folds her arms over her chest.

'Hello, it's Jerome... Camaris's boss from Eton.'

'I remember.'

Augusta and Clarissa emerge from the darkness, faces paler and more pinched. A snotty-nosed Olive follows, trailing a comforter behind her, cheeks streaked with dirt.

'I heard about Camaris... I wondered if I could do anything.'

'What did you have in mind, Mister Jerome?'

'I'm so sorry we couldn't help Camaris resolve whatever it was that led her to leave. She's a lovely person and a great teacher.'

Jerome is talking for the sake of the children. Particularly to Augusta with her heart-shaped face, full cheeks and flame of hair. Now he sees that, despite her colouring, she takes after her mother, with those ice-blue eyes that betray nothing.

'I doubt she left of her own accord.' Naomi's ambiguity is chilling. After a moment, she turns and shoos the girls back into the house. When she turns back, Jerome thinks she's going to confide in him.

'Goodbye Mister Jerome,' she says simply and goes back inside.

On the drive back to Coban, Jerome tries to put the fragments together. Maybe he planted a seed that germinated Camaris's get-away plan. Guatemala is the perfect place to reinvent yourself. Camaris could pop up a few hundred miles away, start over, never be heard of again. But there's something about the fairy-tale ending that ignores the sinister, tenebrous side to this lawless state, that ignores Camaris's fragility.

Two days later, Jerome gets a call from the chief officer in Zone Three. A woman's naked body has been found in the dump. It came in on a rubbish truck from Zone Fourteen near the airport, tied with string into the foetal position, wrapped in newspaper, and stuffed in a large Hessian coffee sack with 'Dieseldorff', a Cobanero roaster, stamped across it.

'The boys at the morgue say she was cute, a *gringa*, mid-thirties, no ID. Nobody seems to be looking for her.'

Jerome recalls Camaris's aquamarine eyes. And the children's. He scrolls down his contacts to Güicho Sierra, the detective that spoke to the school's administrator. Then he puts the phone down deliberately and goes to his window. He watches the children playing in Eton's garden, waiting to be collected. They are Coban's wealthiest – you can almost see the silver spoons sticking out of their mouths. Over the years he's heard stories. Of parents tied up in their own front rooms while thieves clean out their apartment. Of mothers at gunpoint, emptying purses at stoplights. Fathers who've got on the wrong side of *narcos* and disappeared overnight. Siblings held hostage till harried parents pay up.

Jerome rubs his face with his palms. He's burned out. He could be fighting social injustice in South London rather than staying here. Brent and his family will be in Utah by now. Besides, Detective Sierra, hired by Brent, would never turn his client in. And what good would a conviction do anyway?

He remembers Camaris's question, 'Or sedated?' and asks it of himself.

Dorf and the Daisies

'The sun shone, having no alternative, on the nothing new.'
– Samuel Beckett, *Murphy*

It's obscene the way she cleaned up. It was a mess. I was a mess. Covered, I was. And she came and, I swear to God, when she finished, there was nothing left. All traces were gone. I kept saying to her, 'Wait a minute, slow down there, I want them to know—to see—the evidence.' But she didn't take any notice. I called out to Patroclus in the house opposite, breathless: 'Quickly! Come quickly!'

But when Patraki arrived, nothing was left. Nothing. I've tried. God knows I've tried. Once, I wrapped the turd up, oh so carefully, folding the edges of the handkerchief over it, and put it in one of those plastic Tupperwares Ethel loves so much. I hid it. Over there, in the corner, behind the bed. But when I woke up in the morning, it had gone. Not a remnant. Who the hell are you? I recognize you. It was you who sent me the Romeo and Juliet cigar. And the monk's bag.

*They snap and crackle the whole year through. Doris Day never tires of
them and neither will you.*

They keep moving my things, the bastards. There's a whole team of
them. There's what's-her-name from Georgia and the other one who
speaks a few words of English. Sometimes there's a third one. Maybe
that's my wife. I mean my ex-wife. They keep rearranging my stuff.
But once things have been shifted, they are no longer the same. Natia,
or whoever the hell it is, puts this thing here over there, and that thing
there over yonder. Till I can't find them anymore. Things that have
significance for me. Once they're moved, they don't have the same
meaning. Things like the handle of my knife. The Havana cigar my
daughter sent me for my birthday. Or the monk's bag from Sri Lanka.
They've disappeared. God knows where the hell they've gone. My
pipes, for example – if you move them, they change somehow. I know
it sounds like I'm a dingbat, but that's not it. Not easy, getting old,
you know. But what are the options? Maybe George Eastman got it
right. One bullet in the heart and his problems were over; his suicide
note said, 'My work is done. Why wait?' Is my work done? What was
my work? I spent too long trying to work it out... and ended up being
a lousy market researcher, to put bread on the table.

I was drafted before I was even shaving; didn't know my ass from
page eight. I was in Tinian, the island. You've heard of it, right?
Nothing but a hangar, a runway, and cane fields. Location of the
Great Marianas Turkey Shoot, when it all started to go balls up for the
Japs and they lost four hundred and twenty-nine planes. From there,
we sent Little Boy and Fat Man, along with the Greeting to the
Emperor at 8:15 on a Wednesday morning. Necessary Evil, my ass.
Cavafy was right: we invent the bloody barbarians. One day they are
Nazis, the next they are Japs, then Koreans, Vietnamese, Iraqis,
Afghans – and that's just in my lifetime. Who will be next? Let me
hazard a guess: China or Russia. I saw *banzai,* not the thousands that
jumped into Saipan's shark-infested waters or bashed their babies'
brains out against rocks, but enough to haunt me for the rest of my
life. And hundreds of B-29s dropping napalm. There was this one day,
fuck me sideways, when there was just me. I had to fight my way out.
I shot three Japanese soldiers. Three. Then I cut the tapes of their

engraved brass ID tags and gave them to my officer like trophies. Tell me, somebody, how are you supposed to stay sane after that?

Hey Betty Boop! Say, what's the scoop?
Your smile looks better than brand, brand new.
My teeth aren't new, but my toothpaste is.
New Mintodent! Get with it, Daddy-O.

When I was discharged, I bought a ticket to Alaska. That was the farthest place I could imagine. Can't remember what the hell we did. Salmon fishing? That was it – Barney, Johnnie, and I were going to hit the big time catching fish! I ran into a brown mother bear that weighed over three hundred pounds. She was defending her cubs; she reared up on her hind legs and came for me. I will never forget those claws. I shot her straight between the eyes. It was her or me. I've killed three Japanese soldiers and a grizzly bear. Another time, I was walking in the snow with this girl I was seeing... and I started to get frostbite. I couldn't feel my nose. She grabbed a handful of snow and rubbed it on my face. A layer of nose-shaped skin came off in her hand. I came home at Christmas when my mother fell ill. She was born on a plantation in the Deep South. When she eloped with my father to New York, she was excommunicated. My father died. I grew up in Pop's house. My stepfather, Dud, an engineer at Eastman Kodak, was around all the time, but it was just me and my mother really. Who the hell are you, anyway?

I met this redhead in Australia; we got engaged. I promised to marry her, but my mother had a heart attack, and I went home. Pops was dead already. My mother was still working as a secretary at Kodak. She was born in Rochester, grew up there... and never left. No imagination. We lived on rat's ass and handouts. Not a pot to piss in, nor a window to throw it out of. Ethel and I were in Quebec... about to set sail for Europe. I called from the port to say goodbye to her. Found out she was dying of pneumonia. I went home. Amongst my mother's things I found this newspaper cutting after she died. Carefully kept, torn and folded into itself, a yellowed article about a fireman called Robert – a court order to pay child support to a previous wife. This is all I know about my father. Yet I know him. Am afflicted by his legacy. He married again and had three more children. I've got half-brothers or -sisters knocking around someplace. Dead by now, perhaps.

When I was thirteen, I was messing with a Lincoln, off Tacoma. Of course, I'd never driven. It was on an incline, and the damn thing coasted straight down into some old lady's yard. Glided straight through her living room's glass doors. Lucky she wasn't in the living room at the time. Wasn't my car either. Another time, I spent the night in Rochester's science museum. It was a dare to sleep beneath the woolly mammoth skeleton. I was scared shitless and sat wide awake all night in the museum foyer on a wooden bench. On Saturdays, we went to picture shows with newsreels, serialized cartoons like *Captain Marvel*, and movies like *Tarzan, the Ape Man*, *Captains Courageous*, or *Little Orphan Annie*. I hung out with my buddies, smoked woodies.

Look, here's the new Plasterplast that adheres every time.
Better than any other bandage. The proof?
Take an apple at room temperature. Touch the apple with any other
brand of bandage, brand X, Y or Z. None stick. But a Plasterplast plastic
strip with new super-stick sticks every time.

Rochester was the armpit of the world. A little nowhere place, where nothing happened, with nobody of any interest whatsoever in it. The only person of note was George Eastman. Who developed Kodak, the first commercial film-roll camera. He opened a school of music and a theatre the year I was born. When they ran auditions at my school, turned out I had perfect pitch, so I got free violin lessons and joined the orchestra and choir. I soloed tenor on local radio and was chosen to sing at the New York World's Fair. Boy, was that exciting! The World's Fair was put together on twelve hundred acres of reclaimed land in Queens, where Fishhooks McCarthy had dumped the city's incinerated garbage. It was a rat-infested, mosquito-breeding valley of ash till a few businessmen came up with an international event: Dawn of a New Day. The cataclysmic mote in their vision was the Second World War. They had to cancel the Navy fleet, otherwise distracted in the South China Sea. But never mind!

There was this brand-new thing called TV. A thousand people across New York watched Roosevelt in black and white on two hundred sets. View-Masters made an appearance for the first time, electric typewriters and calculators. What a miracle! There was even a time capsule they buried with a Mickey Mouse watch, a Gillette razor, a Kewpie doll, a pack of Camels, and change for a dollar. What use they thought these items might be to humanity in the future, God only knows.

But the highlight for me was the pavilions. I discovered I was pig-ignorant and, come hell or high water, I would see the world. The pavilions were physical embodiments of how foreign governments wanted their countries to be seen by Americans. The Greek Pavilion was plastered with Nelly's idyllic collages, a photographer in cahoots with the Fascist, Metaxas. The Japanese Pavilion's motto was of eternal peace between itself and America, even as we geared up for war. I saw genuine European art for the first time ever – Da Vinci, Michelangelo, and Rembrandt. A theater of Time and Space. And wandered through *Bring 'Em Back Alive*, Frank Buck's Jungleland with an orangutan, six hundred monkeys, snakes, and a trio of elephants. There were even a dozen different girlie shows, from the artsy-fartsy Dalí's *Dream of Venus* to the *Hot Mikado* and *Billy Rose's Aquacade*. When the Bendix Lama Temple failed to draw crowds, they introduced dancing girls to pull in the punters.

Well, thanks for coming by. I really appreciate it. Call again when you can.

I am alone. Worried. I had an argument on the telephone with my son this morning. He's short-tempered these days. I need so little – a bed, one shelf to put my things, a small room at the back of his coach house. I could visit old friends and maybe go for a drive to the Vienna Woods, for old times' sake. But he's gone all funny. Can't be done, he says. Something about his old lady forbidding me, since the troubles. I don't know what he's referring to. Anyway, up yours, Charlie. Your timing is impeccable, kid. I just put yoghurt in my mouth. Yesterday, you called just as I finished eating yoghurt. Funny that. There's less of a pain in the ass or more of a pain in the ass. There's no getting better. Not wiser, just sadder.

When I was in the army, there was this guy called René Partons (we pronounced it 'Reeny Parthoons', as we didn't know the damn difference). Anyhow, Reeny never washed. I mean never. The rest of us would shit, shower, and shave every day, whether we needed it or not. But not Reeny. Once in a blue moon, Reeny'd go to the sink, so help me God, dip his pinkies under the cold faucet, and smooth down his eyebrows. His socks were green, and he wore the same pair of polka-dot skivvies come rain or shine. Rancid he was. The barracks couldn't stand the stink, so one morning we hauled him off to the showers, peeled off his uniform like skin off a banana. We pushed him bare-ass naked under the showerhead, lathered soap on with a brush, scrubbed him down, rinsed him, and threw him a towel. My dear, could you pass me those pipe cleaners?

Hey guys, how would you like to be the ginchiest in your fat city and own a nifty Dean Martin whistle ring, with its own secret tune?

India. Now that was something different. I was there when they shot Mahatma Gandhi. India was exciting back then. Not like now, where the world is all one huge shopping mall and everyone eats the same burgers and wears the same jeans. Back then, people were real individuals. When I came back, I met Ethel, on a three-day voyage to Italy. We wrote love letters. She wanted to get married. Could have been anyone; I just happened to show up at the right moment. What a comedy.

I made that journey overland. Through Syria, Iran, Afghanistan, and Pakistan. I remember these guys sitting on a truck of figs, white jellabiyas tucked up around their waists, no skivvies, balls hanging out; couldn't tell the difference between their balls and the figs. I got dysentery in Hyderabad; passed out cold in the street. A stranger picked me up and took me back to his house. He and his wife kept me for a couple of weeks, feeding me, making me tea, nursing me back to health. Fine, honourable people who saved my life. Finally, I made it back to Australia. The redhead wasn't interested anymore. The redhead died. The redhead was a lesbian. The redhead married someone else. Who gives a fiddler's fart?

Yesterday, I saw it outside in the yard. The box. It was long, sanded smooth, dark wood. Waiting for me. All of it. Empty. I know it's all in my mind… but try telling my mind that. 'Bid us sigh on from day to day,' as Beckett would say. When I see it, it's real. Besnik came by today, the first time in six months. He cleaned my pipe. I'm having a smoke, damn right. Where the hell did my pipe cleaners go? I told Besnik about the box.

Your grandmother, or your mother, wanted to get married. So we did. Only, her family! Jesus Christ. They were bizarre. Really peculiar. Always asking you your opinion or telling you theirs. Saying things like, 'Chrissie wants to know what you think about such-and-such.' Frightening, for crying out loud. As tight-assed as bulls in fly season. Your mother thought frozen smiles and perpetual consternation were perfectly normal. She missed them when we lived in Vienna. We've lived more than fifty years abroad and she still refers to New Hampshire as 'home'. Who are you, again? You think I'm soft as a grape. Well, guess what? I'm softer.

Skip the onion, skip the lettuce, special requests don't upset us. All we want is for you to dig it, your way.

They're doing the three-prong thing. Which is? I don't know. The first one happened. Doctor What's-His-Ass made all the arrangements. It's an injection. You swallow it. You stick it under your pillow, under your armpit. And then you're a new man. No examination. It's like putting something on the table, that's how physically involving it is. They stick it on your back. Up your ass. It's just a pill; so harmless! The doctor loves it. I had it in my mouth for a while, then I changed my mind. Wanted to check it out. But today I was up for it. Now, I'll eat more steak. I'll let you know if anything drops off. I'll send you a copy. Or a piece. Bye, bye, nice talking to you.

Ethel dated a whole raft of men at Radcliffe. There was John, the doctor; he was a good guy. Ethel wanted to marry him, but her father forbade it, as they were distant cousins. Then she went out with a Harvard medical student. But his parents told him to focus on his studies. So, he gave her up. Christ, what a soap opera! Then she dated Dyer, who was studying medicine. That was what people did in those days. Dated. She left Dyer behind when she came to Athens to work as a teacher. He was still writing her letters when we met. He didn't know what hit him when he got the news. Marrying a foreigner? But it was her old man who went fucking nuts; he wrote to the Greek consul, asking them to intervene. Imagine that. Dyer hooked up with a nurse and went to live in California. Years later, they found his body on a beach in the Bay Area; Doc Dyer strangled by a junkie who he'd refused drugs to, poor bastard.

Forty years in market research, up and down the UK, holding qualitative research sessions to find out what dish detergent Newcastle's housewives preferred or which luxury car a Mancunian civil servant aspired to buy. You know those concentric circles on the Nurofen packets? That was my idea, borrowed from Tantric mandalas. Just looking at the packet made you feel better; you could throw away the Ibuprofen! I pioneered market research in England. They'd never heard of it before. The *Financial Times* interviewed me – a two-page spread with a sketched portrait! Hot stuff. 'He had turned, little by little, a disturbance into words, he had made a pillow of old words, for his head.' Sam was a genius!

If you don't give your man 117 Cologne, I will. If your man lives for the thrill, give him 117. The license to kill... women.

Then I met Nina. You'd been born, and before that, your brother, and before that, your other brother. I had the whole kit and caboodle: a wife, three kids, and a marketing job. The full comedy. I was working in the States, some research for someone or other. You know, we have these hearts and they love people. When I met your mother, my heart went *bleep* and I carried her in my heart. Then we had each of your brothers and my heart went *bleep*, and then *bleep* and they were in it. You came along and *bleep*, another person in the soup. And then Nina, one more *bleep*.

Ethel and I were sitting there, once, in this restaurant; she was wearing a cap over her cropped hair, all these keys around her waist.

And she laid into me: she wasn't going to put up with this, or with that, or the other. Men should do this, or that, or something else. That she wasn't having it anymore. She got up and stormed out. This fellow, sitting at a table nearby, came over and put half a bottle of wine on the table and said, 'Excuse me, I know it's not any of my business, but I overheard... and you might need this.'

This puncture needs a real man, but when there's no man to be found, Best Era should be. Why? Because Best Era tyres have a tyre within a tyre. Best Era never gets a flat. Give the dame a chance, buy her Best Era.

We did our Grand Tour of Europe and ended up in Vienna. I wasn't keen on the idea – Austrians being the 'enemy' and all that. But we got off the train at Grinzing by mistake. The next day I met this guy, Charles, who explained I could register at the university as a GI and get a grant. So, I studied philosophy. I studied philology. No, psychiatry. I wrote a thesis on D. H. Lawrence. And we stayed at Charles's Tel Aviv apartment the year after you were born. Your mother wanted to go up Masada, whose nine hundred and sixty inhabitants committed suicide when the Romans laid siege to it. So, we took a taxi through the desert, though it was hotter than a festering fox. It was midday, and the only way up was by camel. The driver said it was too hot for a baby, so we left you with him. Five hours with a stranger. You were still there when we got back. Well... we think it was you...

Our dearest friends in Vienna were Hedy and Otto, good souls. She was this huge brick shithouse of hausfrau and Otto, this wiry man. They were on the bones of their ass, even poorer than we were, but Hedy had a heart big enough for all of Vienna and then some. Otto was a little less kind; he used to say, 'I was born a Nazi, I've been a Nazi all my life, and I will die a Nazi.' Frau Markgraf washed the boys' diapers, took them for walks in the cemetery, and cooked them dumplings. She pumped their legs every afternoon at 4:15 precisely to make them shit. Then I went to India, where they shot Gandhi. It was all so new and exciting to see people doing things differently. I met this redhead in Australia. But I guess things didn't work out. At any rate, she married someone else. The redhead was a lesbian. *Tempus fugit*. Acch. Time flies. Fruit flies.

> *Nuts! Oh crazy nuts! Badboy's take them, and they plunge them in chocolate. Nuts!*

God! What is it all about? I've lived all these years and I still have no idea. Do you think they ask after me? I mean, do you think they ever think about me? My son could make a room light up. I tried to help him, God knows. But he didn't understand. It was all toenail fungus... He said I interfered with his daughter. And so we became enemies. Most peculiar. I had three children, for Christ's sake! Three. Acchhh. You're one of them. You turned out okay; the brains of the eldest, the charm of the second, and a goodness of heart all your own. Third time lucky, champ. Speak to you later.

The first one showed up one day, sat there on that sofa. He brought me a brand-new jacket, new trousers, and shoes. I had to put them on. I couldn't understand why. Me, of all people, who's never given a shit about clothes. Why would it matter? All these things we are supposed to do nowadays. So tiresome. Drink bottled water or else. Eat fruit. Every day, a banana! Fuck me! I never ate a banana before, why now, when I need it least? And the pills. Just to prolong this pointlessness. Most ridiculous is washing my feet. My feet! I never go anywhere. They're my feet, for God's sake. My ass, I could understand; I could hang it out the window and advertise. But my feet? What a comedy! Shit, I need to take a leak.

I go to the window: there's nothing to see. It looked like that yesterday, it looks like that today, and it will look like that tomorrow. I look out at that wall, over there. Same as it always was. Sparrows chirp every so often. What makes you think they're happy? Perhaps they're chirping in pain. Chirping their little agonies out. Children play there. They shout, 'Dorf, Dorf, we love you, Dorf. We don't want you die. Even though you will. Goodbye, Dorf! We'll miss you.' So, watch out; if anything happens, don't forget what I told you. When you find the body, call the police and let them know, okay? You were alright, but you turned out just like your mother. Or was it your grandmother? Or is that me who's just like my grandmother? Who cares?

I hear them singing. All the women come and hang their hats there on that piece of furniture, and then they go away again. Most peculiar. I wonder if they'll come back. And the back window? I look out of that less. I look at my feet and wonder what the fuck for. Cracking ice for grandfather's piles. Ninety. Let me give you some advice, blossom: don't bother. Now, where'd my matches go?

Just remember. It's the pleasing mildness of a Buffalo that's just as satisfying to a doctor as it is to us. More smart guys smoke Buffalos than any other cigar.

They want me to eat more yoghurts with vitamins. My girlfriend, the blonde from Georgia who's built like a tank, brings them to me for breakfast. And keeps giving me water to drink. There's a whole bevy of them wanting to make conversation. Nag, nag, nag. I wish to hell they would leave me alone. Who needs it? Really. Life is too short. And blood tests. What do they do with all that blood? They've been taking it since I was in the army. What for? So, when it happens, they know exactly why. And the latest news is a fire in my bed. A fire in my head. All I want is to warm these bones like Sam McGee. I've lived ninety fucking years, and I don't have a clue. I just want to get out of here now. My needs are minimal. 'I don't know why I told this story; I could just as well have told another. Perhaps some other time I'll be able to tell another.' Samuel was right, you know – we're all bloody alike.

I'd like to teach the guys to dance in synchronicity.
. I'd like to buy the guys some Fizz and keep them company. It's the real deal.

If I piss myself, it might be several hours before anyone comes, which means lying in it. Something is vaguely troubling me, but I can't recall what. To do with my son. Was he here? Or was that part of the dream? Perhaps that's why it's so fucking dark and so damn quiet. Where did they all go? And smoky... wasn't me, pal, though I wish to hell it was. So much smoke and no tobacco. Let's swing my feet off the mattress and lever off the bed.

I can breathe out okay.

In is another matter.

Now is the time, now is the prime time, now is the prime time of our lives. Never be miffed, 'coz life is a gift. Never feel down... and please stick around...

Part Two
Suffering

Ku

Birth, death, old age, and illness are forms of suffering.
Attachment and aversion cause suffering.
The everyday from an enlightened perspective is free of suffering.

How to Preserve a Butterfly

(to Keep it Bright and Beautiful Forever)

1. After netting a butterfly, the best way to kill it is to carefully hold the specimen between your thumb and forefinger. Gently squeeze the thorax; the wings should separate slightly. To prevent it from drying out, a relaxing chamber can be made from a jar with a damp piece of paper inside.

A box of glass Christmas balls.

Circa second half of the 1960s, glass spheres dusted with sandpaper frost, a segment sliced away to reveal their snowflake cores.

Eight gold and red spidery foil fronds that tremble.

Three green crêpe-paper honeycomb bells.

An orange, manic-eyed, Lucite Bambi manacled to twin miniature hinds.

Five balls covered in satin thread: three pine-green, one holly-red, one snow-white.

A polystyrene cardinal with real crimson feathers.

A green wire of plastic flowers that won't light if a single bulb blows.

One midnight-blue tree-topper, resembling a flagpole spear, still in its paper box, labelled 'The Unbreakable Kind'.

The foil tree had been stored in the attic for decades but, like my butterfly collection, must have been thrown out. A real tree would have dropped its needles onto the moss-green wall-to-wall carpet, so we had a fake one. Despite our parents' oft-avowed atheism, Norman and Nina set great store on the arrival of cards, arranged on the mantlepiece over the gas fire between the book alcoves. Drinks in the Square were the big event of December. I prefer lepidoptera over chattering people. My sister, the Termagant (née Ness), nicknamed me Butterfly-Boy, but the pressies were Meccano until I could insist on a microscope or nets.

2. From the top, insert a pin through the centre of the thorax. Affix the specimen by pinioning it onto the spreading board's centre groove and pushing the pin ½" deep. Slide the butterfly up or down the pin until the bottom of the wings are even with the top surface of the board (Figure 4).

One wooden chest of Meccano.

The world's mechanical wonders in your home. The set, bought the year I was born, with black-and-white instructions, was supplemented by later versions in aluminium, zinc, and plastic, accompanied by colour manuals. Sets nine and ten appeared beneath the tree with my name on them, but they were really for Norman. We called our parents Norman and Nina: it was our mother's idea, 'to dissolve barriers'. Everything about Norman, a Yorkshireman, said, 'Stay calm and keep your blockades firmly in place.' *Now Nate, what about the Eiffel Tower?* Staunchly Labour, Norman never forgave Nina for voting for Thatcher. He blamed the Tories when Airfix gave its eight hundred workers forty minutes' notice and shut its factory gates. Meccano's closure marked the demise of the Baby Boomers and rise of Generation X. But at least I got nets that Christmas.

A lanky teenager, with down on my lip, I transferred my obsession with butterflies to girls. Kim, Rhonda, and Cindy; I couldn't think of anything else. The Termagant's once-androgynous friends teased with their kohl-eyed looks and swelling cambers. Around me, they giggled, forgetting what it was they wanted to say. Norman continued to spend evenings prone on the kitchen floor, building Meccano bridges to nowhere.

3. Cut several strips of wax, tracing, or plain white paper about 1½" wide and 6" long. You will use these strips to hold the wings in place and keep them from curling as they dry.

My LP collection and the Ferguson Radiogram.

The turntable stood in the sitting room. When friends came over, Nina discreetly disappeared into the basement kitchen. Not the Termagant or her friends. Genesis. Tangerine Dream. Pink Floyd. Black Sabbath. Deep Purple. Led Zeppelin. Steve Hackett. Fleetwood Mac. Nina snuck me extra pocket money for gigs at the Hammersmith Palais. We shook our greasy locks and punched our fists in the air. Later, Nina bought me a Schneider portable for my room so I could return her discretion, leaving her and my geography teacher nestling on the sofa with a bottle of Mateus Rosé.

Norman stayed later and later at the office. He installed a folding bed behind a filing cabinet and camped, moving there permanently when Nina's new flame showed up. She loaned him money which she didn't have and let him stay over. If Norman minded, he never let on. *I know, Nate, a road surfacer!* My focus briefly shifted from Cindy to Nina's lover. For teasingly brief moments, he reciprocated.

4. Gently insert a sharp pin between the veins on the front edge of the left forewing and pull it into place. Place a strip of paper over the left wing as shown in Figure 5 and insert pins around the forewings to secure them.

Nina's Goblin Teasmade.

Norman would never have addressed something as vexing as

privacy. But Nina persuaded him to build a partition to divide their kids' bedroom; cheap-as-chips, industrial grade hardboard over a frame. The Termagant could still hear everything when her mates slept in my room. She kept the Teasmade. Which was when she earned her nickname, the Termagant, that delicious Shakespearian slur.

The Teasmade, Nina's since childhood, was an encoded talisman from mother to daughter. Despite my resembling Nina more, their bond was tighter. Meccano was Norman's talisman. Even though I'd lost interest. Even though I was sleeping with my sister's best friend. Even though I was smoking dope. *What about a cargo ship, Nathaniel?* Even when Nina went abroad (something Norman had never done) with us. Without him. Or was having an affair. Even when she was diagnosed with cancer. Or losing her wispy blond curls. And the breast that lay over her heart. Even when she began to die. Was dying. Had died.

5. Now do the same with the hindwings. Use a pin inserted at the vein at the base of the hind-wing or use spade-tipped forceps to properly position the hindwings. Affix pins around each hindwing to hold them in place (Figure 6).

Nina's charcoal of me on cotton rag.

Running, butterfly net aloft, sketched one summer in Wales. The fibres impregnated with the scent of wildflowers and grasses, the violent purple of foxgloves and ochre of Welsh poppies, the throb of bees and glimmer of dragonfly gauze. Nina curled over her sketchbook, sunshine smothering us. Norman reading, a shadow in the cottage gloom. Not speaking to her. Not to us. Did he have an internal dialogue? What would it have sounded like? Did he stutter and raise his imperious dark eyebrows? Would it have all made sense in his head? *Let's save for the locomotive next, Nathaniel.*

We could only guess at the Norman narrative. Of raising himself up by his bootstraps. Constructing Meccano high-rises alone in his bedroom, a precursor to studying engineering. Of the first university degree in his family. Courting the tiny artist with sparrow-song for a voice. Moving down south. Fathering superfluous children; Norman just needed Nina. Setting up the Clerkenwell partnership. The distance settling in. The differences. Stop. The loneliness. *What about the twin-cylinder motorcycle engine, Nathaniel? Nate, are you listening?* He had lost Nina. It wasn't supposed to be like this. Stop. The kids had turned against him. Stop. Why didn't he do something? Speak up? Tell her how much he loved her. Or hated her. Something. She was dying, for fuck's sake. Stop.

6. Cross two pins over each other to set the antennae in a "V" position. Also insert two crossed pins to hold the end of the butterfly's body in up in its natural position if necessary (Figure 7).

An inventory of objects invested with me-ness.

With Nina-ness and Norman-ness.

And Termagant-ness.

Though I'd prefer the Termagant scratched off.

I'm entitled to this list of childhood mementos; proof that those halcyon days existed. Carefree and beloved once, I traipsed through wild grass, net in hand, capturing fluttering beauty, binding it to foam. Norman never noticed the carpet beetles in the attic that devoured my specimens. My precious hairstreaks, fritillaries, skippers, brown arguses, silver studded blues, marbled whites, and large heaths laid waste. The rarer brimstones, tortoise shells and commas, painted ladies, and emperors ravaged by a common carpet beetle.

Norman's corduroy jackets were too broad in the shoulder, his leather lace-ups too wide, his stamp collection too dull. I wonder if not writing a will was intentional. *Ah, we haven't made the coal-tipper yet, Nate. Nate?* His deliberate time-bomb that would unravel the affections of the children that felt none for him. Norman's last laugh.

7. Allow the specimen to dry for 1–2 days, or until the wings will stay flat when the pins are removed. Very carefully remove the pins and paper strips and transfer the specimen to the display case. The specimen will be fragile as it has already begun to harden again.

The Termagant's house.

My lawyer says I've rights to the heirlooms and the house, at its current value, taken from me, just as Nina and Norman were. We never discussed inheritance; the Termagant paid the death duties and moved in. Nina always said, 'Look after Ness, she's your little sister.'

There are moments (in a lecture or dropping off to sleep) when memories plague me. Infant Ness sobbing, stung after knocking a bee I'd trapped from its jam jar. Ness, a little older, having a nightmare and crawling into my bed. Ness boiling pasta the night of Nina's funeral when we realised Norman wasn't going to make dinner. Reminders of intimacy. Other families hold together, why not ours?

8. Remove the glass cover from the case and set it aside. Position your insect specimens in any arrangement desired. Start with the largest insects first, leaving adequate space between each specimen. Push each pin securely into the foam in the bottom of the case.

Ness, my cherubic, tough and funny sister with bangs and shrill voice, was only fourteen when Nina died. Her constitution was stronger than mine but still... There was no counselling back then. No family support. Just Norman, with the emotional empathy of a Digestive Biscuit. He couldn't take care of himself, let alone us. He moved back after the funeral but withdrew further, his silences deepening till he disappeared from our lives, as if he'd died when Nina had. We scrimmaged through, but, simply put, Ness and I were orphaned.

University was a relief. I buried myself in books and boys. The Termagent's tinpot hobbies prospered, grew from a viable concern to a solid enterprise. She moved from digs to the family house. Her boyfriend solidified into a husband. Children followed. I became a tiresome uncle, invited to gatherings as an afterthought. Where did Norman's negligence end and ours begin? How much do the

Termagant and I own? Are the little girl and boy who ran hand in hand chasing butterflies the same grown-ups who, unable to face each another, sat either side of a room, our mediators relaying demands and counter-demands? An inventory of shabby relics: all that remains of Norman and Nina. Of Ness and Nate. Of decades of affection and altercation. After half a century, we formally concluded our relationship with the division of goods.

Norman's Seiko chronograph.

Norman bequeathed it: *Take it, Nate, I've no use for it now.* Forgotten in a kitchen drawer at home, it's the deal-breaker. The house, the decorations, the Meccano, the record player and LPs, the Teasmade and the charcoal. The chronograph is the cherry on the cake. Now, when time-keeping is futile. To mark minutes without parents. Without a sister. With no child to build bridges to nowhere with or to pour Teasmade cuppas. Parts of me erased; moments void of history, wafers of soul, shreds of heart, specks of DNA. Some mornings, before I leave, I catch my reflection in the hallway mirror; Norman's empty gaze returns my stare.

9. Be careful handling the specimens as they are fragile. Pay special attention to butterflies and moths, as the fine scales of their wings can be easily rubbed off, destroying their colour and beauty.

EROSION

The hall is being prepared for a ceremony so they meditate in the common room. Some face the wall. The others sit before the windows, drawing the curtains so nature won't distract them. Ocean keeps hers open onto West Allen. The slab of flitting birds is flanged by the dry-stone wall with a lichen-embossed wheel of life. Beyond it, the monks pitch their dishwater to hungry ghosts in the tangle of iron-red reeds. The next stratum of elongated Japanese pine trunks conceals the river with a fan of flattened boughs. Above is the upward embrace of hill where hares lope and deer graze by a copse. On the distant ridge, green and ochre since the snow melted, frets the edgy, churning sky; clouds bumper-to-bumper.

Compartmentalisation is mind-imposed. Rabbits grooming on their haunches outside the kitchen also scan the horizon, turning their ears to sound out predators. The cawing rooks gather sprigs for their nests on the glade, then head for the trees in a clamour. Though it appears to toss and turn on the hills' marge, the sky rests equally in her lap. This synthesis is life. Stillness, sound and movement, textures, light and shade; undelineated, a confederate whole. Just as the generations before and ahead (inherited marrow, progenitor bone, and filial flesh) are wrapped in Ocean's skin. Or the unbroken red line of Zen ancestors spanning back and forward, unfurling in all directions from the Buddha to the meditators and to every sentient being, and back again.

Yesterday, Ocean walked to West Allen. As she swung over a stile into thigh-high grass, a doe bounded ahead of her. She curvetted effortlessly away, clearing the wire in one leap. Ocean's heart soared with her; civilisation was as trivial as a fence. She trailed the muddy track, clambering over gates, gathering grey sheep's wool and marbled grouse feathers from the gorse. At the river's bank her feet sank into the mud. She rinsed them in a rain-filled bath, left for thirsty sheep. The bridge Ocean had crossed the previous summer was rent and hung precariously. A tractor growled downhill and two claggy, dreadlocked collies stopped to lick her hands, wagging their tails. The sheep trailed them to the feed silo with a tremendous bleating.

Six days of meditation ahead. The monastery is perfect. The obstacles lie within. The first evening is difficult. The following day, near impossible. Given silence and amplitude, neglected demons clamour. Each brings their ghouls with them or manufactures them the way children invent night frights to scare them back to themselves. The bell rings at 5.45 a.m. They stumble, fold mattresses and duvets, and jam them into their cupboards. Shower and pad through the refectory, bow to the Buddha painting, up to the hall, shoes off in the stairwell, bow at the doorway, shuffle for meditation mats and cushions, bow to the Buddha statue. Prepare the seat; bow to the wall, bow to the others. Thirty-five minutes facing the wall. Eight minutes of *kinhin*. Another thirty-five minutes at the wall.

They clean the hall. Breakfast on porridge and tea. Ocean works in the kitchen, making bread. In the project room, unfolding *wagesas*. Often in the garden, turning stones to pull spidery weeds. Turning stones is what they do. They build houses or temples with their stones, carve statues or erect cities. They bury their dead, or themselves, beneath them. And call those they value gems. Ocean has brought her own collection; family, relationships, desire, or her lack of it. The way... or how far from it she's drifted. They are here for the precepts. Commitment. Ordination. Confirmation. Getting off the fence. The vows are sixteen; two overlap and are sticky for her. Non-coveting (which implies not setting herself up to be coveted) and not selling the wine of delusion (nor buying it). Not lying, not killing, not stealing, not drinking are child's play in comparison. The jewel, Reverend Oisin reminds them, is within. Uncovering it is the work.

They live the week in silence. Sixteen heads bowed: unfolding napkins; placing cutlery, cup, and wash-stick as prescribed; passing food one to the other; bowing with each offering; reciting the prayer to exclude greed from their minds; eating only to attain enlightenment; lifting bowls to foreheads. They work side by side. Sleep a foot apart. Meditate. Wash hands silently. Without looking up, intuit who's sitting next to them, which monk is reciting, who's drinking tea in the refectory. They get to know their companions better than those out in the world. More importantly, they get to know themselves. Released from the distractions of small talk, the mind delves deeply into itself.

Reverend Oisin reminds them of Theravadin monks who beg each day, accepting whatever lands in their alms bowls without discrimination. He draws the parallel between the bowls and their lives. They can't choose what lands in their bowl. Only what they do with it. They share time silently in the lounge with its stained blue carpet, office chairs, coffee tables with foam coasters. A tray of boxed teas, instant coffee, a kettle, and jug of milk sit on a laminate table. At one end is the Buddha altar, opposite an appliqué triptych inspired by the Japanese pines outside.

By the end of the second day, tiny shocks flicker from Ocean's lungs to her serrated tonsils, pressure building at her temples. Chills run between her shoulder blades. The third day she can't keep food down. High on hunger, she can't sit, let alone stand. Reverend Aibreann gives her a wainscoted room in the attic. She feels like a tall water tower, bricks collapsing, one by one, water gushing. She tries to hold back the cascade, but nothing stems the flow. All that remains is anguish and hopelessness. She sleeps for twelve hours. And again, another dozen. She wakes to meals left at her bedside; only the changing oblong of sky through the dormer window indicates passage of time.

The day of ordination Reverend Aibreann knocks on her door. She showers and dresses for the first time in three days.

'Do you wish to become a Buddhist?'

'I do.'

They each kneel before the master, the razor taps each scalp three times; Buddha, *sangha,* and *dharma.* Each agrees to all sixteen precepts.

'I will. I will. I will…'

Reverend Fionn recites prayers over lunch of potato pie and broccoli that she can't keep down. Palpable emptiness lifts her; suddenly meditation becomes untroubled. Pleasurable. 'Practice is enlightenment,' Master Eamon says. A ceremony follows in the novices' hall. Opposite her, a portrait of Throssel Abbey's founder, Jiyu, shifts in the candle light; a baby morphs into a young woman, turns into an old man and transmogrifies into a skeleton. Chanting 'Namu Shakyamuni Buddha', they stumble through a dark maze of red silk corridors that twist, double back on themselves. The master offers incense. They offer pieces of paper on which is written all they wish to let go of. Two celebrants chant to shed greed and delusion. The monks accept the papers, setting fire to each and dropping them into a cauldron. Once ash, they stir them and scream, shrilly and abruptly, faces contorted. Maybe problems are no more than wood pulp, compressed and rolled thin, easily torn, shredded, or cremated. Everything, even stones, are just for the time being.

WHORLS

The primary shape of the universe is spiral.
Without beginning or end.

Each time the piglet snorted the terrier jumped so hard all four of his paws left the ground. Pink, four times the dog's size, with fine white hairs and blinking eyes, she was tied to a tree with twine.

Soon after dawn, Neri showed up at la Doña's house with the steel wheelbarrow, a wooden table, six sticks of firewood, a small pot and a large cauldron. A few minutes later Grandfather Servillano knocked on the wooden door; they shook hands. Grandfather's white straw hat shaded his fine-boned features. His stiff white sleeves were rolled up along his wiry forearms, his shirttails tucked into the belt where his *machete* hung. He carried four knives, folded in a Hessian sack, under his arm.

La Doña wasn't at home. Her mother offered the smoking fire to them, pulling her pot of corn from the brazier with a martyred expression. She didn't approve of slaughter in her back yard. However, she'd carved out her role in life as a dependent and knew how to hold her tongue. Servillano examined the fire indifferently. He asked for kindling.

'There's none.'

He wandered off, scavenging amongst the coffee trees behind the lilies, dahlias, and *velo de novia*, leaving Neri to the widow's disfavour. Servillano returned and, after much snapping of twigs and shredding of newspaper, he placed a sappy piece of *ocote* at the heart of the firewood and struck a match. It caught; smoking, crackling, roaring, then settling. Neri filled the cauldron with water from the spigot and heaved it over, splashing dark spots on his suede moccasins. Servillano settled it on the brazier. Without asking, he tried the lid of the old lady's pot, but it was too small. Disappearing again into the undergrowth, he came back with a piece of corrugated steel as long as his arm. He hacked the *lamina* down to size with his machete till he had himself a lid.

He told Neri to bring the wooden table closer, then settled the legs in the dirt till it was level. He fanned the fire. Neri smiled at Doña Ana's boys, who'd abandoned their game of football to watch. The younger, not yet at school, was small and sullen; his big brother was contrastingly sunny. Neri wanted to get this dreadful thing over with, but Grandfather moved at his own pace. He never made haste; a poor man can't afford mistakes. Neri had not worked the land like Grandfather, though as a child he'd spent hours in the old man's company – a realm inhabited by spirits, punctuated by earthquakes, and coloured by Civil War. But Nerito was a man now, and his world was palpably different. He spent hours on buses spluttering into the smoggy City and his studies were peppered with exams in hot, dirty classrooms. The things hoped of him bore no resemblance to those once expected of Servillano. And yet, he responded to life's demands as Grandfather did, with silent fortitude.

Chaos is the fundamental reality of life: we are an accident. Non-chaos is a fiction.

Servillano stoked the fire for so long the boys lost interest and returned to their ball game. He laid out his knives with care, placed his straw hat on the nearest aloe vera and, pulling a faded handkerchief from his trouser pocket, knotted it tightly about his scalp. All at once, it was time. Neri's hands shook as he tried to untangle the blue nylon strands of the rope harness, then sawed at it with his machete. The piglet began to squeal. The boys dropped their football and gawped.

Neri felt the black glare of the old lady at his back. Picking up the warm, squawking creature he braced her in his arms like an infant. The whining terrier danced between his feet.

The moment Neri set her down, the piglet made as though to escape, and he had to hold her fast. Servillano tied her hind legs together with twine. The piglet hobbled as though dancing a jig. The smaller boy began to snigger and, despite himself, Neri laughed – until the old lady glared at him. Servillano gripped the creature between his calves and, picking up the axe, brought the blunt side down against her skull. She shrieked. The boys froze in horror. The terrier barked and wagged his tail at this new game. Servillano struck between the animal's ears as she struggled and yowled. He whacked her again with all his strength. The interval between each blow lagged. Seven distinct thuds followed; each time Neri cringed as though it had impacted on him. How long it took to extinguish life.

A helix is a staircase that leads to the Tower of Babel. Creativity is at the eye of the whorl.

Heaving the scuffling shoat onto the table, Servillano had Neri hold her rump still. With one swift motion Servillano cut her throat. The blood collected in a yellow plastic bowl placed just below the table. Bright, primary and frothing, it dripped, dripped, dripped. Neri felt hot and cold in turn, his eyes drawn to the steaming, bubbling, crimson goop. The piglet squirmed as Grandfather reached into her throat cavity with bare hands, scooping gore into the bowl. The animal wriggled, wilful to the last. The old man pressed on her belly, massaging her blood towards her neck. Neri turned his face to look at the boys whose arms dangled, their mouths slack. In the kitchen doorway the widow shook her head in silent reproof as the pig turned a latex pallor. As Servillano enlarged the cross at her throat, she rasped her last laboured breaths.

Servillano pulled the lid off the cauldron and indicated they dunk the shuddering animal, headfirst, into the boiling water. She came out bone white, lips curled back from her teeth in a fearful grin. With the smallest knife he began to shave the wax creature, pouring boiling water over her oyster flesh, scraping her smooth with his knife. The hairs came away as cleanly as lathered stubble in the barber's chair. Servillano flicked off each trotter nail with deft, glinting flashes. Soon, the piglet lay sleek and ivory, from the tip of her snuffler to the end of her sinewy tail, nipples stiff, huge ears standing out. Washing down the table, the old man made a cut from gullet to anus and tugged the innards neatly into a bucket. The terrier shimmied around the bucket till the old lady grabbed him by the scruff and locked him in the shed.

When Doña Ana returned from Antigua, her basket brimming with relishes and accompaniments, the boys had gone indoors and Neri and Servillano were washing everything down. The butchered animal lay neatly curled in a plastic tub. Servillano had knotted his reward, the head and heart, into a black plastic bag and tied it to his handlebars. The terrier whined wearily from the barn. Neri couldn't look the Doña in the eye.

We twist through this progressive explosion of imaginations. We are the sphinx and the labyrinth.

That afternoon, Neri was walking down Tercera Avenida towards the plaza when he bumped into five school friends heading to the bullfight. He couldn't think up an excuse. Everyone was headed in the same direction on foot, by bike or pick-up, eating *chuchitos* and sipping *granisadas*. The crowd around the pitch was deep. The young men clambered onto a pick-up beside a green fire truck. He couldn't see till he stood on the cab roof. The bleachers were four thick: dozens filled the gap between them and the fence, and others dangled off the rough wooden palisade. On the other side of the pitch the trees were hung with unfamiliar fruit: he screwed his eyes to make out the boys that sat amongst the branches.

The bull was a huge fawn animal with a massive frame and cashew hump between his shoulder blades. His eyes were large and soft, his ears smooth and a velvet curtain of dewlap draped from his neck. He stood very still at one corner, the flank between his ribs and rump heaving. Four matadors and dozens of bystanders, encouraged over loudspeakers, baited him. A tall gaucho in a cowboy hat hopped from one foot to the other. A bare-chested drunk waved his t-shirt above his head. Several boys shadow-boxed. Others, hooting and whistling, climbed the tree-trunk in the middle of the ring, hanging from its knots. The matadors shook red rags. The bull looked from one to the next and back again. Lowering his head, he cantered nonchalantly toward the tree. A kid, scrambling up the trunk in the nick of time, lost his trainer. The crowd roared.

The bull stopped to catch its breath. Those hanging on the palisades slid down and kicked him. He ignored them till a string of firecrackers exploded at his hooves. The crowd tittered. Angered, the bull lowered its head and went sweeping along the fence; the men pulled themselves up and out of danger in a wave. A small wiry matador led the bull on with tantalising twitches of a red banner. With a jolt, Neri recognised it was his old best friend, Wilton.

Each time the bull lowered his head Wilton twisted this way and that, avoiding butts. Neri's pulse thudded as his friend aggravated the bull, taking bigger risks; his sympathy moved from animal to man and back again. The bull, drawn to Wilton's flag, missed it, jamming his head between two logs. The crowd guffawed as bystanders caught his tail and tugged it. Maddened, he rushed at them, knocking an old man from his perch and trampling him underfoot. The crowd gasped as he turned, running roughshod. A second and third turn hushed the flabbergasted onlookers. On its fourth turn the bull was diverted and the unconscious man dragged beneath the fence. The whistle went up from spectators on the near side of the pitch and two firemen emerged from the green truck with a stretcher and first-aid kit. They lifted the deathly pale victim to the stretcher, wrapped a bandage about his head, and carried him into the ambulance.

To trace the coil is the daily observation of the people and the land.
Scrolling tendrils set in motion by the primordial generator.

Neri left. He couldn't bear to find out who would go down next. He wanted to walk to the hills at the edge of town, but dark clouds were gathering so he headed to the centre. Several foot-pedalled merry-go-rounds and a painted Ferris wheel were crammed into Segundo. At the corners of the plaza were Biblical friezes: dummies labelled 'Shadrak', 'Mishak', and 'Abnetenango' roasted in eternal cloth flames rippling over an electric fan. The smell of spun sugar, fried chicken, *tostadas*, and pizza hung in the air. Half a dozen musicians in blue suits played rapidly and out of tune. Moors and Conquistadors, in flowery dresses and straw hats, swayed on stilts. Boys set off home-made bombs. Mothers bought *dulces* and rides for their kids. Thieves picked pockets.

As large drops of rain began to fall, Neri was drawn by the yellow light of a house that had opened its front room as a makeshift bar. He ordered a Gallo. Other locals followed him, moments later.

'Only one casualty, *hombres*, not bad, eh?'

'Yeah, that Wilson got off lightly, *graçias a Diós*.'

'Reckon the bull spoiled his looks, though.'

Time and space unwind out of Hunab Ku corresponding to heavenly bodies.

Neri stared into the darkness. Thunder and lightning cleared the plaza, hushing the musicians. In moments, the plummeting beads of rain turned to sheets, transforming the streets into rivers. The water swirled and brimmed at the step. The white face of the old man formed in its eddies: silence must have been welcome after the bull had gone berserk. The man's features morphed into the piglet's: throat slit, face poached, coiled cosily in the tub, flies gathering. The water spun, the image distorted, reforming into how he imagined Wilton's face now: his nose bent this way, a raised laceration from ear to hairline, or perhaps from cheek to throat, a hollow eye-socket sealed shut.

The next day Doña Ana served her family suckling pig. She was disappointed by how little meat it yielded. The morning after, the church was crammed with mourners for the old man's funeral. He'd bled to death at Hermano Pedro Hospital the previous night. He left two widows, with a clutch of children each, who discovered each other when called on to pay burial costs. Wilton was let out of hospital the same day, permanently disfigured. Later that day, Neri returned to university, sleepwalking through his last year of lectures and failing his exams. He remained the rest of his days in the City. He found a job as a driver of a four-by-four for a drug lord who appreciated his discretion and nerves of steel. One year to the day of the bullfight, Servillano died in his sleep.

Surviving fright and disaster, transforming misery into poetry is an attempt to master chaos.

GAIT OF A BARROW BOY

He said his name was David when we first met on the stairwell. A neighbour told me it was Frye. Some months later, he reckoned it was John. When I ring the council on his behalf they say, 'We have a Dave J down at number 37.'

'That's him,' I say.

He walks twice a day. No matter the season. Whatever the weather. Too intentional for strolls, they aren't calculated enough to be reconnaissance. Neither casual nor leisurely, 'ambles' would be misleading. Perhaps 'forays' capture them better. The first is before dawn; even on the longest winter night he's up at five. His second is in the late afternoon. Circuitous routes choreographed long ago, signposted by refuse points and council bins.

On the night shift as a lad, he had lifted wooden boxes of apples or hessian sacks of potatoes and swede, toted two bushels on his head or pulled half a ton. He'd shifted orange nets of carrots or wooden crates of leeks, cauliflowers, and lettuces. Stacked mushroom boxes, knocked root vegetables free of sod, or trimmed leaves. Untied ropes or unrolled icy, soaking canvasses. He grafted among men in waistcoats, long aprons, flat caps, leather belts and leather shoes. Among tough old flower sellers with celeriac complexions, quince-sharp humour and russet hearts.

Lanto, as he was called, started as a nipper. Tad died when he was a gwas. Ma was at her wit's end with five lads when Great Uncle

Llewelyn, an auctioneer, offered to apprentice him. Covent Garden had just two Taffs; the rest were East Enders, practically one family – thirty-three porters were related by blood. Lanto lodged with Uncle to start, but Aunt Hettie wanted him out from under her feet so he was packed off to Bruce House, a warren of dormitories on the corner of Drury Lane and Kemble Street, its dire cubicles infested with drunks and vermin that nicked or ate everything.

John, as he became, hardly had a copper left once his digs were settled for, but he sent what he could till Ma was in the fords of the river. When he wasn't working he read, earning himself the epithet the Walking Dictionary. He kept his knowledge clandestine, like his names, polyonomy a defence mechanism. Plenty of other young men kept themselves to themselves but as time wore on they became fruiterers, greengrocers, or auctioneers. They found what they were looking for, or it found them; they got sweethearts, tied knots, and formed families. The Walking Dictionary stayed alone.

In seventy-four, the council gave Dave Johnson the keys to a bedsit, assigning him a place in the waning capital of less than seven million. Though few play a role in history, history dispassionately stamps its mark on them. Nails in the Sick Man of Europe's coffin were the oil crisis, miners' strikes and dock closures that brought the country to its knees with inflation at twenty per cent. John's fate was sealed when the market shut its gates after three hundred and twenty-five years. Local dissenters stood down developers' plans to install Barbican-like slabs on the piazza. Alternative enterprises breathed new life into Fowler's arcades. One by one the porters found employment elsewhere, at Borough or Spitalfields. All but John.

When I opened the bakery I'd drive once a week to Borough Market for boxes of salad and fruits. And when it closed its doors, Nine Elms. The only woman, a girl really, amongst restaurateurs, chefs and greengrocers, I haggled with vendors over crates of tomatoes or blackberries at inky dawn. I exchanged hand-scribbled receipts torn from blue carbon copy pads in exchange for thumbed notes with cashiers in Portacabins, page-three girls sellotaped to the walls. Borrowing a trolley, I loaded crates into the VW's trunk and drove through vacant streets back to Bermondsey. The rest of the day I hefted seventy-pound sacks of flour, cut armfuls of dough out of mixers, or trays of pastries into ovens, mopped floors with steaming buckets of bleach and water. I'd dropped out of college to work night shifts with a baker. Stepping into his world, I'd been absorbed, our lives seamless. Spliced to him and the business, we worked, ate, and slept together, breathing in sync. People around us got it on, fell out, went to prison, or died but, it seemed, nothing would part us. Nothing distracted me from him except, finally, myself.

John lives six metres away from me. Yet I know almost nothing about him. His bedsit layout is identical to mine and he has a similar view. He gets the afternoon sun some minutes later than I. He tends to the window box of ivy and geraniums hanging off the balcony outside his front door and I to mine. When I knock to bring him home-baked bread or cake he opens his door just sufficiently to wrap his head around the door; he never lets anyone cross the threshold. He's never changed his baseball cap, V-neck or trousers in all the years we've been neighbours. In summer, he sheds his parka to the V-neck with snowflakes across the chest. When the council installed boilers and central heating to flats, he declined. Over his bald pate, anchored by the thin locks that sprout above his ears, is an armour-like plate of a shiny greenish-blackish material. The disc adheres to his head permanently; over time it has thickened.

He has no phone nor television, just a wireless. Though he archives them in stacks, he doesn't read the papers anymore; his tortoiseshell frames hold obsolete lenses. With a hard-bristle broom he sweeps the narrow channel running between the newspaper towers, opens his front door, and brushes the detritus onto his front stoop. A tawny female blackbird visits to peck the crumbs. One night, an entire baguette sat there till morning. When it rains, John leaves empty tins outside his door to collect whatever drips off the roof. He emerges with a single red glossy rubber glove on one hand and a rusty cake-tin in the other and sweeps the rainwater off the railings into it.

A friend's kid screeched on the walkway: 'Oh no, oh no, *he* lives on *this* floor? The hobo! The hobo! Run, run.'

'That's my neighbour... and I'm fond of him. He may be eccentric, but not deaf,' I say defensively. Perhaps we are not so dissimilar. Were my circumstances a fraction more left-field I can imagine myself into his skin. I am hard-wired not to infer security from life. Whether I lost it somewhere or had it wrenched from me, I can't say. When I have found myself without – without love, friendship, work, or a home – it seems congenital. When I find myself with, I am astonished.

John's sea-borne lilt is unmistakeable; his small frame rides imaginary waves. In the restaurant-lined side streets of the piazza he makes the best finds, though, over the years, the dreck has deteriorated. The supermarkets dispose of their waste covertly these days; wheelie-bin binges are a thing of the past. The more nutritious leavings of Rules or Food for Thought in the seventies declined to refuse from Costa and Prêt in the nineties, and now to half-eaten Tesco sushi or off-scourings from Pho or Five Guys. John garbage-picks without judgement. Home by nightfall, he keeps a bare bulb lit for an hour or so in winter. But usually he retires with the sun.

I also walk. I'm not foraging for refuse. And I gave up seeking nature here long ago. I'm rummaging for humanity. There are few traces amongst the stagnant-eyed office workers that swarm in and out of Holborn. Little evidence in the glassy looks of shoppers with their clutch of laminated paper bags. No hint in the out-of-towners' laughter coursing from the theatres as they climb back into their coaches home. Less in the elemental cries of pissing drunks or the cackle of slutty counterparts. On occasion, I glimpse it in a forgotten pensioner, shuffling along the pavement. Catch a hint in a vagrant who takes shelter in the cardboard charnel houses in the alley below.

Tonight, John saunters back along Long Acre, swipes his fob and gamely climbs the stairs, melodious courtship cat-calls echoing off the stairwell. He turns sharply onto the fourth-floor balcony to his splintered and weather-beaten door, with its tarnished 37. From his left pocket he pulls on a rope, tied to the chain affixed to his belt, and levers the key into the brass lock. A slight turn to the right... the cylinder is jammed. He tries again. And once more. He eases the key from the lock and polishes it on his sleeve, spitting on his fingers. He strives with his left hand but the bolt won't budge. The door stays shut.

His voice rises, feral and urgent, to the pitch of a feline before copulation. But though he strides up and down the balcony, gesticulating and looking wildly about him, no one responds. He returns to the key and works at it again. It has opened, day after day, walk after walk, without fail. The heat of a blister building, he rubs his fingers against his blackened trousers; when he goes to spit on them they are bloody. He sucks their tinniness and wipes them on the newspaper in his carrier. On the other side of the sash window, newspapers gleaned from other walks are stacked up, a tower-block landscape in miniature. But now they are separated from him by the panes and front door. Weariness sweeps him. The sun has fallen, its warmth vanished. The balcony is part of an extrinsic domain, a vast unknown sweep of hostile world.

He hears footsteps on the landing.

I turn the corner, into him.

'I can't get in! Can't get in. No way.' His face is ashen and there is blood on the ground.

'Shall I try?'

The barrel has broken. When I hand back his keys my fingers are sticky with his blood.

'I'll call the Council. What do they have you down as?'

'John Davidson.'

I throw the shopping on my kitchen floor, put on a pot of water on the gas for tea and find the phone number for City West.

'We have a Dave J at number 37?' the receptionist says suspiciously.

'That's him,' I say. When the repairs department call back, they ask if he has ID.

'I doubt it.'

'We can't let him in without ID,' says the voice of officialdom.

'Look,' I reason, 'he probably doesn't have ID. He's been living in that flat for decades. He has some mental health problems and he's frantic.' There's hesitation at the other end, as the voice struggles with the dilemma of a call-out conflicting with home time.

'Ok, we'll send someone in the next four hours.'

When I go back outside with a cup of tea the Walking Dictionary is gone. I look over the railings but there's no sign of him. Perhaps he's joined the rootless legions that shift from one place to another, walking till he forgets his name or any version of it.

His Father's Land

The first time Eugenio saw José he waved.

'*Buenos días*. I'm José Mariá Amado Alvarez.'

'Pablo's grandson?' Eugenio lifted his brim.

'You remember him?'

'I grew up with your father and his brothers.'

'All I recall of *abuelo* is the sting of his cane... for eating his strawberries,' recalls José.

'He was a hard man,' Eugenio agreed, 'All his sons left. Your father was the last to go.'

'My uncles made their fortunes in Málaga... my father stayed poor in Lanjarón.'

Eugenio came up to José's shoulder. He was as skinny as a boy, limbs tight as wire. His cotton shirts and trousers soiled yet ironed. But it was his face that was most striking, alert as a child's. Though his hair was thin and grey, his eyebrows were as black as coal. He smiled easily. When he pushed his straw hat back to raise the brim, his glittering chestnut eyes met José's.

Though a head taller, José was still of small stature. Balding, with finely cropped light hair, he had pale skin and a deferential hunch. He reminded Eugenio of Pablo: the same build, something about the eyes.

'You are visiting?'

'No, I'm here... for good.'

'Nothing left now.'

'The house is comfortable. But...'

'The land needs work. The trees are good.'

'You think?'

'The drought's been hard on them but their roots are deep. Let them drink. Have you family?'

'No, I'm alone.'

'So am I. If you need eggs or milk... or to share a glass of wine, stop by.'

The teenage José liked to read. And to sleep. Reading and sleeping were his two obsessions. He let authors unravel their plots and his subconscious untangle his dreams. He thought little of the future, not because unknotting it was beyond him, but because he had no ambition. Paco was going to work in a bank. Manuel would take over father's restaurant. Enrique would build a plumbing empire in Málaga. José just wanted to read or sleep. When he finished school, however, he couldn't put off his future any longer; it had arrived.

Eugenio removed the suction cups from his cow and straightened his back. Not quite sixteen litres. She'd dry up soon; her last birth was difficult, she wouldn't have another. He thought back to his old herd of thirty that had produced six hundred litres. He'd supplied Capilerilla and all the villages close by. These days he had only one cow. He patted her fondly before rinsing the milking machine.

To complicate matters, Rosa was in love with José. She insisted on marriage the summer they finished school. He had no job, he protested. Not to worry, she reassured him, her father would give them a small loan to start something. José had no interest in business but being a shopkeeper might allow him scope to read and sleep.

Eugenio carried the stainless-steel pail upstairs to his well-ordered kitchen and placed it on the fire. Then he went back downstairs and, filling a bucket with maize, sifted it into the pigs' trough. Five snorting swine lifted damp snouts and, squinting at Eugenio, scrambled for position. Hairy pink backs shook free from the swarming flies a moment. The smallest mounted its neighbour in desperation. Eugenio ducked under the stairwell and into the barn next door. He pulled hay from the bale for the mule and, stooping down, climbed into the coop. The rust-feathered hens fussed a moment then ignored him. Finding four warm brown eggs, he folded them into his sweater and climbed upstairs for breakfast.

By the time José and Rosa were wed, only Manuel remained in Lanjarón; Paco and Enrique had left and, with them, all of their friends. Rosa prevaricated over her father's loan. What could they do in their small village celebrated for pure waters and wind-dried ham? There were already a dozen shops hung with haunches like flowstones. And a massive resounding hall housing curative baths. Hotels every step of their way and more cafés than they could shake a *jamón* at. Rosa favoured a baby shop but she indulged José's whim. They opened a bookshop.

Eugenio cracked eggs into a pan and, removing the pail of simmering milk, put coffee on to boil. Lunch might be the mainstay but it was a long time till two. When Diana was alive she made almond biscuits and good bread. But there were only so many hours in the day. Eggs did him nicely. In the parlour he folded back the lace cloth and set his plate carefully on the wooden table. The framed faces in the photographs occupying it smiled at him as he ate.

Libros Libertad was a triumph of caprice over reason. It remained untainted by customers, attracting neither tourist nor local. The former were unable to read Spanish, the latter preferred not to. José sat doggedly for two dusty years amongst bookshelves waiting for someone to step over the threshold. Instead, Rosa walked out. She preferred her old life to this one with José.

The photos were of sons and grandsons, taken before they were men. His eldest lived in Barcelona and visited little these days. His second lived in Bubión, below, and ran a construction business. The grandchildren wouldn't be there much longer: they were leaving to study in Granada. Well and good, Eugenio thought, swallowing the last morsel of egg. Farming was impossible; no one could make a living these days.

José closed the bookshop. He could have gone home to his mother's but he moved instead to his father's land. His grandfather had inherited it from his grandfather. The villagers of Lanjarón considered this lamentable. In the face of their disapproval José declared the change suited him. In Lanjarón he'd been perpetually disappointed. Up in Capilerilla existence would unfold like a dream with only nature itself to contend with. Secretly, he was terrified.

So Pablo's grandson had come back. Pablo had been the village elder throughout Eugenio's childhood. Certain things marked him out from the others. He'd married a girl from Bubión. He kept books in his house. If there were disagreements between neighbours, they consulted Pablo. And one thing more; during the Civil War when the mountains were overrun with Communists only three families remained in Capilerilla. Pablo's was one.

José drove up to Capilerilla, taking the hairpins slowly. Herders pastured their goats on what were once orchards. Wild rosemary, thistle, and mallow had overtaken tilled fields. The almond and olive trees dropped overripe fruit on the ground. Farmhouses lay in ruins and the old roads that led to them had crumbled.

Back when Eugenio was a child, every house was filled with a family. Today, there were just twenty-three old folk in Capilerilla, of which just four were men. There had been a primary school, a church, a weekly market, a butcher and Eugenio's dairy. Nowadays, those who remained went down to Pitres and bought things sheathed in plastic at Covirán. The UHT milk came in Tetra Paks, *salchichón* arrived shrink-wrapped, fruit was delivered in cartons from Almería. Even the wine came in bottles.

José had just boxes of books; the furniture went with Rosa. Carrying them to the house, he felt dizzy. Perhaps it was the altitude. He sat on his back wall overlooking the valley. The wild flowers were alive with grasshoppers, as long as his little finger, which jumped and spread their tawny wings. Shiny black beetles rolled balls of mule dung. Rust ants marched along the wall. Clumsy beetles with enamelled blue wings zoomed into him. In the trees, he spotted hoopoes and jays and an eagle circling for prey. They belonged to this place, but José?

He unpacked a little, built a fire and made an omelette. Throwing a blanket on the couch, he settled down for the night. For the first time in his life he couldn't sleep. There was an insect outside that sounded like his mother's sewing machine. José got up and went in search of it. The closer he got, the stronger the vibrations grew, till the earth shuddered under his feet. He parted the grass with his torch but he never found it.

They wanted better lives. That's why the others had gone. Eugenio left twice. To Granada after the Civil War as a child. And in sixty-one, when his second-born was sixteen days old, on a holiday visa. He went with two others from the village to Düsseldorf to work in a car factory. After three months, they got papers. Every month they sent money home. Home, where the clouds never sat still. Where work changed according to the season. And Diana waited for him. Eugenio came home when she fell ill. He bought the house, the garden, the fields and the cows with what he'd earned abroad. But he couldn't buy her health. His brothers had moved on like the clouds blown by late summer wind. And then Diana, all of a sudden, like mountain fog.

The house was built of stone with ceilings of log and cane, and a roof of *launa*, the spongy local soil that glittered like fool's gold. The sculpted cone chimney was capped with a disc of slate and a basket. The front door opened to a parlour and kitchen. Until he died, José's father had kept it well. Now it smelt of lichen and ghosts. José plastered the walls with limestone. He built shelves and filled them with the books he'd never sold. He pruned the wisteria that hung over the front door and the vines on the veranda's pergola. And he filled the pots on the porch with geraniums. Decorating helped him close a chapter.

Behind the *casita* was an old orchard; apricot, cherry, *níspero*, and fig. Below were two terraces of unkempt land. To survive, José needed to be self-sufficient. It could be done, he told himself: his great-grandfather had fed an entire family. But José had to start from scratch. He spent three weeks just walking. The higher tier of land would make a fine garden; it was close to the house with an *alberca* full of water.

José was a gardener, not a farmer. He created concentric semi-circular beds on the crescent step. First he put down tarps to smother the wild grass and weeds. Then he broke up the soil with a hoe and fork. He carpeted each bed with hessian, anchored with stones. He laid tiny paths just wide enough to walk along with small grey pebbles sifted from the soil. The whole thing was watered by a network of skinny black pipes that snaked from one bed to another. Tiny holes, at the turn of a tap, leaked droplets of water, every six inches or so. The seasons turned. Eugenio bit his lip. The curved rows proved whimsically impractical. The hessian rotted away. With no fence, the wild boars dug up all that José had planted.

On a parched autumn evening, a year later, Eugenio sat down to his supper of *salchichón* and wine. There was a knock on his door.

'*Buenas?*'

'*Buenas tardes*, Pablo.' José looked hard at the old man but he hadn't noticed his slip. 'Come, share my supper.'

He brought another plate to the table, sliced *salchichón* onto it, and poured José a glass of syrupy wine.

'This is from the pigs I slaughtered last Christmas.' He held the *salchichón* up for José to admire. 'The wine's from two harvests ago.'

José nodded his head in appreciation and chewed at the sausage. They ate in silence. When he'd finished Eugenio said, 'Did I ever show you my Spanish/German dictionary? Look, it's still in the newspaper I wrapped it in... here's the date; June 5th, 1961!'

'It's an antique, Eugenio!'

'I'm an antique, *joven*! Living history... the things I've seen up here in the mountains. The stories I've heard... my grandfather told me he slaughtered Moors in Morocco.'

José tried to smile but instead his shoulders shook. Eugenio realised he was weeping.

'What's wrong, son?'

'More than a year has passed... and I've got nowhere. In spring the wind blew down all my frames. The frost killed my tomatoes. It's been the driest summer ever. This morning... the boars came again...' he choked back a sob.

'Poor Pablo. But this is nature, no? We are not God who can make paradise in six days. Ours takes a lifetime of trial and error. I'll stop by.'

José took the old man's bony hand in his and squeezed it.

Eugenio showed José how to dig a patch of unbroken earth and put down potatoes; backbreaking work. The ten-foot furrows were just a spade's width, perhaps ten inches deep. Half a dozen had him breathless. Eugenio buried potatoes in the earth, gnarled shoots up, and covered them with soil. They used dried weeds as mulch, packing thick sheaves along the furrows to stop new ones springing up. He might confuse José for Pablo, but Eugenio knew what to plant when and how. As José worked beside the old man he began to think.

He thought he was learning how to farm but slowly he realised he was unearthing other things.

'Time to pull up those dead ones.'

José reflected on his past.

'Today we'll sow the cabbage and cauliflower, a few lettuce, and onions.'

He considered life in Capilerilla.

'Tomorrow, asparagus and, between the apricot trees, garlic.'

And speculated on the seasons ahead.

This unravelling of nature was better than any dream or book. It gave rise to real beauty. It wasn't the fancy sort bought in stores; it emanated from the Pico Veleta itself. It whispered in the leaves of the white elms, the sour cherry trees, and the figs. It cascaded in the water that poured from the falls and was reflected in the reservoirs. And radiated from the earth itself. It gathered, on hot afternoons, with the flies and shadows, under whitewashed rooms suspended over the village paths. And bloomed with the geraniums in the clay pots lined up on front steps and balconies. It nourished Eugenio's pigs, slaughtered each year on the twenty-seventh of December for *salchichón*. It emanated from the tough gold stalks of hay tied into neat oblong bales for the mule. From the beets, fed to the spotted cow that gave milk. And the grapes, crushed into sweet wine. It shone in Eugenio's eyes, shaped his words and mellowed his speech. And little by little it seeped into José. The spirit of *su tierra*, his home land.

Eugenio bore no grudges. He neither fretted over drought, nor over the quitting of the land. He expressed no bitterness over losing Diana. He never groaned when he left his bed at dawn, nor grumbled when he returned long after sunset. He wished for nothing other than what he had. Increasingly he grew befuddled; names, bottles, packets of seeds swapped identities. The few remaining old folk in the village were scant help; most were themselves bent in two and forgetful.

One clear August afternoon, two years later, there was no sign of Eugenio. After dinner, José filled a pail with ripe figs and climbed up to his place by the light of a waxing moon. The front door was ajar, a chat show rumbling loudly on the TV in the parlour. Eugenio's balding pate rested on the arm of the wooden couch. José called softly at first. Then with more force. When Eugenio failed to stir, José understood. The old man had taken his last siesta.

This also awaited José, but he grew to fear it less. The trees bore red and ochre fruit. The onions, sweet as apples, waited on the soil to be pulled. José fried tender broad beans in garlic and olive oil. Ruddy lettuce leaves, strong and crisp, filled his salad bowl. The tiny white flowers of the strawberries fell and hard green fruits appeared that reddened until they glistened like rubies. Later would come tomatoes, cucumber, and peppers.

ABSENT WOMEN

Just where the island Thirasia's hip protrudes (and fifty fearsome beast-heads sprout), two rocks jut up. When I asked my *yayá* if she could see the rock men she told me, without looking up from her sizzling *loukoumades*, that they were rock women: Zaforá and the spinster, Yeorgía, who adopted her. Zaforá, head wrapped in a scarf, bore a basket of firewood on her back. Other times Yayá said Yeorgía was Maroulia, my mother. Hidden in the ruins of the cave beside ours, crouching at the open doorway, I would screw up one eye then the other, squinting across the caldera, whispering: 'Zaforá, Yeorgía, Zaforá, Mamá, Zaforá, Yeorgía,' till the figures blurred, names jumbled, identities smudged.

After it rains, Thirasia is not of this earth: her colours glint, the sea between us slick as oil, the feathered clouds so low I could reach out and touch them. On dry summer afternoons the island is barren, foreboding even, with her woman's curves and head of winding serpents. She lies curled in sleep on her right side, folded in on herself, misshapen centaur breasts sagging. An exaggerated auricle drapes her neck, where the outline of something man-made lies. A monastery, perhaps?

'Long before you were born, Dimitri, a basket washed ashore after a storm,' Yayá once told me. 'In it was an amber-haired girl. Yeorgía, the old maid, raised her as her own, naming her Zaforá after the bitter-honey crocus once abundant here. Zaforá grew into an enchantress, all blazing hair and a complexion of freshly strained yoghurt, causing havoc in the village: every man in love with her. Fathers and sons vied for her favours. The priest swore to leave his wife if Zaforá would have him. The donkey-man stabbed his betrothed on her account. Boys her own age fought over trifles on the off-chance she'd look in their direction.'

'What happened to her, Yayá?' My grandmother was absorbed in gouging the seeds from fist-sized tomatoes. Long before soap operas had employed the art of suspended drama, Yayá had it down to a fine art. Overcome with emotional investment in a story, she'd freeze at the critical juncture and all attempts to thaw her were useless. Her sagas spanned weeks, sometimes months. I pieced them together the way other children solve puzzles.

I miss her. In her flowered, patched pinafore, thick wool stockings darned at the heels, a headscarf knotted beneath her sun-creased face. On saints' days she wore the same black skirt and cardigan she put on for special occasions since Pappou's funeral. Most of all I miss her stories, delivered in instalments, without deference to the child I was, nor respect for beginnings and ends. It was she who insisted the island opposite was inhabited. Locals were as incredulous as if she were suggesting life on the moon. 'On Thirasia? How would they survive?' they asked. 'What would they eat?' 'How would they build their houses?' When I proposed, 'As we do,' they shook their heads like I was a fool.

There's always been the sneaking suspicion I'm not all there. I don't sleep behind a stack of chairs like Panos or shuffle along, like Vangeli. But my origins are besmirched. Yayá tried to keep that story from me as long as she could. But in *nipiagogeio* the kids asked: 'Why do you live alone with your yayá?'; 'Is she really a witch?'; 'How come you have red hair?'

One morning Yayá was telling me of saffron's potency against the Black Death, with a digression on a fourteen-week war named after the flowers' stigmas, when I screwed up the courage to ask about my parents. She raised greasy hands from a pot of celery and pork and looked me in the eye.

'Dimitri, are you sure you want to hear that story?'

I nodded.

'Well, your father, Theodoros, you can see from that picture in the alcove how handsome he was; you don't look a bit like him... such a good, gentle, honest boy, just like his father before him, God rest their souls. All the girls adored Theo. But he cared only for Maroulia; they were earmarked for each other. Ask anyone.

'Before he went to war they were engaged. As a conscript, he worked the kitchens and when he returned home, the first visitors were showing up. There was no taverna in town. His father left him a house with a terrace and caldera view, so Theo set about buying tables and chairs. With me in the kitchen and him front of house, we did well from the start. Once established, he went to Maroulia's father to ask for her hand.

'You can imagine the blow when her father said no. The old sea-captain, Doukas, beat him to it. Now let me tell you a thing about Doukas. Forty years at sea and he had a woman in every port. His first wife died of heartbreak. You know that Venetian house next to Kaliope's? Well, that was his, as was the Maritime Museum and the Captain's house below the bakery. And the empty lot in the centre of town, not to mention two chapels and several houses in Finikia. Though he was old enough to be her grandfather, Doukas got down on his creaky old knee. Those were the days of the Hunger, Dimitri. She agreed, thinking of her parents. And they consented, thinking of her. Of course it made them all miserable. What to do?

'Everybody and his mother were invited to the wedding, even your father, though wild mules wouldn't have dragged him. Maroulia's silk wedding dress was stitched in Athens and overlaid with Belgian lace; her chiffon veil was from a voyage to China. A tiered English wedding cake was ordered from a Cretan patisserie and five goats were slaughtered. Theo's broken engagement was forgotten and the wedding was all anyone talked of. It drove your father half mad.'

Yayá switched on the mixer to whisk eggs, drowning out any possibility of continuing. I'd learn no more. But I had developed my own strategy – resurrecting burning questions on other stories, set aside. The moment she switched the whisk off I asked, 'Yayá, whatever happened to Zaforá?'

'Zaforá? She told Yeorgía she'd only marry one of her own, from the island opposite, within sight but not reach. So she stayed alone.

When Yeorgía died, Zaforá's auburn curls turned ashen before the ninety days. The only thing that would have saved her was a bulrush Moses of her own. But one gusty night Zaforá went missing. Days later, they found her dress in the same spot she'd been washed up as a baby. Run along and play! If I don't pay attention the *galaktoboureko* will be ruined.'

Thirasia's physique is layered, like filo pastry, one strata over the next: sienna, rust, ivory, nephrite. Her high eastern shoulder slopes down to her western tail and slips into the Aegean, forming a natural harbour tapering to the barb. The sun sets within spitting distance of her tine. The seagulls, indifferent to her nooks, are more likely to perch on our ruins, than on her ridged keels. Perhaps Thirasia's inhabitants are frugal folk who throw few scraps away. I hold my breath as the dragon's chest expands and falls. She might, after all these petrified eons, shake her scorpion tail and extend her black, hinged, membraned wings and rise.

Yayá was boning cod.

'Tell me about the wedding, *Yayá*.'

'Which wedding, *agápi mou*?'

'Maroulia to the Captain.'

'*Panagia mou!* That *pappou* would have been better suited to giving a bride away than taking one. Maroulia was like Aphrodite beside the Keres, so beautiful was she compared to her bridesmaids as she stumbled through the ceremony, pale as her organza dress. The church filled with the metallic fragrance of crocuses. The gun shots could be heard as far away as Imerovigli and enough rice was thrown to feed two dozen families. The entire village followed the *bouzouki* players to the town hall. *Retsina*, from the Doukas' vineyard, flowed. The *Kalamatianos* was exuberant; but those of us who loved her had heavy feet.

'When we got home in the early hours, Theo wasn't there. Nor when I woke before dawn. When I went to church, Thea Areti was lighting a candle. She whispered that Maroulia had disappeared before the festivities were over. Some guests, the worse for wear, had made themselves into a search party, but...'

With chapped hands she stripped the tiny leaves of wild thyme from its branches; it was the moment to change tack.

'But Yayá, did they never find Zaforá?'

Wiping away tears with the back of her hand, she sighed. 'A corpse washed up months later... they said it was hers. They didn't want to bury her in the cemetery; she wasn't from here and had no family to pay for last rites. In the end, the church rustled up a simple headstone and performed a hasty service. A handful of old men gathered for *koliva* as your Great Uncle Babbis began to shovel earth on her. His spade slipped, shifting the body on its side, and Babbis caught this glimpse, between what was left of her shoulders, of black pleated wings fixed to shafts, like a bat's. That's when I knew for sure it wasn't your mother, Dimitri.'

'Really, Yayá?'

'Theo Babbis told me so. Now, unless you're going to help stuffing these tomatoes, Dimitri, leave me in peace.'

I imagine how we must appear to the villagers of Thirasia. Sometimes I think I see a daub; a farmer, perhaps, following a hidden path to a vineyard on the fertile southern slope. Or a couple of red-headed children running between rocky outcrops. But they could be wildcats or mountain goats. At this distance, who can tell? It's too far to swim, but a fisherman could row there. None do. Each is tethered to his own watery holding, unfurling nets in late afternoon to draw them up at dawn, writhing with life. What keeps me here is harder to gauge.

All my life I've heard only malice spoken of those islanders: that their soil is poor; that the wind that caresses our escarpments whistles violently over theirs. When ill luck comes our way it is the island's evil dragon, Kampe, who cast the evil eye on us. It's said most of the inhabitants died during the Hunger: just a handful of half-feral, inbred redheads remain. Our villagers contend that should you be foolish enough to cross over and set foot on so much as one of those basalt rocks you'll be struck by a malady so acute you'll never make it back.

Our village is full of farmers, sailors, shopkeepers, priests, wives, and children. Surely their village is also. We have a history of volcanoes, earthquakes, Venetians and saffron gatherers. Like as not, they share a similar past. They probably pass their days doing the same things as us, tending their vineyards, cultivating tomatoes and melons. Their trees bear figs and mulberries. Their *yayás* probably cook chickpeas, rubbed to loosen the skins, bake *tiropita* and pick *hirovoski* on their cliffs. Their *kourabiethes* might be as crumbly as ours, their *ouzo* as fiery. If Zaforá was anything to go by, their women are goddesses.

Yayá was plaiting *tsoureki* and boiling eggs in beetroot juice.

'Did you ever see my father again?'

'Each morning I woke to our empty house and prayed to the Virgin Mary to return my only son to me. No word came; only rumours slipped from loose tongues. But five years later, Maroulia showed up on our doorstep with you, a small bundle, in her arms. She was mute and too weak to stand. I nursed her myself, spoon-feeding her with saffron rice, the cure for melancholy. But she'd lost her will. The last day she pulled herself out of bed to a chair by the window. She sat, staring, past the flowerpots, sleeping cats, and you at play, her eyes fixed on Thirasia. I couldn't read her expression but something there had a hold on her.

'Dimitri, brush these with egg white. Careful, don't splash.'

Yayá lay down that afternoon for her *siesta* on Great Friday, thirty years ago, and died. My work as postmaster keeps me occupied. Alone many years now, I'm neighbour to all, loved by none. Being the only villager with red hair would be misdemeanour enough but being born out of wedlock to an eloped couple is unspeakable. Isolation becomes habit. So much of who we are is a fulfilment of others' expectations.

By full moon I scrutinise Thirasia's shadowy contours for a tell-tale flicker of candle or gas lamp. The occasional glimmer seems more firefly than human. When sleep is impossible, I stumble over to sit in the same chair my mother spent her dying days in. I stare through the darkness where the monstrous she-dragon, Kampe, lies in wait. On good nights, I'm on the island opposite, with my father. A light at his window, he holds a vigil. I raise my glass of *ouzo* to him.

'*Yamas!*' he coughs, spits, clinks his against mine.

We drink and speak of how things might have been. We never speak of what was.

On bad nights, when *tsipourou* has numbed me past caring, I see his wiry body twisted in a blanket. Emptied bottles, overturned glasses and overflowing ashtrays lie about his mattress. Next to him, a pale naked woman sleeps, long saffron hair spread on the pillow like a flame. Her limbs are too long, her waist too narrow, and breasts too voluptuous to be human.

She steps out onto the balcony, towing something after her. She taps a pack of Karelias against her palm; a match flares. She turns toward the moon, exhaling smoke. Her draped *peplos* slips down, revealing black wings, folded along her back. She drags behind her a segmented tail that thins to a hypodermic barb.

Shortcut to Heaven

They are shut out when Ainsley seals the door. The sun remains burned on his retina. Days later he will conjure up the textures, rough cinderblock or velvet bougainvillea. And colours; the amber of his bottled urine, the red earth scattered with rusty tools, the cobalt sky. Yet right now he craves the dark room. Everyone does, even without knowing it. Stopping just short of the mattress, he reaches out till he touches the prickle of the wool blanket and sits.

The last few days of preparation have been intense, but glitches persist. He rigged the solar panel system and fan; washed bedding; stitched swathes of plastic shower curtain. On the outside, he can tweak the plumbing or fetch fruit from Pana. Inside, he's a prisoner. But Ainsley is on the verge of a breakthrough on his mission to retrieve beatitude. He lies back and inhales the blanket's oils. This weariness, that unfurls back across generations, is ancient. His body is a mechanism that functions better under orchestrated conditions but even the finest-tuned slumber brings only passing relief. He hangs sheets of black plastic over his bedroom windows. No electronic lights glow in his room. He wears earplugs.

Rapture, experienced on one single occasion as an adolescent, haunts him. Bliss, in the body of a fifteen-year-old; prone, running fingers through blades of grass, sipping cool air. For a quarter of a century he's been searching for the elusive portal back. To chart steps that leave no trace. There has to be a way in. But heaven, more slippery than a bar of wet soap, is hard to grasp. Ecstasy, the natural human condition, sours in everyday life to suffering. Ainsley's childhood was muted. Beyond his home, he found the schism was greater than he'd thought. He wandered from one state to the next, from mobile homes to soup kitchens, community yurts to adobe huts. Hungry-eyed, drifty girls shared his bed, harbouring appetites he couldn't satisfy. Doors opened, couches unfolded, dinners were cooked. But beneath their charm something lurked. He wandered along a hall of mirrors; his soul, convex, concave, fractured and warped, reflected back at him.

Solicitous hosts lost patience. Children, excited by his wackiness, presently grew bored. Two or three harboured a suspicion Ainsley was taking advantage. He failed to notice. When he did, their small-mindedness offended him. A trailblazer with revolutionary work of magnitude to accomplish, he might even be a contemporary bodhisattva, dragging every last human into liberation. So what if he didn't pay Tokyo's gas bill? If the laptop he borrowed from Mia got a bug? Or he devoured Duke's kilo of peaches?

Ainsley has sampled Tantric Hinduism, Buddhist meditation, crystals, stones, shamanism, and shiatsu. He's read Gurdjieff, Herbert M. Shelton, Arnaud Desjardins, Immanuel Velikovsky. He is structuring his way. Callous to anything but the Grail, he's knocked on ashram gates and realised teachers' doors. And dismantled a few. He hit upon darkness: profound rest that allowed consciousness to recover. An ancient idea tried and tested by hermits. Unable to face another winter, he bought a one-way ticket to Guatemala. Baptised in warmth as he stepped off the plane, he peeled off his wool sweater and left it on the tarmac. Neither pollution nor poverty dampened his elation. He found his way to Lake Atitlán, where both were less conspicuous.

Ainsley's piercing eyes, acetic brow, hollow cheeks and humble demeanor mask an ego that propels him. His credentials are indoctrination in original sin, a rock-star twin brother turned Tantric guru. And a father who sends him a couple of hundred dollars a month. It's a license for sagehood. His conjecture has form: thick walls, a fan, compost toilet, and shower. Darkness envelops him in security and unconditional love. Here, there are no demons. No dilemmas or dramas. Silence wraps around him like a Madonna's arms. No difficult concepts, nor harsh doctrines, no acts of faith. No awkward positions, tricky mantras, or esoteric instructions. Hibernation strips off the psyche's layers, one by one, a lover undressing her *inamorata*. Outer skins fall away, followed by the softer, intimate membranes until the core is reached. Unhooked from gross matter, the soul repairs itself.

Ainsley recognises the rest of the world as chronically exhausted at best, psychotic for the most part. Deprived of dreamtime. When animals get sick, they crawl into a grotto to heal but humans persist in denial of their physical unease and spiritual confusion, clinging to their egos like life rafts. When dissatisfaction overwhelms, they try to escape. But the organism can repair. Respite is the primary condition of healing. It's like falling through a trap door of consciousness. Ainsley's conjecture is founded on three tenets: darkness, silence, and slumber. Forty-eight hours of tenebrous salvation restores a lifetime's lack of sleep. He will prove it by emerging rehabilitated with all his faculties but none of his fears.

Ainsley lifts the latch on the door. At first just a crack to let his eyes adjust to the light. Some hours later he steps out. Cinderblock the texture of puffed rice, the bougainvillea's pile so soft he could sink into it. Those colours; amber of bottled urine, red earth scattered with rusty tools, cobalt sky. It is enough. Much more than enough. He craves nothing.

THE UPTURNED BOWL

It was only after Auntie Maya kissed his forehead and left him at the gate that Upali started to sob. Auntie was the last thing he could claim as his own. As the tuk-tuk bore her away, the taciturn monk echoed Lord Buddha: 'Which is greater, the tears you have shed while wandering or the water in the four great oceans?' to which, of course, Upali had no answer. The surly fellow led him to the dormitory, pointed to his bed and left. On the white sheet lay a folded square of saffron material to make a robe of. There were nine more beds, ten tables, and four bare white walls. Upali put the banana leaf filled with Auntie's vegetable *kottu* on his bed. He had no appetite; he'd fed his roti to Kanthaka that morning.

From the balcony he watched flying foxes swoop and cut as dusk settled. Further along, he discovered a room filled with statues, photos of monks, and scrolls in wooden boxes. Climbing the steps, guarded by colourful gods and devils, he sat before the domed stupa. Which of the forty-thousandth-of-the-Buddha's-body was inside: a tooth, a rib fragment, or a smidgen of navel ash? Auntie Maya had told him that before Lord Buddha died, a disciple asked him what form a shrine should take. Gautama placed his folded robe on the earth, with his upturned begging bowl on top and rested his umbrella against the bowl.

Behind the stupa he found chillies, curry, tomatoes, *brinjal*, and okra flourishing in the shade of a jackfruit tree. Jasmine and *pansal mal* grew beneath the stalactite-trunk of a bodhi tree wound with a rainbow of flags; a light breeze ruffled its glossy leaves. A brilliant lorikeet bobbed on a branch whistling *twi-wit-wit*. Inside the *vihara* he sat on tiles decorated with elephants, horses, lions, and bulls pivoting the wheel of life. A huge buddha reclined behind a lace curtain, his serene lady face propped on a plump yellow arm, framed by black curls, eyes coyly lowered, huge earlobes drooping. Saffron robes hugged his curves. A mirror at his soles reflected back the magenta designs inscribed on them. On a long table, a dozen saucers of frangipani petals weighted the air with their fragrance.

Upali fell asleep.

He was an ordinary Sinhalese boy living in a small town, known for its saltpans, on the south coast of the Sacred Island. Each day, his father, a Ratnapura gem-setter on Bazaar Street, left the house as Upali ate breakfast, returning late at night. Ama took care of him, his little sister, and everything else. Asita and Upali spent their mornings at school, in pressed white uniforms, reciting lessons in English, Tamil, and Sinhalese. Afternoons they played in the shade of coconut palms and pawpaw trees. They had two ribby ginger dogs, with big heads and white eye-patches, four speckled chickens, and a milk-cow the colour of jaggery. In one corner of their home a shrine stood, to which they offered incense and petals. Opposite was the bed they all slept in. The *mahout* next door let them ride his elephant before he led it to the beach. In dry season, they watched father play cricket.

That morning, they'd gone to the market just before six. Monks were chanting, cross-legged outside stupas. Malays, in long white shirts and brocade caps, were returning home from the first call to prayer. Hambantota's Christians gathered for mass. Tamils brought petals to offer Shiva. Lining the street were wooden boxes brimming with the day's catch, piles of yellow coconuts, small dark watermelons, and hands of green bananas. Women in their best saris or chadors bought bags of white rice for biriyani from shops along the seafront. Tuk-tuk drivers pulled over to eat freshly fried *hoppers*. Father bought them a ginger beer; they fought for sips from the brown glass bottle, bending the straw this way and that. Ama was filling a vendor's scales with okra when a noise, like a vast body of water rushing down a colossal drain, brought everything to a standstill.

They looked up. Before their eyes the Indian Ocean, subservient only to the moon before, pulled away. A moment of dumbfounded silence was followed by a whoop as hundreds ran across the sands to collect the stranded fish into their arms. Father was one. Asita laughed out loud.

'A miracle!' Ama murmured.

How could they know the sliding water was an intake of breath before a giant exhalation? Mythic waves, like monkey armies and King Ravana's sprouting heads, belonged to Ramayana storybooks.

'Fishes, fishes, fishes!' cried Asita clapping her hands, 'So many slippy fishes!'

'But where did all the water go?' Upali asked.

Ama was silent. He tugged on her arm.

'Ama, where...?' His mother's face was drawn in a taut grimace he mistook for a smile. She was squinting into the distance, one hand on her full-term belly, the other folded over Asita's hand. Upa followed her gaze. Two storeys high, cutting out a slab of sky, lifting the horizon, it came, a wonder without history or implication. Upali's eyes dropped to where father stood on the sands. Letting go of Asita, Ama cupped her hands around her mouth and yelled. Others also screamed and flailed their arms wildly. Those that had run into the breach couldn't hear. A rushing noise replaced the sucking sound, drowning Ama's cries. One by one, the fish-harvesters looked up, dropped their catch and ran. Father, with his batsman's sprint, bolted towards them. He scooped Asita up, her fist still full of okra. He grabbed Ama's hand. She, in turn, dragged Upali. They headed towards the mosque. But when it reached them, moiling and churning, its force broke their grip. Each was propelled hundreds of feet forward.

They didn't understand, even as it washed over them.

Elephants had marched inland before dawn. Furrowed-brow macaques chattered complaints to their winged neighbours minutes before. Peacocks, sharing the topmost branches with egrets, kingfishers, and cormorants, kept a bird's-eye vigil. Crocodiles, iguanas, and salamander froze, still as dead wood. Birds took wing while roosters drowned. Tuk-tuks and tractors were overturned. The *muezzin* was swept from the mosque. The church bells swung, dumbly, underwater.

Upali was unsure of what happened. When he came to, a hush had fallen across Hambantota like sand flung before a coffin. For months after, he would hear only the reverberations of the ocean's cudgel. In the next hours, he saw stunned survivors clutching a toy, curd bowl, or coconut grater; all that connected them to the past. Dazed, they slept-walked through a puzzle-town of scattered pieces, muddled forever. He discovered Ama's body, half a block from their house, curled beneath a jackfruit tree, one palm cradling her belly, the other fist full of earth. He never found Father or Asita.

Days later, an old temple spinster discovered Upali. When the second wave slunk back, Madam's home was still standing; not a plate or cup broken, everything rearranged. She lost nothing, not even little Kanthaka, but gained this young boy, who had wandered exhausted into her garden and coiled up beneath her aloe. She was too frail to bear his weight, so a neighbour carried Upali into Madam's yard. She fed him and he slept for hours on her porch. She woke to find him in her yard; arranging, dismantling, and re-arranging a clay bowl, stick, and sodden mat into the shape of a stupa. There was nothing to do but look after him until a relative claimed him.

His father, tall and lithe, was one of the dead.

Asita, not yet five, a second.

Ama, and the child in her womb, two more.

The school building and his teacher, Madam Sirimavo, were no more. Gone were the ribby dogs and cow the colour of jaggery. Ama's sweet voice and curry belonged to the past; flown were the *kotturuwas,* his father's goodnight hugs no more. Next door's tusker had stampeded, joining his wild brothers. The *mahout* spent his days under a guava tree talking gibberish. Upali's best friend, Diyon, went to live with an aunt in Tissamaharama, which may as well have been the other side of the world.

Upali missed so many things his loss of speech hardly registered.

The tsunami's kick was acute, the damage chronic. Images of corpses (against walls, on car roofs, tangled in the branches of bodhi trees, buried in saltpans) were seared in memory. Ghosts like undeveloped negatives lingered; portraits of needle-mouthed, big-bellied *petas* or radiant *devas*. Life froze in its frame that day and, though it rolled once more, its colours were blanched. It is possible for pummelled stones to never recover. For houses to be bruised, temples battered, roads raped. Hambantota bore its ruins like scars.

Auntie Maya cared for Upali doggedly. She coaxed him to the new government school and the US Aid playground. She stroked his brow when he had nightmares. He fell asleep lipreading her familiar chants and the lessons she intoned, handed out by aid agencies for him to memorise. Perhaps she thought one day he'd ring them back at her, like the hammer and anvil of a coppersmith echoing its mate. Those silent phrases still replay when his mind wanders from meditation. Her wisdom ran through his days like the heat of her *sambol*. It was Auntie Maya who taught him that suffering is caused by attachment. That the only escape is through right understanding, thought, action, livelihood, effort, mindfulness, and concentration.

She left out right speech.

When Upali woke, it was dawn. His body was numb and he was still in the temple. A very old monk sat meditating before the shrine. Skinny, with high cheekbones and white fuzz on his pate, he turned after some time and smiled. 'Welcome. You have come on a long journey from your many births. We will help in your struggle to escape *samsara*. But first... breakfast! Madam told me your favourite is coconut roti? Jayakumar makes the best you've ever tasted. Come.'

Upali followed him into the refectory of seated monks passing a pot of tea along the table. A few looked up as he passed. The head monk took his place and waved him on to an empty chair at the far end, beside a boy with a mischievous expression: 'Who are you?'

Upali bowed his head and looked into the bowl of his cupped palms.

Empty Pockets

'Sorry, darling, simply too big a risk,' Ma Pru texts.

'Still happening?' Emil, known for his spunkiness.

'Not sure we can make it.' A prep-school friend.

'Feel crap. Might have to pass.' Naz, my clubbing partner.

'Sorry, hon, got the blues.' The cameraman who worked on *Blackfish* with me.

'Emi was sacked. Licking our wounds at home.' The producer.

'Yuwa has a sore throat. Apologies!' My Nigerian ex.

Turning fifty isn't joyful under normal circumstances. Today it feels irrelevant. All that planning for a party to end all parties; the room above the Colonel Fawcett, the soul band, caterers, invites, the fight with the pastry chef over less sugar in the chocolate mousse. I've put it on hold. I always felt empathy for Mrs Dalloway, but at least her do wasn't cancelled. There *will* be a party I tell my friends, the band, Colonel Fawcett, and the taciturn pastry cook. Who knows when. But there *will* be a party.

Tonight I'll salvage a get-together for whoever can make it.

A documentary I worked on two years ago marked the centenary of the last pandemic, blamed on rural Chinese shunted in containers to labour on the Western Front. But Americans brought it to Europe. Kindled amongst malnourished soldiers, it smouldered across trade and shipping lines, igniting three infernos that year. Spain, the only country with an uncensored press free to report on it, gave the flu its name. A third of the world was infected. More than three per cent of the population reduced to dust.

Suddenly there's not much to do. I've got fine cheese, crackers, a spinach pie, half a dozen bottles of wine and some weed, to kick off. I revise my playlist and put clean towels in the bathroom. By one o' clock I'm done. I go out. The streets are deserted. On the almost empty bus, a small number of passengers are wearing masks, one or two have a scarf wrapped around their faces. The odd person in a café stares into the middle distance. I get off at Old Street and walk towards Bank. There's no queue for the Sky Garden; I'm ushered up to the thirty-fourth floor before I ask myself why. I order a G&T at the bar and step through glass doors onto the balcony. The distant city numbly curls around the Thames: Tower Bridge, the Gherkin, the Shard, the Eye, the Houses of Parliament. Pruned of people, its buildings and icons empty, arteries stilled: the City is abridged, a skeleton.

Sobered, I descend. I stop by Waitrose for a sandwich, ominously reduced to ten pence. The headline 'Loved Ones Will Die' contrasts with the one seven days ago: 'First Coronavirus death in UK'. How rapidly things change. I sit by an installation, *Forgotten Streams*, marking an underground river that once flowed through the City. Other days, the title might inspire a faint nostalgia, a reimagining of Shakespeare's or Pepys' London, teaming with hawkers, duchesses, and rogues. Today I eat my cheap sandwich wondering what else we will forget in months to come. Will we forget what it feels like to get lost in a crowd of Saturday shoppers on Oxford Street? To pack our bodies in rush hour's underground anonymity? To sweat in one collective transpiration at a rave or Pilates class? Will teenagers not know the dubious pleasure of house parties or a one-night stand?

How far can Britain go? Will we, like Korea, ban international flights? Could we, like Iran, prevent concerts or, like the Japanese, close schools? Might we copy Italy, anchoring people to their districts with police check-points? Forbid our locals to watch the world go by from a café pavement as in France? Or go as far as China and haul away those with temperatures to enforced isolation? Dystopic scenarios like this are grotesquely far-fetched, risible even... except they are already happening. I came of age against the backdrop of

AIDS, which changed how we thought about intimacy. Will I grow old in a world where we keep one other at arm's length? Spanish influenza took place in another era. We understand contagion better. But is the price of progress hysteria? The less accustomed to mortality we are, the more fearful we grow. For most of the world, infirmity, scarcity, and poverty is normal. So far, less than a hundred people have died in this country. It is viral information, not the virus, that haunts us; a loss of reason, almost a neurosis. SARS-CoV-2 has caught government and big tech's imagination, run riot on social media.

I make my way along Cannon Street. A couple of stray tourists, dragging noisy wheelie-bags, stand out for being the only ones. Tottenham Court Road is hushed; the homeless, druggies, and bedlamites trailing blankets, pushing trolleys, or sitting on cardboard boxes outnumber the shoppers. Soho feels out of kilter, passers-by mute or too boisterous. A clutch of tipsy Essex girls fills Old Compton Street with hysterical laughter, ventriloquising the general mood. In Covent Garden, I stop in Neil's Yard to stock up on moisturiser. My favourite shop has a sign on the door: 'We put our customers first and have decided to shut till further notice.' The place I stop for a latte has a sign at the till: 'At this time we are only accepting cards, not cash.'

On the empty Northern Line home, it occurs to me I haven't seen a single elder or infant. Indoors, I clamber into a hot bath and weep. For myself, of course. My family. For my corner of northwest London. For the world as I've known it. For the staggering scale of whatever is to be unleashed. I climb out of the bath and rub steam from the mirror to find my mother staring back at me. The sweats are coming more often these days, and I think of Clarissa Dalloway, so young yet 'unspeakably aged'.

I put on the dress I was going to wear. Given I'm staying home, it looks ridiculous. A gift from Laurie, who I've hardly thought of. More a steady Richard than an enigmatic Peter, he and I followed the script of divorced man and middle-aged woman; when he broke it off my relief was palpable. Eat your heart out Mrs D: women *have* changed. The Yves St Laurent number, come to think of it, isn't right. An AllSaints t-shirt and 501s are more me.

They come. In ones, twos, and threes, till my house is throbbing. Childhood friends, those I've known since my twenties, work colleagues. Single, in couples, gay, lesbian, black, white, Jewish, and not. Twenty-somethings to fifty-somethings, with kids, without, in television or the arts, locals, Londoners. My sister and my cousin. Most hesitate to hug; they do a little dance instead, knock elbows or mime high fives. Others cling, as if for the last time. The vibe is good, noisy, assertive. We party. We drink. We smoke. We talk. OK, we talk about the virus mostly. Even when we talk about other things, it always comes back to that.

Aileen bounds up the stairs full of laughter, hitting hips.

'Already been in bloody quarantine two weeks since my bunion operation – I'm dying of boredom.'

'Our daughter and her boyfriend, on their gap year, are stuck in Colombia. Could be worse,' Adam and Jules.

'Fuck, I'm supposed to be flying to Madrid this Sunday.'

'We're meant to be going home for my niece's wedding in a fortnight.'

'Our daughter is stuck in a Paris bedsit; as of Monday neither café nor library will be open for her to study in.'

'Doubt I'll make it back to Vancouver, before my ma dies.'

'What about music festivals,' my cousin adds. 'And Passover? Our chairs will have to be four feet apart at the Seder.'

'Eleven plagues to recount instead of ten!' my sister adds.

Emil comes over to my side, edgier than usual. We talk about Denmark's reaction and how slow we've been. His sixteen-day tour for high-flying techies was cancelled last night. Today, he was fired, along with a thousand other freelance tour operators. At least Dave's still in work, I gesture to his stolid partner, with his full beard, tattoos and piercings, drinking ale at my table. Emil shakes his head.

'Dave's hospital documentary was pulled this morning.'

As we smile, crack jokes, do lines, and pass a spliff, there is the nagging sense of facing an apocalypse. We have no idea what this scared new world implies.

'Remember that thing Ma Pru used to say, sis? "If the wind

changes, your face will get stuck?" Well, feels like the gale roiled, span, and flung us down. The clocks are stayed and wherever you are is where you're going to be for some time. Imagine you're a Wuhan factory worker... stuck at home for a month. Or a domestic in Delhi? Destitution is around the corner.'

'In a difficult marriage in Rome? *Merda!*' adds Jules.

'Alone, like me? Game over,' sighs my cousin as she rolls a joint.

'Living with narky teenagers in Madrid? *Mala suerte.*'

'Illegal in Athens? *Dískolo.*'

'Or a luvvie? Universal Credit.'

'A nurse or a policeman? A job for life,' grins James.

'Like IT! Wow, wow, wow! Or big pharma!' Florian fans his fingers.

'Pandemics are as old as the earth – like forest fires, clearing dead wood for new growth. Perhaps this one will incinerate our collective karma?'

'James, the optimist! Considering how shit we've been to the world, we must be on borrowed time.'

'Karma, like God, is dead,' says Florian, 'Long live tech! I reckon there'll be some new war fought between the almighty companies we'll be more reliant on than ever if we can't leave home. Big tech will get even richer and vilely powerful. We'll be driven deeper online and further from ourselves...' Florian is interrupted by my sister bringing in the chocolate mousse.

Everyone sings 'Happy Birthday' and Emil pretends to wash his hands. I blow out the fifty candles. I make one wish with my eyes squeezed shut; this bad dream will end.

'All day,' I say, 'I kept feeling like Meryl Streep in *The Hours*, time slowed to a Virginia Woolf-like stream-of-consciousness. But all of this makes Clarissa's dilemmas quaint.' The lines have loosened my tongue. It's as though the entire world has filled its pockets with pebbles, is wading into the river. Time to jettison the ballast.

Cane Stalks

There was A time when Kap would have resisted a wild goose-chase into La Libertad's boonies. But since his wife had left, the several hours' drive to report on sugar-cane production was a welcome distraction. When he'd put to bed circular projections over his failed marriage his thoughts turned to his countrymen, born with AK-47s in their hands and Hail Marys on their lips. Three decades of civil war had segued into the drug war. To the trinity of national emblems that every *pre-primaria* child learned (the winged *quetzal*, the *monja blanca* blossom and the *ceiba* tree), they should have added a national motto: 'Shoot first, pray after.'

Kap spent the afternoon with the nervy Los Cocos foreman, who explained his boss, Don Otto Salguero, was at a funeral. He took him on a tour of the offices and plantation, but Kap sensed he was unwelcome. The foreman didn't even nod at the *graneleros* as they toiled, clothes stiff with sweat and syrup. An inexhaustible resource, these small men who spoke little Spanish earned two dollars for every metric ton of cane they cut.

As Kap's head hit the pillow that night he realised he'd left his iPod somewhere. Shortly after dawn he showered and headed back to the *finca*. Oddly, there was no guard at the gates. Desperate to piss, he parked and made toward a long shed across a field of cut cane. On his way back, he tripped on something, too soft to be a stone, amongst the dried stalks. A face, caked in blood, stared past him. Staggering to the pick-up, gaze trained on the ground, Kap glimpsed a decapitated body and two more heads.

He pressed his backside against the *picop*'s door and hunched over, hands resting on knees, to steady himself against the horizon's sway. After a while, he stepped up into the cab and slumped over the steering wheel, cradling his head in his arms. At the sound of grunting he looked up; a bloody *campesino* hobbled toward him, waving. Reaching the bonnet, he threw his hands across it like a drowning man clutching at a passing log.

'*Qué pasó aquí?*' Kap demanded. What happened?

'*Qué horror! Qué horror!*'

'*Pero ¿quién hizo esto, muchacho?*' Who did this?

'*Saber... saber,*' cried the fellow. Who knows?

'*Pase,*' ordered Kap. Get in.

The *campesino* swung himself into the wagon. Kap drove to Don Salguero's house but the maid didn't know where he was. He went to the refinery, then the police station. A police van followed them back to the cane fields. In the next hours, officers from La Libertad and the rest of Petén arrived. Kap watched as they dragged the bodies into one heap. Twenty-eight. Two women and three children. Nameless labourers hired by the season.

The little man, in his black gumboots and soiled clothes, told the police he was from El Quiché. The others were from the mountains, peripatetic labourers, hitching from cane to coffee harvests to their own subsistence *milpas* and back. None had finished third grade, paid taxes, nor knew a thing about the man who hired the man who hired them. They couldn't read the papers. They hadn't heard Salguero's wife and father had been killed a week before. Nor that they were found with a note, written in blood, pinned to the bodies: 'Otto Salguero I am coming for you, Z200'.

When the gangsters showed up the *campesinos* told them: 'We know nothing.' But the Zetas started hacking at them anyway. They fell like cane stalks, their blood soaking into the dry soil they'd just cleared. The survivor said: 'They came, took our *machetes* and killed us, one by one. Except me.' Knifed in the thigh, he'd curled up and passed for dead. When he came to he was so terrified he didn't move for hours. As the last moans subsided and he was sure the Zetas were gone, he crawled to the shed to take refuge. By dawn's first light he saw the carnage. And not too long after, Kap. There was a piece of card, pinned with a rusty nail to a corpse, which the police read to him: 'What's up, Mister Otto Salguero? I'm going to find you and kill you.'

By the time the paperwork was done it was dark. Kap wanted to drive home but his head was throbbing so badly he checked in to the hotel once more. After sporadic sleep dominated by depleting nightmares, he bolted a breakfast of black beans and eggs, reading *Siglo XXI*'s lead story; Salguero, the trafficker, had escaped the Zetas, disappearing without a trace. The President placed Coban in a state of emergency and was sending in the army.

On the drive home, Kap stopped to buy a green coconut at the roadside from a woman with a transcendent smile. Taking long draughts of milk through the plastic straw, he kicked the dirt at the tarmac's side with his toe. The lush tangle of vegetation and sumptuous unfurled sky reminded him that while he might not, this place would survive all hells.

PART THREE
NO-SELF
MUGA

Beings and things are empty of self-existence.
Attachment to self or others is the cause of human suffering.
Realisation recognises no such self exists.

Mu!

*A monk asked, 'Does a dog have Buddha nature or not?' Jôshû
said, 'Mu!'*

I pass through the winged gates of the monastery, climb the path that circumvents the monk's hut, and take the wooden ramp that leads past the kitchen to the shrine. Suzy goes wild as I pass her: only her chain holds her.

What brought me here? I know nobody. I flew to Yangon via Bangkok, then took a series of busses north to Kalaw. I'm without Eva, who is visiting her father in a latitude just six degrees north, ten thousand miles away. I don't know if he will bring her home. Our displaced tussle is being mediated over poor connections between failing states. Being here paradoxically grounds me; I am so restless, rootlessness settles me.

The road to the monastery is glutted with vivid colours, the scent of baked earth, and lush swaying foliage. Stilts push through the soil, supporting homes. The wooden *mohinga* stall is crowded by school children in white shirts and green *dhotis*. Their mothers, hair tied in brilliant scarves, walk home from the fields, bamboo basket straps around their foreheads. Lines, descending in size, of barefoot, saffron-robed monks snake past me, receiving alms, black bowls tucked under their arms.

White begonias, lychees, mangos, and a glass of water have been offered at the Buddha shrine. Unfurled below are a sequined patchwork of fields of sesame, corn, and lentils. Here and there, acacia, mimosa, tamarind, and *thanaka* grow. Slender red paths trellis about the handkerchief meadows, curling up and down the valley. I sit, legs crossed, below the stone shrine, listening to the calls of *yahunas* and babblers.

We spend every summer in an abandoned island village, where my parents have bought a quake-wrecked cave. We run down the three hundred and sixty-four steps to swim in the sea, crap in a traditional dry toilet, bathe under the stream of a can filled from a well that collects rainwater from the patio. My days are spent exploring ruins that line the cobbled streets in the company of strays. My mongrel, back home, is never far from my thoughts, but I shower displaced affection on the street dogs. Most nights are spent in the taverna, dancing.

Lagging behind my mother, struggling with bags of shopping along marble paths, I have my first lesson in carnivory. The local butcher overtakes me running, a half carcass of a lamb slung over his white-coated arm. From neck to shank, through shoulder, rib, loin, and leg, through cleaved vertebrae, the exposed cavity of ivory skeleton, fat and crimson gore is laid bare. Shorn, headless, its forelegs pruned, it resembles my dog, stripped of fur, and, though I'd rather not think of it, my own torso.

But what keeps my eyes glued to the marble paving slabs ahead, is the drip, drip, drip of warm blood. The butcher, short of breath, dumps the corpse on his huge wooden slab, and I make the visceral connection between slaughtered animal and my mother's dinners. Born in the twenties, she grills chops and steaks or moulds mince into meatballs; something dies for every dinner. She and my brother, the family gourmand, compete over who can stomach the bloodiest fillet.

Some journeys nudge you off your habitual path; discrete, numinous moments build slowly. I know, a month in, in the tranquillity of that valley, that this will be one. I walk, one step after another: content, mindful, and at ease. It has taken many visits to the monastery to get me to this place. Each day I've benefited from Sayadaw's teaching. He makes sense of my hesitant questions and confusion; he listens, nods, and smiles. Knowing all this will pass is enough. I get to where the walkway forks, up to the kitchen or down to Sayadaw's hut. I usually walk up around the kitchen but, today, I take the path down.

Everything is still, sultry; Sayadaw is napping. Under the cabin floor, in the shade, Suzy is dozing against a wooden stilt. I consider turning to avoid waking dog and master, but I'm already too close. I pass her, thinking I've made it, when suddenly a rush of wind buffets me off the path, onto my side. In that fleeting moment she travels with me, her teeth sunk into my forearm, and her glazed eyes meet mine. We are conjoined like twins or lovers. Sated, she turns and slinks back to her dugout. I look down at the viscid blood that oozes down my left forearm arm and seeps into the red earth. My pulse slows, my left side freezes. After days of sitting, moments slip by before I manage a pathetic howl. Sayadaw comes running down the wooden steps, half asleep, robes flapping: 'Suzy! Suzy!'

Sayadaw guides me up the steps into his hut and I sink onto the wooden floor, flooded with nausea. The room is so muddled it looks like it's been burgled; my eyes rest on a pirate DVD, Sylvester Stallone, abs flexed, revolver slung around his neck. Sayadaw pulls one drawer out after the next, his movements jerky.

'Hold it up, hold it up,' he cries; his fear shocks me.

He finds sachets of saline and pours them over the gashes with shaking hands. He sees what I haven't; the second wound from Suzy's lower jaw on the underside of my arm. He shouts out his door and the cook comes running. He gives curt instructions and stuffs money in her hand. Taking my good elbow, she guides me to her moped and kick-starts it as I scramble on. I cling to her with my right arm as my left bleeds all over her plum jacket. She drives, avoiding the potholes, to the Golden Lily Guest House. The blind Sikh landlady on the balcony calls her sister, who panics but gives the cook directions. We arrive at the surgery, where some twenty people are sitting quietly outside on benches in the wide dirt street, waiting. A feverish baby lies on her mother's lap. Ailing men lean on their wives' shoulders. There is no hint of impatience. Their capacity for selflessness demands it from me.

When the doctors arrive, a husband and wife, they see us in turn. The consultation room is just large enough for an operating table and two plastic chairs. The husband asks the cook questions in Burmese and me some in English. He cleans the wound and dresses it with copious amounts of white lint. He tells me he'll order the rabies vaccine and to come back tomorrow. Over the next three days, he cuts away the infected flesh; a dog's mouth is the foulest of all animals, he explains, second only to humans.

The days in my room pass slowly. I practice one-handed yoga. I read or write. Take showers with plastic bags wrapped around my left arm. Have conversations with travellers on the veranda. Some Croatians arrive, just released from a police station for camping in a forbidden zone. An Italian takes me to a school to teach English. A Japanese-Hawaiian makes friends with me. The Sikh sisters make me special breakfasts of eggs and naan and bring me fruit. One of their sons spends hours explaining Myanmar's complex history and lends me books in English, some forbidden under the regime.

I'm twelve. Another long Oia summer. My brother returns from spearfishing, vexed he failed to catch an octopus or anything 'worthwhile'. He has a large snail, almost a foot from tip to outer rim. He puts a large pot of water on the stove and rummages for a length of rope in the back room. He explains how he'll drop it into the boiling water. When the water boils, the snail will extend his foot, and his girlfriend is to tie the rope and yank it tight. As they are distracted, pouring wine, I slip into the steamy kitchen and snatch the snail. Hightailing it out of the door, I flee down the steps to the sea. My brother catches up and grabs me, taking the snail back. On our walk home, he identifies my inconsistencies. I eat cows, pigs, and chickens so why not snails? I stop eating meat.

Over those many solitary hours, I discover meditation. From Myanmar, it's difficult to talk to Eva; there's either no electricity or no connection. Freakishly, the few days before Suzy bites me, Eva is bitten by a *pizote*, a raccoon with a ringed tail, while exploring Mayan ruins. The implausibility of a near simultaneous bite on the other side of the world confounds me. I'm sleepless, worrying about not being there to kiss away her tears or hold her close. Beyond logistics is my brush with mortality. The flesh around my wound is rotting.

A local tells me that half of Myanmar's dogs are infected with rabies; I have no idea if the inoculations have been in time or will be effective. The nearest city, Yangon, is eighteen hours away and hostile. From there, home is another twenty-four hours away. Cossetted by meditation, I'm mostly placid. The demarcation between life and death is less credible than the borders drawn between Myanmar and India. Everything is less than real; my belief in things is suspended. Suzy has reminded me that we're all animals, guided by base instincts to sleep, eat, and bond. If I surrender to fear, I'm no different than Suzy who attacks, slinks away, forgets.

I mention to another traveller that Sayadaw doesn't know what's become of me. He walks the two hours to the monastery and back to tell him that I'm okay.

I am thirty, married, living in a two-up two-down in Hackney. I've given up my managerial job at a charity to write theatre reviews. To support myself I become a freelance sub-editor. Around this time something shifts in my relationship though I can't put a finger on it. I am in love with what we could be and in despair with how short we fall of it. Coming home from long commutes, I cook. One night we fight; he throws his drink at me. Sticky with pineapple juice and coconut milk, I run a bath, which he gets into.

I plough my right fist through the bathroom window. Glass shatters like blown sugar over the knuckles and lodges in my wrist. My neighbour makes a tourniquet with a leather belt to stem the bloody fountain. The ambulance drops us at Homerton Hospital. The junior doctor says it's too late to remove the glass as he stitches me. If the shards stay put, I should be okay. Some months later I discover my husband is having an affair with a trainee. In hindsight, the slaughtered lamb, adultery, and animal instinct coalesce. The viscous threads of delusion and emptiness knit.

On the third day, the wounds are clean enough to stitch. The doctor plunges a syringe full of anaesthetic six times around the wounds and holds my hand while her husband makes the stitches. They work side by side, wordlessly. It seems impossible the gore will knit back. He laughs when he catches me staring at his handiwork. She shakes her head. Plunged into darkness by a power cut, he continues to work by the light of his headlamp. He makes nine stitches on the brachioradialis near the crook, five on the flexors halfway down the forearm.

These unasked-for mother-of-pearl hieroglyphics, on my left forearm, are Suzy's indelible mark. The glass-scored bow and fletched arrow-tail, on the inside of my right wrist, a token of my shattered marriage. Each time they catch my eye they are a nudging reminder of how driven we are by desire. Of my emptiness. Or lack of it.

Footprints

Clinging to the rail to prevent himself from being pitched into the aisle, he doggedly took in the glittering reservoirs, abundant jungle, and pellucid sky that lay beyond the glass. They arrived in Dalhousie after dark. The old man hesitated before he stepped onto solid ground. He stopped at the first hotel for *kottu* and sweet tea. Refilling his bottle with water, he knotted his *lunghi* tight about his waist and followed the trail of huddled vendors drinking tea beside their stalls of hats or slabs of sweetmeats. He wondered who bought all their wares, since he appeared to be alone. But as first one, then several pilgrims overtook him he realised there were many.

Soon, the sandcastle silhouette was lit with flickering bulbs. Behind him a ripe moon filled the sky with preternatural light. The Yatavara *bhikkhu* who'd sent him was right; this place was sacred. Only a couple of miles from his village, Elkaduwa, he was a foreigner here. A sinewy octogenarian, he'd not spent much time around people. His hair was matted, lips and teeth stained with betel, his dark skin cracked and dusty. Most remarkable were his cupped, clawed hands. He had a wife and children once, but they'd left for Colombo or the next life. Alone in the forest, he cut Vs in the bark of rubber trees, collecting the fishy sap that leaked into coconut shells pegged beneath.

Pilgrims were already stumbling back down Sri Pada. Some threw their feet down haphazardly as if drunk on arrack. Groups of boys, sporting knit hats or towels against the chill, sang in brash voices. One bounded past, narrowly missing him, and tumbled headlong into an old lady in white, who fell like rice beneath a scythe. Her withered husband stood dumb over the crumpled heap of her. The rubber collector fumbled in the folds of his *lunghi* and pulled out a blue handkerchief. Helping her sit against a step, he tied it around her bleeding elbow. She raised her dark violet irises to him in gratitude.

When the boy crashed into her, she raised her arm, saving her face, but not her elbow. She shut her eyes against the pain and her foolishness. She might have stayed home, selling rambutan and Chinese apples. As soon as they'd started climbing she'd had second thoughts. A strong, wiry woman, her exercise was limited to the steps between piles of wood-apples and coconuts. After an hour, they appeared no closer to the yellow rectangle of light encircling the giant footprint. Her feet ached and she withdrew into herself.

She and her husband had walked the entire way from Wayagama. They'd left Tilak behind to mind the shop. He was a fine boy but he'd had enough. Since the troubles started, visas to the Middle East were as hard to get as lotus root, and someone suggested Peru. He had laid hands on a tourist visa in New Delhi. When she fell ill, he held off. But when a stray South American backpacker bought a pawpaw and mentioned Lima as a fine city with plenty of work, Tilak said it was time.

Part of her knew he was right. The shop had been buffer against the usual chaos but war, poverty, and inflation had grown dire. If she were Tilak, she'd be on the next plane. Her husband cared more for his betel, areca nut, lime, and tobacco than his arthritic wife and ambitious son. Life without Tilak was hard to imagine; she would have to sell and buy fruit and keep accounts alone. Last week, as she washed clothes at the falls, her neighbour told her to take her woes to the Buddha. So she bought herself a white skirt and set off with a lunch box of rice.

After all her doubts, as she felt the rubber collector's gentle hand on her arm, an astonishing peace filled her, as though she'd already reached the summit and the Buddha himself had smiled. She closed her eyes. When she heard a child squeal she opened them. A haggard man sat on a bench beside the path, his children leaping and laughing, mimicking frogs in the undergrowth.

'What's that?' the eldest asked.

'A sleepy worm,' answered his sister.

'Look, Thanththa, look, *loku akka* has a worm on her heel!'

Their father peered at the rubbery cylinder coiled beneath her anklebone.

'A leech.'

'Oh, Thanththa, take it away.'

'We need a little lime or salt…'

'Here:' the old lady pulled a tiny jar from her blouse, 'some Siddhalepa balm.'

Thanththa dabbed ointment at the leech's head. Recoiling, it dropped to the ground, leaving a bright stream of blood.

'Thanththa, look how red it is. Look! Look!'

On the stones, the leech flexed and stretched, a rubber vein with a life of its own. Her father ground it to a pulp with the ball of his bare foot.

'Thank you, madam,' he said passing back the salve, 'very kind. I hope you haven't hurt your arm too badly.' She beamed a smile back at him. 'We lost their mother last year – she always wanted to see the Buddha's footprint; I was busy; no time. But here we are.'

He rose and the children scrambled after him.

They skipped up the steps, the eldest leapfrogging and croaking ahead. Not long after, they stopped to rest beside a cluster of stalls. Thanththa bought four plump black mangosteens. The children shone the skins on their t-shirts, stripped them of their fleshy leaves and wheel-of-life navels. Tearing away bitter red pith, they popped the sweet white cloves into their mouths and spat out the seeds.

A solitary *bhikkhu* appeared dressed in dark rust robes. Handsome, with a square jaw, pronounced nose, soft eyes framed with thick unshaved brows, his skin shone. Thanththa offered him a mangosteen. He accepted with a nod, putting it in his saffron cloth bag.

The *bhikkhu*'s pace was steady, his cloth bag swung, umbrella in one hand. He was thinking of his brother, who'd made this pilgrimage before he died.

'Have you come far?' asked the father of the three children.

'From Anuradhapura,' the monk replied.

'The sacred city.'

'I live in the Lankaramaya temple.'

'First visit to Sri Pada?'

'Fourth. And you?'

'First. My wife died last year. We've come for her.'

'The world is full of suffering.'

'And you, do you suffer?'

'I lost a brother in the war and my mother,' the *bhikkhu* replied.

'Did you choose to be a monk?'

'I was chosen. My elder brother is a doctor, the second died in the war, and the third, an accountant. It fell to me.'

'Funny... we poor folk think it's just us that don't have choices. I'd rather be a *bhikkhu* than a tuk-tuk driver, but it wasn't my calling.'

'It seems appealing, the ordered life: respect, a seat on every bus, alms. However... our Sacred Isle is so troubled... But let's take each step with the Buddha; the same he took two and a half thousand years ago. You'll find great peace.'

The *bhikkhu* followed a group of city boys in baggy jeans, designer t-shirts, sharing headphones, smoking. They laughed and sang, racing, jostling one and other, occupying the path's breadth. They reminded him of his brother, unfettered. But what immense suffering lay ahead of them. Reluctant to disturb, he remained a pace behind.

'Look at Siripala,' joked one, 'in such a rush. Wants to get back into Pushpa's arms.'

'Not just her arms,' another chimed.

'Who can blame him? I would run up the peak and back to...' his voice trailed off as he caught a glimpse of the monk's rust robes.

He stuttered an apology.

'Try to keep your thoughts pure.'

The monk fished in his bag for the mangosteen. Instead his fingers found his prayer book and, thinking how much more value sutras would be to the boy than fruit, handed him the book.

Siripala spent the next hour in silence. Heady with exertion and altitude, muscles fluid, he used the metal handrail to pull himself up the last flights of stairs. First light glowed at the horizon and groups of women in white descended, chanting. At the summit, pilgrims covered the steps and walls like snow. Siripala recognised a group of students he studied with at Colombo's science faculty. Amongst them was the girl he loved. He wove through the crowd and squeezed in between her and her best friend. Just then, gold-rimmed puffs, heralding sunrise, gave way to the sun's oyster pinks and blood-oranges, flanked by monumental stacks of goose-grey clouds. He turned to his beloved and planted a gentle kiss on her full cheek. She took his hand in hers.

Once the sun had risen, they began the climb down. Giddiness heightened by tender feelings made everything radiant; old people, young men, mothers, and children glowed. She let go of his hand just once when they stopped to drink water and let the shaking subside in their legs. A small child, in her mother's arms, woke up and began to sob. The girl reached into her denim pocket and pulled out her mascot, a bronze elephant the size of a two-rupee piece. She held it up to the child, who eagerly closed her plump fist around it. The weary mother nodded her thanks and continued on her way.

A Rāmañña Nikāya *bhikkhu*, feet planted firmly at the roadside, was offering blessings. He called to them. The mother had only the bus fare home in her blouse, but she couldn't refuse. The monk mumbled a prayer and wound the orange string twice around her wrist, tying a knot. He held the mother's wrist and blessed her. Before she could pull the twenty-rupee note from the folds of her sari, her daughter lifted her arm above her head and dropped the bronze elephant into the alms bowl. The monk grinned broadly.

When the crowd thinned, the Rāmañña monk wrapped the alms, which would be used to repair the steps he trod, in a cloth and placed them in his bag. Some thousand steps up, at the path's edge, sat the beggar Keerthi, without feet, polio legs twisted. He'd climbed up on crutches at dawn, as he did every day. The monk lifted the bundle from his bag and wriggled his fingers in amongst the notes. He pulled out sixty rupees, enough for a plate of rice and curry, and gave it to Keerthi, who nodded thanks before nimbly hobbling to the nearest stall to order breakfast.

The stall-holder was hoping to make a barefoot pilgrimage that evening to the Tooth Temple in Kandy, open just once every six years. He would join the patient queue of pilgrims that curled around the lake. They would shelter under the arches, passing the night on the pavement, awaiting first light to take their place in the line once more. His trip was in the balance; he must sell all his rice and curry today or he'd not have enough for the journey. But if the day started with old Keerthi setting foot in his stall, he was in with a chance.

Us and Them

Ben

Ben is released from the transatlantic vacuum between Louis Armstrong and Yafo just before midnight. He steps out of the air-conditioned atmosphere into the mystery of a starry sky and inhales deeply. As the driver shouts and shoves his hold-all in the back of the cheroot for Jerusalem he feels, at last, conspicuously foreign. The highway climbs beside a cliffside graveyard, which dispels his fears of inauthentic beginnings. The passengers are dropped off, one by one, at the city outskirts.

He checks in to the absurdly well-appointed Leonardo Plaza Hotel, tips the bell boy, rolls back the coverlet and, without ado, falls asleep. He dreams of his father, long before his sapping invalidity. Benjamin Senior has his little boy's hand in his and they're walking through Lafayette, where Ben buried him a year ago. Soundlessly, his father points towards the family plot and squeezes Ben's hand. Ben runs ahead to discover a granite headstone and lilies. The epitaph is unfinished, the third verse evaporating at 'Bring me my arrows of desire...' He stoops to rub the stone with his cuff, to reveal the next line of Blake's poem. Instead, he finds James Fenton's lines: 'This is us and that is them. This is Jerusalem.'

He wakes at the first call to prayer. From the balcony he watches

"

clouds curl, cordial in a glass of water. The crows circle pines, their cries growing more insistent as the flock assembles. The earth-diggers' judder on a site beyond the Arab cemetery is intense. When he'd mentioned it last night to the receptionist, she explained they were digging foundations for the Tolerance Museum.

'Whose tolerance? Mine?' he asks, but her perfect lips stayed pursed.

In the dining hall he barely touches the excessive breakfast and drinks two cups of Turkish coffee. There's a print-out plan of must-sees and an annotated map in his hold-all. But he leaves without either. Naked without his customary briefcase, he walks briskly to the city walls, vulnerable but inexplicably vital. Hesitating at Jaffa Gate, he turns back to admire the view and is overwhelmed by the gravitas of history and religion. He considers calling his lover, Ryan, who was suspiciously understanding of his 'pilgrimage', but doesn't. Passing through the arch, the city closes in as he follows David Street and takes a left down Greek Patriarch Street. Drawn along an alley with niches of carpets, spices, juices, and religious keepsakes, he scents his line toward a courtyard in the shadow of the Omer Mosque. His quarry is the Church of the Holy Sepulchre; the first thing on his abandoned spreadsheet of 'Things to Do'.

He steps into the dim vestibule resonant with the low tones of Russian, Greek, Romanian, Serbian, and Georgian. His eyes adjust. Visitors fall to the flagstones before a large, damp slab of jade and rust marbled stone. Ritual is anathema to Ben's Mississippi sensibilities, but not prostrating would appear hostile. He gets down on his knees and touches his forehead to the rock. The image of his father, head-bent, at the dinner table, saying grace, comes to mind. The stone emanates an immutability stretching back to Emperor Constantine.

Searching the walls for unforthcoming clues to the temple's history, he finds himself appreciating the basilica murals. Two millennia later the stones are yet lit by votive candles, scented by incense, warmed by the heat of pilgrims' bodies, and resonant with supplicants' prayers. Guides gently lead subdued retinues, drawing attention to a detail here or a stage of the cross there. Visitors move in shoals, dispersing around statues and reconvening. Ben finds his way up a staircase to the bedrock behind glass which, he overhears, is where Christ was crucified. He wishes he could share this with his father, to whom it would have meant so much more. Ben recalls reaching out to close his father's eyelids and swallows at the stricture in his throat.

He joins a queue behind three Ukrainian women who take photos of each other with their iPhones, touching the spot where the cross was raised. He bends down, disappointed to find metal, not stone. Descending from Golgotha, he passes through the Chapel of Adam, where the first man's skull is purportedly buried, and steps out into the courtyard. Many more skulls have piled up, century after century, in hope of holding on to this territory. His visit falls in one of those momentary hiatuses prior to and post troubles flaring. Fragments of the Book of Ezekiel flicker, parroted hysterically by a boy sitting next to him in Tanakh class; 'Son of man, cause Jerusalem to know her abominations...' the word 'harlotry' justification enough for its repetition.

Ben gets lost in the web of streets. In a covered yard, foreign men sit at ease, drinking tea and talking. Feeling a rush, he steps in and orders a tea. Remaining some time, he's lulled into a limbo broken by the arrival of a large, talkative family of London Jews. He rises but has second thoughts; his attention is caught by the father. Throughout the second call to prayer he watches the Londoner, his small physique and large gestures. Men come and go. A remarkable looking Bedouin arrives after the third call. Before the fourth, a woman toting a Hasselblad. Ben gets up to leave as she does.

He will bump into the photographer again.

Amy

The driver, having flirted outrageously the entire ride, drops Amy at Jaffa Gate, where her partner Mo, her three children, mother, and sister, are waiting. She is hoping this first visit to the Holy Land since visiting a *kibbutz* as a teenager will make her feel more Jewish. Or will rub off on her kids. Much of what Amy has seen and heard in the last twelve hours resonates: large voices, unsolicited frankness. Other things jar: archaic outfits and dramatic outbursts.

'What the hell are you wearing, Amy?' Lizzie squeaks.

'Lavender and cerise.' Amy looks down at her full French Connection skirt and Gap tank top.

'I'm not talking co-ordination, I'm talking appropriate,' her sister protests. 'Showing your belly-button? Really?'

'Why on earth not?'

'It's a matter of courtesy, dear,' her mother waves vaguely.

Amy's colour rises; she's forty-five, but her mother and sister still gang up on her.

'To whom?' Mo winks at her.

'People's sensitivities,' says her mother.

'What are you saying, Mum? That I should dress differently so that the men won't ogle me... or women won't be bothered by the fact their men are letches? Perhaps they'd realise the rest of the world has moved on from screwy hang-ups.'

'Absolutely. To higher things; décolleté and navels!' Lizzie snorts.

'Let's head into the Old City, ladies,' says Mo. He orients himself with his phone and they follow him through tiny Torah streets inhabited still, it appears, by Moses' descendants. When they are certainly lost, Amy stops an old man with curled sideburns and a fur *shtreimel* and asks directions in schoolgirl Hebrew. The old man answers Mo in English. As they follow his directions, Mo whispers into Amy's ear, 'You're such a hottie, he just couldn't look you in the eye.'

'Would he have been so keen on you if he'd known you were bi?'

'As long as I'm circumcised...'

She giggles and pinches his backside.

At the Wall, the first thing Amy notices is the other wall, dividing men and women. She grabs her daughters' hands and they walk, flanked by her mother and sister, toward the stones. Women approach meekly, bearing folded papers of prayers to tuck in the edifice's nooks. On the other side of the *mechitza*, boys are being bar mitzvahed; elders sing, play, and dance. Women stand on plastic chairs, peering over the wall, watching their sons.

'Why is Daddy going the other way?' asks her youngest. Several answers flash through Amy's mind.

'Welcome to religion, honey,' is the one she utters. Lizzie rolls her eyes.

They approach the Wall and, squeezing between supplicants, Amy touches her hand to the stone. She's flooded with images: King Herod, violent outbreaks, burning books, and the screen. The phrase 'the navel of the earth,' comes to mind, and her own vexing midriff.

After, Lizzie suggests they visit the Hurva synagogue but, though they follow the street signs, they never reach it. Lost and tired, they find themselves outside a mosque.

'Let's have tea here,' Amy says brightly.

'Are you nuts?' says Lizzie.

'Not at all,' says Amy, stepping through the wrought-iron gate to the tea house. The family follows hesitantly.

'Shouldn't you put a scarf on?' Lizzie hisses.

'It's that kind of muddle-headedness that led to the Holocaust. The idea that one culture pollutes another... Islam needs us, just like Israelis need Palestinians.'

'Don't be ridiculous, dear, you don't know what you're saying,' says her mother, who has spent her whole life trying to smooth out the wrinkles.

'Mummy, I'm hungry!' the smallest child says.

'Let's order,' suggests Mo. 'Nothing like a cuppa!' Amy smiles, relishing her connection with Mo, the father of her children and ally. Fish-out-of-water bisexual Jews, they've re-drawn their map of Eden. She picks up on Mo's alertness and locates a well-proportioned American male that she also finds attractive. She leans over and nuzzles her lips onto Mo's. And, though they know the entire cafe is watching, he doesn't resist. The gods are playing, she thinks, gleefully; they are dancing through us.

Said

Said's existence is as perilous as quicksand. People like him don't stray from lives that hold them fast. Said has never made a pilgrimage, though he's driven plenty of others. In Nabq, he takes tourists in his four-by-four, 'no fear' lettered on the rear windscreen, to the desert, or to the foot of St Catherine's Monastery. A handsome, smooth talker, he shows photos of previous girlfriends on his phone to prospective ones. It works wonders. Some of the girls are daft enough to invite him to their small Dutch or German towns to stay with their families. He visits. And always returns. He has three grown children and a wife that feeds him when he shows up.

With the troubles, visitors evaporated and he turned to drug and arms smuggling, which suits him better. Prison suited him less well and he found himself crying like a bitch, long-distance, to blonde girls in cold countries, suddenly lost for words. But today he's free. And not working till tonight's job back to Sinai. By chance, he picked up an English woman and dropped her at Jaffa Gate. Said parks and intends to sleep, but he's restless. He watches the juice-sellers and women. The avenue through the gate is wide and inviting. Its alleys, stepped with stones and ramps, are flanked with niches, each with its own merchant. The road opens and he has a clear view of the Dome of the Rock, where Mohammed began his Night Journey with the Angel Gabriel. From here, its gilded cupola contrasts so strongly with its slate-blue walls, it seems aliens crash-landed it on Temple Mount.

He follows his nose to the Arab quarter, messier with its crowded alleys, overweight shopkeepers, and dirty children. Butchers' boys throw punches at each other and titter. A pot-bellied man burns wood in an empty oil tin. Groups of weary African American Christians rub shoulders with disorientated blond Orthodox Serbs. State police shout, 'Hello, hello,' at stray tourists who try to enter the mosque. Old men smoke shisha and play cards outside a hardware shop. It's a defensive, rather than indigenous, quarter. He finds himself outside the Quran School, where men in plastic chairs drink tea. He orders tea and settles himself.

There are few foreigners there. Amongst a large group is the woman he dropped at Jaffa Gate passionately kissing the man next to her. She reminds him of foreign women he's pleasured in the past. The kiss over, her eyes fall on him and she giggles recognition, elbowing her partner. A fatigue hits him and Said closes his eyes. He conjures a lofty scene in his mind: fountains scented with camphor, rivers flowing with honey, where ivory horses drink and women bathe.

'*Falak al-aflak.* The garden,' he thinks, 'Home of peace.' When he opens his eyes he finds another's smouldering on him. They belong to a fine-boned, pale-faced woman who's raising her camera to take his photo.

Photographer

The photographer drags herself out of her lover's bed at around one. She doesn't wake him. Barefoot, she pads down the iron stairwell to the kitchen and makes coffee. She opens the rusty shutters and light pours through the metal window frame; blinking, she curls up in the armchair. In a tree beyond the window a couple of wood pigeons groom each other's necks with their beaks. She picks up her camera from the coffee table and frames them.

She descends stone steps, pitted by centuries of use, that curl down to a ground floor hall where a motorcycle leans, draped in a tarp, reflected in a tall mirror. She takes a shot. The metal door opens onto a narrow strip of pavement beyond which cars, bikes, and busses zip. She passes the falafel shop and the pita bakery. Drawn downward by the slope's pull, she comes to Mamilla's arcade of boutiques that leads to Jaffa. She inhales on the large sweep of overpass before plunging into the alleys of the old city.

The uneven lines and warm colours are suffused with sunshine. She treads lightly. She cannot feel her feet touch the ground. Everything is rendered fabulous in the aftertaste of love-making: nicotine kisses, the pull of twisted hair, indents of nails still in her flesh. The see-saw echo of resistance and acquiescence. Smoothing the mind's jagged edges and rediscovering its downiness. Wanting to give. And receive. She turns a corner and almost walks into an Orthodox

Jew speaking to a couple. The photographer's eye is drawn to her exposed belly and studded navel; she aims her lens and snaps.

She continues, everything conspiring toward enchantment. The setting sun, glistening off Jerusalem stone. Its warmth. The guttural Arabic and bubblier Hebrew that envelops her. It's starting to get dark when she stops at a tea house full of men smoking, talking, or napping. She orders a glass of tea, watching the sweet-seller across the way unwrapping bags of brightly coloured candies.

The sculptured head of a Bedouin who sits, still as a lizard, eyes half-closed, catches her attention. He opens his eyes just as she is reaching for her camera to capture him. The shutter falls a fraction before his eyes narrow and he turns his chin away. The fourth call to prayer starts up. In its dissonant perpetuity she dies, ascends, and is reborn. Moments like these brand themselves on her mind. An American stands up, at the same moment as she, but he lets her pay first, his attention fixed on a man sitting with a group of tourists. She walks home to the man who will still be in bed, waiting for her. He will tell her that these days the Old City is unsafe for Jews like him.

Some months later, at the Photographer's Gallery, her photographs hang side by side; *Pigeons Grooming, Draped Motorbike, Hassid and Barbell* and *Portrait of a Bedouin*. Words projected on the wall read: 'But the Jerusalem that is above is free, and she is our mother. – Galatians 4:26.'

A stranger walks up to her. She braces herself for the usual small talk.

'I was there when you snapped him,' he nods at the portrait. 'A moment before the fourth call to prayer; I'd been watching him the better part of the afternoon, trying to decide what brought him there.'

'The photographer observed through another's lens,' she says: 'And did you decide...?'

'Tea, like the rest of us.' His face creases into a smile.

She wonders if they will become friends.

Conversion

for Father Paolo Dall'Oglio

It's as if he's stepped out of Turnham Green and into the Bible's onionskin. Perhaps the Book of Ezekiel or Haggai, and these men are Daniel or Jeremiah. They pray in Syriac, chant in Aramaic, speak Arabic to one another, as though they live on the other side of an abyss of two millennia. He steals glances but, with their steel-wool beards, granite faces, and knotty feet, they're too remote. Whereas I'm familiar; European, soft, and fleshy. He wants to know my story.

When mass is over, we'll carry dishes of olive oil, red oregano, labneh, goats' cheese, apricot jam, and flat bread to Abraham's Tent and he'll sit beside me, as if by chance.

And ask.

We're used to talking; to each other, our souls and God. We're descendants of a long dynasty of philosophical debaters; Isaac of Antioch, Rabbula, Shem'un Ququyo the potter, Jacob of Edessa. Masters of poetry who composed our liturgy of *madroshé* and *sogitho* – dialogues between the Virgin Mary and Gabriel, Mary and the wise men or Cain and Abel. Conversation broadens the spirit.

He'll place my accent at once. Ask more questions. Be flummoxed by my answers. I've been a monk for over two decades. I did a Master's in history, was a winemaker in Oxford, and a political adviser in Westminster – making me a man of his world. He'll wonder why a Syriac Orthodox monastery should be flourishing in a Muslim country. I'll explain we're a stone's throw from Christianity's seedbed. He'll ask about the brothers' origins, about the black saint after whom our monastery, Deir Mar Musa, is named. And of our relationship with the Bedouin.

He won't ask, 'Why did you become a monk?' That would be an admission of spiritual inclination, nudging him nearer to the cross-legged, anachronistic Semitic-profiled brethren that surround us. An honest question might lead to others. What you don't raise in conversation reveals much.

Mark, Matthew, or Peter? Biblical names have grown more fashionable, Christianity less so. Let's call him Peter. Peter will drink chamomile tea and, after lunch, wander up the steps to Al-Hayak, along the riverbed to the goatherd's house and past the cave retreats. For an hour or two he'll mull over the life of an ascetic. If his admiration is aroused, he'll consider that this may be the solitude he's looking for. If he's the wry sort, he'll dismiss it; no head-burying in sand dunes for him, Peter's a man of the world, needed at the bank or media consultancy. He'll stand on the terrace, captivated by the desert, before bidding me goodbye and returning to London, where I'll become a vaguely aching memory or coalesce into anecdote.

Conversion, like conversation, is complicated. What you can't describe is most important. Mine began when I fell sick in a hostel in Damascus. Something I ate; I don't remember what. Confined to a dorm with its view of the mosque and sprawl of old city, I had time to reflect, a luxury I'd rarely indulged myself in. After months on the road, I was still going for the sake of it; a bad habit. Well into my thirties, I'd structured life around dodging responsibility; never staying in a job or with a woman too long. This was my fifth journey to find myself in as many years. Perhaps my illness wasn't food poisoning but triggered by a poorly assembled life. By guilt over my autistic brother and my father who'd spent a quarter century caring for him. By my last girlfriend, Loretta, yearning for children. An accretion of shame for those I let down.

Days later, and a little stronger, I left Souk Sarouja after breakfast and hopped on a *service* at Abasyn Garage heading north to Homs. Through a small slice of window, I watched ugly city blocks blur into suburban high-rise, then to rock, to a sandscape strewn with unfinished buildings, twisted steel rebar clawing at the sky like the barbed legs of upturned roaches. Metaphors for my life; projects thrown over and abandoned. Snowy peaks fringed the roadside. On the hard shoulder stood carts of pomegranate and oranges. Vendors waved wet fish at oncoming traffic.

I got down at the turn-off to Nebek. The town's façades were more stylish, its cars newer than in Damascus; its level streets were full of affluent returnees from Saudi or France. I stopped to eat shawarma and *maamoul*. The smiling shopkeeper estimated Deir Mar Musa was twenty kilometers away and suggested a taxi. I started walking around midday. Sand and rocks spread out before me, the sculpted hills sparged with litter. Sunshine glittered, but the air had bite; I pulled my scarf up and my hat down, leaving just a slit for my eyes. It took three hours to reach a mine and a fork in the road. I could carry on along tarmac or follow the shadow of a path a mute miner signaled towards, over the Qalamoun mountains. Snow fell as I began to climb.

I grew anxious. My breath came short, my armpits itched. Something held me to the path – a bullish stubbornness or the first inklings of embryonic faith. I put one rounded peak, then another, between myself and the mine. I'd understood just two words of the miner's Arabic: 'hill' and 'house'. The sharp wind cut through my flimsy clothes; I decided the walk was an allegory. I supposed there was a monastery somewhere ahead. I had it on the word of the Korean girl in the dorm, on the smiles of the portly shopkeeper, and the gestures of a miner. I imagined perishing, freezing limb by limb, my fingers already numb. With less than an hour of sunlight left, time was of the essence.

As I came in sight of two lonely houses my mind closed over an idea, like a fist over a talisman: pilgrimage. I believed the house the miner mentioned was the lower of the two and I headed towards it eagerly. A pick-up was parked beside a pen filled with two dozen long-haired goats. Painted on the shed wall were a cross and an arrow pointing downhill. There was no sign of the goatherd bar footprints along the dry riverbed, which I followed. Though the cleft brimmed with shadows I was protected from the wind and the shale was easier.

Spotting the old monastery nestled in the crags was the closest I've come to an epiphany; my shoulders shook. Deir Mar Musa al-Habashi looks like a fortress. Following the cliff's curve, hewn of the same ochre rock, the sixth-century thief-turned-Christian, Saint Moses the Ethiopian, built it. For close to a millennium, monks lived here until it was abandoned a century ago. An Italian Jesuit, Father Paolo, stumbled upon the ruins in the seventies and dreamed of building a bridge to Islam through unreserved hospitality. He constructed some cells, a hen house and, with a growing strength of brothers and sisters, a new monastery on the other side of a chasm spanned by a steel bridge. They ran a cable over the reservoir's cracked mud to the crags to send food to those on retreat.

As I drew close, I noticed a small fissure in the rock, I ducked into the cavity. It widened to a terrace overlooking yellow flats that erupted in stark mountains on the horizon. I dropped my bag and stood, awestruck. After some time, the voice of a young Syrian woman interrupted my thoughts. Leaving my rucksack and boots outside, I stooped to follow her through another doorway, beneath a hanging rug, into a beautiful church. Frescos of red devils, bearded priests, fishermen and their catch covered its walls. In its alcoves stood darkened Orthodox icons, alongside vivid Bedouin oils and pressed flowers. Candles burned beside two silver-bound Bibles resting on lecterns on the floor. The stockinged congregation and barefoot monks sat on carpets, skins, or cushions, cross-legged or leaning against columns, Arabic Bibles and Psalm books beside them. Some read the Gospel, others meditated. One read the story of Jacob robbing Esau's inheritance. Then an exceptional, tall, bearded man with a resonant voice started to talk. I had no Arabic back then, but I gathered Father Paolo was speaking of the troubles in Gaza. Switching to English, he mused that people fight over land because it represents a mother's love, which everyone seeks. Then they took down stringed lutes, a drum, and a tambourine and played, sang, and danced.

*Kyrie eleison, kyrie eleison, kyrie eleison. Ya rabo rḥam, ya rabo rḥam,
ya rabo rḥam.*

Outside, trays brimming with food were being carried up the wooden steps to Abraham's tent. The assembled sat down along two mats stretched out on the floor laden with bowls of labneh, olives, and oil accompanied by rounds of flat bread warmed on wood stoves. Two large kettles of tea simmered. Once I'd dulled the sharp edge of my hunger, I began to listen to the symphony of Italian, French, Arabic, and English spoken around me.

As well as half-a-dozen monks, there was a rosy-cheeked Czech who told me he spent his days building guest rooms, a Slovak new-age traveller who'd completed a week's retreat, a plump Russian practitioner of alternative medicine, and an Italian environmentalist piloting an eco-project. A Lebanese journalist was talking to Father Paolo about the waning numbers of Christians in the Middle East. Instead of being far from the world, it seemed this was its centre. As we finished our meal, I looked up and found Paolo's eyes on me. He asked me my name and if I'd stay.

'If you do, you can help translate my annual letter, Andrew.'

It was a day unlike any other. My clean cell delighted me, so different from the dorm in Damascus. Sweet air and clear skies made me giddy. The brothers' gentleness touched me. After the service the following morning, I left. My things were in Damascus; I had a ticket home in a fortnight; I needed perspective. These were the reasons, or excuses, I made to myself.

The moment my head touched the pillow at Al-Saada, my fever returned. The concierge, Khalid, called a doctor, who administered drugs. Days passed. It wasn't a doctor I needed, it was an angel. As the illness subsided, I experienced a powerful sense of expectation and peace, something I'd not felt since a child. I wrote emails to Loretta and my parents explaining I'd stay at the monastery some time.

On my return, the monks greeted me with unsurprised affection.

I started work at once. I helped Father Paolo translate letters and set up a website. Peeled carrots and chopped onions. Washed stacks of dishes that stretched out along the kitchen counter and swept out dormitories. Taught myself to greet the steady flow of guests and answer their questions. Without compassion, Father Paolo reminds us, we're no better than animals. Stray Italian tourists snap photos during a service or the odd Spanish student grumbles his cell is cold. People bring their expectations with them; the unhappy are met with discomfort; those seeking find transcendence. Our task is to welcome them all. Father Paolo puts his hand on my shoulder and murmurs: 'Humility, Andrew, humility.'

My original fears of stagnation were dispelled early. Our predecessors were rigorous scholars. Mar Musa monks are the first real intellectuals I've known. They debate on a daily basis. Not one speaks less than four languages. They discuss sciences and arts in astonishing depth and have a fierce grasp of history. Well-worn steps, dug into the mountain, lead to a library housing a literary collection that would shame most public libraries.

But the biggest revelation is compassion. Before, affection had seemed like weakness. Friends needed entertaining, my lovers satisfying, my parents understanding. Now, God is revealed in everyone. The maker is there, somewhere, in the string of visitors. Deeply buried in the psychotic Armenian refugee who tries my patience. With small effort, the sacred can be discerned in homely Sola, an aspiring nun, who mothers us, like it or not. The divine is firmly rooted in the stern, wiry Abouna Boutros, with his impish humor. Writ all over the earnest Abu Jihad. Positively flowing from kind Sister Houda, with her quiet wisdom. Ever-present in the eccentric, bombastic Father Paolo, and his grand absurd vision that, against all odds, we are realising. These are my companions: I have no wish for others.

Ascetics are an endangered species; our need of each other is great. I wake each morning before dawn with forgotten enthusiasm. I have no regrets. I have lived almost half my life here. Entire weeks pass without revisiting the past. I no longer fret about the future. Miracles happen; I see them every day. Life brims. With care, gnarled trees yield olives in the desert. Sustained on dry grass and benevolence, goats give us labneh and cheese. Tended by Boutros, our gardens flourish; we enjoy greens, tomatoes, cucumbers, and herbs. Visitors bring gifts of chocolate, coffee, and books. They help us build rooms, protect our fragile habitat, preserve ancient tombs. Strangers come to Deir Mar Musa and find the Spirit here, working its magic in the desert. Prodigal sons and daughters, like me, return. Even Peter has come, all the way from Turnham Green.

Peter has finished his walk. He's been standing for some time on the terrace, contemplating the sifting dunes peppered with Bedouin tents that melt into mountains and sky. He doesn't notice me, hanging sheets. He lifts his gaze from the horizon, where the sun is sinking, only when a large Italian family fill the yard with their voices. They gave him a lift from Nebek here this morning and have offered to take him back.

Peter turns, seeing me for the first time. His face is softer, his eyes bright. He watches me work, lifting, wringing, unwinding, shaking out, and hanging.

'Ready?' the tanned father smiles at Peter.

'No... I... actually, I've changed my mind. Thanks, but I think I'll stay a while.'

FIFTY-ONE ROLLS

Ensa comes slowly onto her knees and sits back on her heels, elongating her spine and stretching her fingertips onto the rug beyond her mattress. She pees, hovering over the icy toilet seat. And puts water on the gas to boil. Preparing half a cantaloupe, a pomegranate, a pear, she spreads butter on a roll and eats slowly. Being on the fringes can bring you into the core of life.

Pappus called this place the focus. Menaechmus did the earliest work on conic sections. But his theories didn't stand up to later discoveries. Knowledge is this, a temporary hypothesis, fragile and subject to revision. Archimedes explored the method of exhaustion. Apollonius gave the parabola, arms reaching to infinity, its nomenclature. And Galileo had stuff to say about acceleration and the gravity of parabolas.

The sash windows frame her view. The building opposite, almost identical to hers, is swathes of red brick, white pointing, black lead pipes. The chimneystacks sit atop the crest of the frosted white, seal-grey slates, six pots apiece. The sky is a solid slab of absolute grey marble. Across the juniper-green metal railings, Tibetan flags flutter. Lavender, ivy, heather, and marigolds brush the windowsill. The occasional seagull, pigeon, or thrush cambers before the granite backdrop; birds and flags apart, the scene is static.

From this, Ensa's life is stitched. On the windowsill a clay pot contains three orchids, trailing wilting ivory flowers of mournful elegance. Self-preservation is an expression of distress; Nietzsche was quite right about that, but it's not power that's the life force: it's simply change. Youth, convinced of its eternity, stays ignorant of decay's immanence. But she's past that bend, beyond the axis of symmetry, on the downward limb, a whole different ball of wax. Perhaps her trajectory is spiralling through a cross-section of a three-dimensional dome. Or she will have to discover it anew like Schatz's oloids or Hirsch's sphericons. Today she nurses the benediction that she will forget the self.

Taking down a stainless-steel bowl, she empties a kilo and half of brown flour into it. Grinds sea salt, a pinch of muscovado, a small hill of yeast, a slug of sunflower oil, water from the tap. She blends the ingredients with her right hand, left anchoring the bowl as dough forms. She rolls out three ropes on the Formica, chops them into discs, and moulds each into a sphere, arranging them on greased trays.

While the first batch bakes, she showers. The top rack browns fastest and she throws the rolls into a paper bag and puts the next tray in. She dresses; cords, long-sleeved T, cotton sweater, wool cardigan. She rubs cream into her face and looks at it. When she's awake, like this, it is beautiful, the complexion clear, the eyes alive, the features fine. When she isn't, she barely recognises the dull-eyed stranger in the mirror. There is no way to level this dichotomy. Without vertices or vortexes, no trajectory.

Wrapping a scarf around her neck, pulling on fingerless gloves, she slips a fiver in her back pocket and her front door keys. With fifty-one rolls under one arm, and some old Wellingtons under the other, she steps out into the gelid Christmas morning. Blackbirds have dug up the bulbs she planted yesterday. She stops to sweep up the scattered earth.

Martlett Court is possibly at its most lovely in the full frore of mid-winter The steamy lit windows on the walkways seem cosier than in other seasons. The branches of the mountain ash are bare; their scarlet berries scattered and smashed on the paving stones. The streets are preternaturally quiet. The familiar dispossessed that sleep opposite the derelict Bow Street Police Station are not there, though a couple of their homes are folded and leant against the wall. The Royal Opera House's revolving doors are still. Not a laptop glows in a single café. A few displaced tourists stray into the piazza, deserted of shoppers on smart phones or entertainers on soapboxes. Fowler's uncluttered neo-classical façade is accentuated by the desolation. Covent Garden station's metal accordion gates are drawn. Marks and Spencer is dark.

The man in Amorino's doorway sleeps, so she does not disturb him. In Jones Bootmaker's recessed entrance is a cardboard screen, but nobody's behind it. The rolls warm her body through her coat and she shifts them under the other arm. Down Saint Martin's Lane toward Trafalgar Square, two squatters are leaning against a wall. The woman is not more than twenty, her fine features pierced and framed by dreadlocks, her long shirt and leggings thin against the wind. He is tall; shaved temples crown Slavic features, hazel epicanthic eyes, nostril pierced by a screw. Ensa asks them where the squat is.

'We've been evicted,' they answer. His is a mellow Brummie accent while hers is RP.

'Eight o' clock this morning,' he adds.

'They sent bailiffs in.' She nods at the gate, where a stocky man in a bullet-proof vest shifts from one foot to another.

'The bailiffs had no papers, the cops kicked us out, illegal-like. It was me who called them in the first place.'

'All our stuff is in there.'

'The judge ruled we could stay. We could go back in, the judge said, but we'd have to hire our own bailiff.'

'We don't even have a blanket.' She starts rolling up.

'The company that owns it, Greencap something-or-other, is registered in Jersey. They filed accounts last year; valued themselves at nine quid. Five carpeted storeys in central London with a bathroom and all! You should see the view from up there. Nine quid!'

'We sat on the balcony for eight hours yesterday.'

'Ten, Mouse,' he says.

'Ten. It was rented out to the Royal Bank of Scotland,' Mouse adds, falling into a PR patter after three days on national TV, 'who were bailed out by the government, which means taxpayers' money: we're only taking back what's ours.'

'More than thirty thousand homes in London are empty. Not to mention offices like these.'

'I brought some bread for the lunch,' says Ensa.

'The others are just getting some tables; we'll be up and running in an hour,' says Mouse.

Ensa continues walking. The first rough sleeper she comes across has put his piece of cardboard at right angles to the pavement. He is a large, restless black man under a blanket that's too short for him. He pulls his blanket up to his chin, tries to catch the other end with his toe and pull it down over his feet. The moment his feet are covered he yanks it up again, repeating the sequence, in serial reiteration. She hasn't the courage to disturb him.

On Garrick Street two men approach, one with a twisted ankle, limping badly. They are bearded, carrying their belongings and zip-locked packed lunches and trailing sleeping bags. They hesitate at her offer, so she tips the open bag so they can see into it and smell the bread. They speak to each other in an Eastern European language. The older man's face dirt-filled creases are so deep he could be one of Van Gogh's potato-eaters. He puts his hand in and takes one roll, though she gestures he should take another. The other also takes just one.

On Endell Street, three Scousers have bedded down beneath the overhang of Nuffield's brown-brick seventies building, where the swimming-pool extractor is pumping out a warm chlorine haze. A young, fair-haired girl with freckles and clear blue eyes sits between two guys.

'I need these two. First, because I'm one of the few women out here. Second, because I can't handle the lights; I'm epileptic.'

'What size shoe are you?' asks Ensa.

'Five and a half,' says the girl.

'My kid's Wellingtons, they're as good as new, could you use them?' she pulls them from her rucksack.

'Cheers!'

'Have a good Christmas,' they call.

Further down Endell Street two Glaswegians with sanguine complexions prop up the doorway of the sports centre. They raise their Tennents to her.

'Our hands aren't clean.'

Ensa shrugs.

'God bless you,' calls the fatter one and the other, 'Thank you, darling.'

They call again, waving goodbye, even as she turns the corner into Shorts Gardens. She makes her way through the back streets to High Holborn, scanning the pavement to differentiate between refuse bags and human beings. Outside the Aldwych Theatre a bald man wearing glasses is lying on his belly on a blanket, stirring a small brown vial with a stick with one hand and holding a paperback in the other.

'No, thank you, my dear, not hungry. Very kind.'

The other side of the crescent a young man has occupied a double doorway and is spreading out all his donations on a blanket below a tree decorated with tinsel and bows.

'Too much food, look,' he shows her. He opens a bag packed with instant noodles, cakes, and biscuits.

'Where is everyone?'

'Over at Crisis. I don't go though, no, not me. You might find some of us along the Strand.' His eyes are hyacinth-blue.

There's nobody at the east end, but when she gets to Ryman's there's a guitarist in his sixties, with fine white hair setting up. He looks in the paper bag and shakes his head. A small knot of itinerants by Charing Cross Station take the bread, which has dropped to body temperature. Down Villiers Street, she hands one to a plump Pole and on Northumberland Avenue to a freckled man in his sleeping bag, who thanks her gruffly.

She swings back up toward Trafalgar Square, filling with tourists. Outside the old RBS building, a couple of tables are out with sandwiches and salads, sweets and beers. Several Love Activists, uniform in their non-conformity, shaved and dreadlocked, are hanging out. They wear brightly coloured, layered, comfortable old clothes and boots that have walked places. A muzzled pit bull called Zeus barges into everyone.

A ditzy, chapped-skinned woman who introduces herself as Phaedra starts a conversation. She lives on a barge in Richmond with ten others, 'escaping the madness' she says, between bits of a crayfish sandwich that 'might be a bit dodgy'.

'Did you ever read Rousseau's *Discourse on Inequality*?' she asks. 'He said whoever was the first to mark out a piece of ground, claim it as his, and find people stupid enough to agree, was the founder of civil society.' Ensa smiles. 'And if someone had been smart enough to pull up the stakes or fill in the ditch, mankind would have spared a multitude of crimes, wars and murders.'

'So true.'

'You are lost, says Rousseau, if you forget the fruits are everyone's and the earth no-one's.'

'Woah! I want a copy.'

She leaves the remaining half bag of rolls with the rest of the food.

As she walks 'home' she considers the word and its Indo-European root – *kei,* to settle down. Settling. What does that mean? Allowing sediment to sink to the bottom. Getting stuck in the parabola's trough. She remembers previous homes that ended up scrambled or undone. The second house her parents were evicted from when she was an absent teenager. The council flat she abandoned, after ten years, when she left the boyfriend whose name it was in. Her first house that she quit when she divorced the husband she bought it with. Dwellings that ended with evictions, no water, or a murder on the doorstep. Arguments that led to throwing-out or walking-out. She was lucky; her nights in the street were few.

Her current place is one room with oiled oak floors, a sash window at each end and all she and her daughter need within its four walls. Their sanctuary for more than two years, longer than she has stayed in any one place for almost twenty. Her mother had talked her into this flat. She was afraid it would tie her down, make a citizen and hypocrite of her. But for now, she has stepped from wandering into domesticity. From drifter to taxpayer. From outsider into urban dweller.

She did everything to let in light. Discarding furniture, replacing it with rugs, cushions, winding wool around the lamps, painting the walls; a friend covered the strip light with a stained-glass window. She felt unwonted loneliness in that room at first. A deeper, more desperate alienation than she'd ever met before. Inclement weather trapped her in its narrow confines; she cursed as she dried clothes on radiators, fell asleep to the whir of the washing machine or put on a coat reeking of last night's dinner. When folk stayed the night they were like puppies in a basket, clambering over each other.

Slowly the strangers in the block grew familiar. As she presses her fob to the scanner, she thinks of Jeff at number four, who'd died last year, telling her about walkways filled with offspring who didn't know their own mothers. She passes Scheherazade, the kindly insomniac who stands sentry on the building; nothing escapes her notice. Next to her lives Wendy, a gentle-hearted spinster. Beside her, the eccentric Colombian, Esperanza, who tutors her daughter in maths out of the goodness of her heart. In number one are the Scotswoman, Jane, and her grandson, Tyler, with his warm, easy prattle.

She walks the first flight of stairs. On this level lives the thespian Sabrina with her theatrical voice, who invited them to a birthday party on a barge. And the silent, stocky guy, who pumped up her bike tyre when it was flat. Next to him, her big-hearted Ghanaian neighbours, Ben and Anna, who kissed her in Saint Paul's after midnight mass last night.

On the second floor lives the bald, toothless set designer, Bob, who gave her daughter his keyboard and kept his dead cat in his fridge till the it reeked so badly they had to hold their breath on the stairwell. And the plump and powdered Clem who smiled indulgently when her daughter, invited for tea, ate every last chocolate biscuit on the plate.

The third floor houses Arben and Ismet, her child's Kosovan schoolmates. And Joe, the octogenarian Irishman, who does high kicks whenever he sees her. At the fourth she passes the crumb-strewn entrance of the recluse who sent them a Christmas card in his Welsh cursive. And next door, sublet to Moscovites, who return in the early hours in luxuriant furs, miniskirts, and bling, trailed by noisy men.

She puts her copper key in the silver lock. Each time it turns she doesn't quite believe it. As though she's dreaming someone else's dream, one that only Rumi's sleeper could have faith in. She hangs her coat on the peg, unlaces her boots, sashays across the floor and does a little leap and a somersault. Because she's quite possibly the parabola's vertex itself, in motion, arms stretching to infinity. And because that's what she imagines the men sleeping in the stinking alley below would do if they were in her socks.

THE GREAT HUSH

It happens in a matter of weeks. At first Benito hardly notices. It falls like forest dusk; the grosbeaks' harmony fades and the high-pitched file of the grackles is silenced. But perhaps it's less like nightfall and more final, like the disappearance of woodpecker vibrations.

Nestled in a canyon, a couple of hours' drive from Condesa where Benito was born, is the small town of Chignahuapan. Its people are gifted at hand-blowing *esferas de Navidad*, glass Christmas baubles, which they decorate in as many ways as their imagination allows. Those with cruder brush-skills daub earthenware, hanging knots of brown mugs and piling stacks of large-handled pots on their doorsteps. The potteries jostle with guesthouses that line the main street, an extension of the Chignahuapan–Tlaxco road that cuts from the southwest toward Zacatlán. It follows the Sierra Madre, extending a thousand kilometres from the wetter peaks of Veracruz to its drier ridge at the Texan border. Repeatedly cleared by logging and grazing livestock, the balance between humankind and nature grows ever more fragile.

It was exactly the Chignahuapan–Tlaxco road that the Gutz family drove along almost sixty years ago, when Benito was little, in their *vocho*, one of few Beetles back then. As Señor Gutz cruised down their street, he tooted the horn, echoing the VW ad that parodied the Apollo moon landing.

'I'm ugly, but I get you there!'

'No, no!' his baby sister, Araceli, cried, 'You're not ugly, Papito!'
'Yes, yes! Ugly!' Benito yelled. Mamá giggled.

Out of the city, the siblings drank in the world beyond their Condesa lives through the open car window; the barefoot women with baskets balanced on their heads, men in sombreros bent over crops of maize or village boys balancing a pole across their backs, a pail of water rocking at each end. Caught the clip of donkeys' hooves, thunder of wooden cartwheels, vendors' parrot-calls, or *mariachis'* frenetic beat. The streets grew broader, the buildings sparser, the sky unlaced. They could not know then how that landscape would dwindle, encroached on by miles of sprawling half-built homes, how that same sky would fasten down on them.

Benito would attend the Colegio Alemán, study medicine at UNAM and stay on as a professor. He returned to Chignahuapan for family weekends with his first, and only, girlfriend Paty. Araceli drove up with her fiancé, who became her husband, and soon with their kids. When Paty broke their engagement, Benito's visits tapered, till absence yawned over two decades. Benito's fears, felt foolish in these more tolerant times; he might so easily have brought Max up to stay. But it was easy to forget how Mexico lagged back then. After Papito died, Araceli inherited the other house in Vera Cruz. The *casita* by the thermal waters was Benito's. One weekend, while Max was rehearsing, Benito took off, intending to return the next morning.

As he drove along El Nigromante, 'The Exorcist', which ran a level west to east, Benito was struck by how much he'd missed the place. He slowed past the town's best bakery, La Garita, the Azomalli General Store, the Santuario del Honguito, and the clutch of guesthouses and *cabañas* that lie closer to the river's mouth. The moment he arrived, the house laid claim to him, like a father to a prodigal son.

He'd pushed away all the memories. Of neighbours' chickens pecking in their yard and barefoot children running on the red dirt. Of clouds, kept in check by the mountains, composing themselves around their peaks. Of the sky's immensity. How Araceli carpeted their hideaway house with cascading tangles of bromeliads that swathed the oaks they called old men's beards or witches' hair. Locals sold its tresses to factories that stuffed car seats with it or made it into swamp coolers. He recalled an old *campesino* knocking on their door with the gift of a rabbit, kicking paws braced. And the aroma of the stew Mamá made of it, with *nopal* leaves from the scrub beyond their garden. How sulphurous steam rose from the brook into the clear mountain air. And the *magueyes* that threw their flowers up, higher than the roof, till a *campesino* would slice them open to drain the honeyed sap. He'd all but forgotten Papi's tales of Tlaloc's linear rivers taking new twists when he got drunk on *pulque*.

Now he fell in love with the house as passionately as he had with Max. Waking at dawn that Sunday, Benito strode down to the hot springs, skinny-dipped, returning to a breakfast of mushroom *tlacoyos*. He followed the familiar path to the waterfalls, past sheep, cows, strays, and hillocks of sweet fermenting fertilizer. Coming back in the late afternoon, every aspect of the run-down *casita* charmed him: the adobe walls, shuttered windows, clay roof, overgrown yard, and stone *pila* with its cold-water spigot. Unspeakably happy, he delayed his return to the city, sending Max a conciliatory text that his childhood summer home was brimming with surprises.

On the drive back Benito considered relocation, triggering five years of toing and froing. The only place he truly unwound was Chignahuapan, far from the city's restlessness and reminders of work undone. Benito bought several *manzanas* at the outskirts close to the thermal waters. He began discussing an idea with an old architect friend, Ulises, who grew so enthused he bought adjacent land. But there was a twist. In real life, there is always a twist. One evening, as Benito discussed selling his Condesa flat with Max, a moment of truth arrived.

'I can't.' Max's eyes locked onto the dilapidated Art Deco façade across the road, as if he'd only just noticed it.

'Can't?'

'Leave... I've still work here, my mother's here and...'

'And?'

'I've met someone, Benito... I'm sorry.'

Benito examined Max's profile carefully. Max, implicated in his life at every turn, had imagined himself into another's. Benito had considered such a thing happening and told himself he would be fine. But rehearsals are just that. Stepping into the street to buy tortillas or vegetables from passing vendors, Benito felt distanced from his own life, like a cinematographer filming his own biopic. Unresponsive to long slants of morning sun hitting his pillow, he pulled himself out of bed late in the day. After Max had left, things got easier. Benito drove up one weekend to Chignahuapan. Arriving, he fell into a deep sleep. The following morning, he set to work tidying, washing linen, and stocking the larder. Things he'd never addressed were resolved that day. By evening, when Ulises came around with a bottle of tequila, Benito had moved on; Chignahuapan would be his new home. He sketched his plan on a sheet of *oficio*.

Benito had thought of himself as a professor, a partner to Max, a citizen of the metropolis. But up here in the mountains, survival tasted different. He rebuilt himself, assumption by assumption. He courted the small community, forged alliances, and spoke with builders and carpenters. Land was bought, woodland cleared, foundations poured, wood cabins and clay roofs constructed. Four years later, the sign 'La Misión' went up. He took on staff. Fair and plump, Ixchel was his forthright and dependable cook. Her Junoesque daughter, Monserrat, along with the tractable Maria and Martha were housekeeping. The self-effacing *campesino*, Jesús, in his rubber boots and baseball cap, chief concierge and gardener.

Word spread slow and sweet as honey. A storm struck the electricity tower the first rainy season and La Misión was without light for six weeks. Ixchel, adept at magicking local dishes and replicating foreign ones, conquered her savage fear of the espresso machine. Married to a sour drinker whose chickens contracted scissor-beak pox and rabbits died of myxomatosis, she ploughed her hope into La Misión, as if wed to it. Monserrat was persuaded to change guests' towels each day. Jesús trailed Benito like a famished stray but fell to pieces if a customer complained. Subtle differences in approach were needed: some visitors wanted privacy, others craved attention. By the third year, La Misión was flourishing. Benito took himself off each day on walks along dirt roads that led from the town to the falls or the mouth of the Almoloya.

Till 2020. Towards the end of February, a dozen or so returnees from Italy brought it back to the country with them. The eighth case appeared in Puebla, a hundred and thirty miles southwest as the *chachalaca* flies. Being a people steeped in faith, they paid little heed. At the start of July, Los Tres Tristes Tigres' 'El Corrido de Coronavirus' topped the charts as Mexico's death rate soared to sixth highest in the world. By the end of the month, it was third. But it was the lesser mentioned footnotes that bothered Benito; the uptake in suicide, a burgeoning dependency on technology, children schooled on television, scads of teenage pregnancies. The great hush that had fallen over all of them.

The owner of the thermal baths is the first to come down, expiring within weeks. Few mourn the man who cordoned off the source, charging locals to bathe in their birth right. However, the virus slips silently from house to house, neighbour to neighbour. The deaths are few the first month, a couple the next, then a few each fortnight, till they lose count. Everyone watches for signs: a feverish flush, the rasp of a cough, burning sinuses, blandness, an overriding exhaustion. The roads empty. Visitors thin to memory. La Misión hasn't had a booking since New Year's Eve, the prelude to a barren unknown. Ixchel and Jesús barely lift their eyes to Benito's, knowing that he will have to let them go. He keeps them close; his survival is as woven to theirs as theirs to his. The day he can't pay them any longer will be the day La Misión closes for good.

When Monserrat knocks on his door in tears, he guesses before she can get the words out. A builder she's known all of five months, working on the house across from them, is the father.

'Do you love him?' Benito wonders if this is even a question.

Monserrat looks at him through tear-bright eyes.

'I think so,' she whispers, 'but how can I know? I mean... if it will last?'

Benito nods. He suspects most of us are conceived this way, growing up as a moment of passion recedes as in a rear-view mirror, the distance lengthening. Though Paty had taught him a great deal, conception's emotions are sealed off from him, abstract.

'What is it, Monserrat, that you want from life? I mean... what do you hope for?' He's wise enough not to project.

'I want to, just, you know, be normal. Finish school. Keep

working for you. Maybe study... engineering.' She surprises herself with this last.

'So, it's not the right time, then, to be... a mother?' he asks, gently. 'Do you want me to talk to Ixchel?'

Monserrat heaves a huge sigh. 'She'll be so angry...'

Benito promises to talk the fury out of her.

But when he goes to the kitchen that afternoon to find Ixchel, it's empty. Just a few coals, tossed from the fire, still glow on the dirt outside the back door. There's no sign of Jesús either, so he walks down the drive and onto the road. The building site is quiet but for the builder's radio.

'*Buenos días?*' Benito shouts up at the open window but no one answers.

He continues along El Nigromante, past closed pottery shops, shuttered *hospedajes*, and dark restaurants. The houses are stilled as though under a spell, the pavement empty, the road quiet. A sweet smell of yeast wafts from the empty La Garita. The spry notes of a funeral march crescendo and a procession overtakes him at a clip. The hearse, chased by half a dozen masked mourners, is trailed by musicians playing trombone, sax, and guitar. In the hospital yard, a stir of discharged invalids and relatives await paperwork. A handful of subdued patients queue, as harried chemists dispense drugs. A truck loaded with oxygen tanks rattles past. The *parque central*, with its pretty white colonial church and dusty fake Christmas tree has had no market since the Día de Reyes. Defeated, Benito takes a battered white taxi back. He barely hears the driver's muffled low-down on the shrinking supply and exorbitant price of oxygen.

When he gets home, Benito disrobes. He steps into the shower and stays till the pestilence is rinsed from him. Ever since Biblical times, he thinks, epidemics have dogged us; but this time technology has cowed us into unthinking terror. Roosevelt's words, 'the only thing we have to fear is fear itself', seem a prophecy. Since his late thirties, when every gay man he knew had embraced chat rooms, and later Grindr, he had resisted. His friends nicknamed him *el hobbitcito*, after *Homo floresiensis*, the large-footed, small-brained hominoid destined for extinction. After a few years they started to ignore him. Max compensated for his reclusiveness, while Benito sadly watched his lover turn into a tech-addict. Like a security blanket, Max's phone went everywhere – from bathroom, to kitchen, to work, even bed. Max's thoughts never disconnected from the miniature, myopic world of fashion, music, and muscle curated beneath the surface of his glass screen. His newfound world packaged everything into safely distanced soundbites, aligning Max's opinions with his cohort, coached into generic oversimplifications Benito found unbearable.

But this was child's play in comparison to what happened of late. Though Max was no longer part of his life, Benito was in touch with their theatre friends. Accustomed to late-night parties and busy social lives, a rift grew between those who persisted despite warnings and those who retreated indoors. Benito observed the schism from a distance. Away from the city a decade, he'd finally grown into a hobbit, more Gandalf than Bilbo Baggins, with dark ridges beneath his eyes and a sun-burnt complexion flecked with moles. Yet for all his estrangement, the urban, lesser hermits seemed more isolated. Though they still posted their dinners or dogs in sweaters on social media, their internal lives had stalled. The disease arrived to fill the vacuum. It was not the plague that was destroying them, but a collective receptivity for escalating drama. Craving to fill an intolerable lack, first one, then another welcomed COVID-19 in. Benito imagined nature as the great equaliser. The passing of strangers, as inevitable as it was tragic. Yet who wrung hands over the fifty million lost to the Black Death, or twice that number to Spanish flu? Mexico had barely missed a beat when Ebola struck Africa or Zika Brazil.

Benito sinks into the armchair he's placed by his sitting room window, wrapping his parents' large bedspread around him. From here, the forest carpets the mountainside down to the Almoloya. The all but full moon is rising, casting silver light on the peaks. He sits as still as the mountains but his thoughts bubble like the spring's mouth. When he wakes, the sun is high and has warmed the room. His mind is clear. He descends, floating almost, to the empty breakfast room but the kitchen is locked. He walks back up and out, follows the red path to the end of his land; Jesús is still nowhere to be seen. Retracing his steps, he comes back to the road. The building site is still. The *comedor* shuttered.

He walks towards town, pulse fluttering, heart billowing.

'Ixchel? Monserrat? Jesús? César? Ulises?'

Up on the hill, sheep graze by the church. But there are no voices, no music playing. He walks past the *pulquería*, the tortilla-seller, the butcher, and gas shop. There are no children on the street.

'Araceli? Mamá? Papá? Max? Max?' his voice high and cracked.

'Ma-a-ax?'

He wakes with a start. Ember-red, the moon is sinking behind the mountain. Benito limps stiffly to bed. Under the covers, he grows attentive. He listens. The silence is profound. Overwhelming.

Perhaps, at sunrise, the tank won't gurgle without Jesús to water the plants.

Ixchel's hum won't drift up from the kitchen below.

Maybe the Almoloya's mouth has dried up, the river's swirl halted.

What then? What then will carry him?

Chalco Millonarios

I open my eyes on a rough-whipped, burnt-meringue ceiling and register the throb of reggaetón. Sunshine scalds flowered curtains, secured by a safety pin. The room's still air is musty. There is an old wooden crate, an empty cupboard with a broken door, some dusty rubbish bags piled in the corner. The queen-size I'm lying on has no sheets, just a torn yellow seventies coverlet. My eye-sockets feel scorched and my temples thrum, my tongue is dry and swollen. My hands are tied behind my back. Anxiety and nausea roil in me.

School had just let out for Christmas. We'd left Marylebone in a big rush, my half-sister crabby because we woke her up early. Mar forgot my passport; she ran back to fetch it. I was the last to check in. The dumpy, tired-looking air attendant sat me in the back row. All three cabin staff talked at me at once: *Hi, Niko! If you need something just let us know, ok? Where's your boarding pass, honey? Do you want me to stow your jacket up here?* I kept my parka and headphones on, put my head in my arms and fell asleep. Flying's no big deal; since my parents split I do this six times a year – three half terms and three long holidays. When we touch down in DF, I stumble into arrivals, but Dar isn't there. I wander out into the sunshine to text him. I need to stretch my legs, so I cross the street and in half a block I'm in a mess of houses. Then...

What the hell? I lift my scalding head, swing my trainers onto the dusty floor and stagger to a metal door. It opens onto a yard filled by a rusting grey Chevy with a broken windscreen and Estado de México licence plates. Two mongrels, one small and black, the other lumbering and ginger, appear from behind the pick-up. The little one scraps like a shadow-boxer, sparring on her hind legs, flattens herself to the floor, pants and wags her tail. The ginger mutt, slow and rheumatic, leans against me, standing heavy paws on my feet. A single aloe grows in a broken bucket alongside several dead ones in tin cans. Two crooked blue *pilas* lean against the wall. Adjacent rooms of unpainted breezeblock form an L around the yard with upstairs rooms open to the sky. On the fourth side is a huge metal gate.

The dogs follow me, the little one jittering around my feet, the larger careening against my thigh. I push on the gate with my shoulder; it's locked. I duck under the washing line. I check out my puffy black eye in a bit of broken mirror that sits on an upturned bucket between two white plastic chairs. A door is open to a toilet with a lit bare bulb and a sink with thirties-style taps. I need to piss but I can't reach my fly. The room next to the one where I slept is littered with a few bits of manky, broken furniture. The third metal door leads to a tiled room with chairs around a table, an empty dresser, and high glass cabinets. Stairs from the yard lead to the upper rooms, open to the sky, littered with dog shit; the outer walls have no windows. Something grunts nearby – a pig?

Through barred windows upstairs I look into a wide, careless street of shabby block houses painted in lime greens or strawberry pinks. The house opposite has a spray-painted mural of a plump black kid, elbows down, fists up, peering between boxing gloves. A car inches along, its megaphone broadcasting a distorted invitation to buy *tamales*. A gas truck pulls up and the mongrels embark on a chorus of howling. Two men approach, and a key turns in the metal door below. I step back down into yard. One of them is very fat with a gold tooth and oily black hair. The other is slight and wears a hoodie.

'Sleeping Blondie's woken up. *Chido!*' His Spanish is thick. 'This job. Uh-oh. Who would do this? A cross between robbing-banks and baby-sitting. Everything ready to go fuckity if you lose concentration.

Puta madre! Flaco, pass me those *sopecitos* and the *caguamas* before I die of thirst. We brought you lunch, Blondie.'

Flaco waves some plastic bags at me. I stare.

'Who are you?'

'Señor to you. Shut up. Eat,' Gordito says.

They put bags and four litres of beer on the table. Gordito indicates an empty chair. They noisily chew *chalupas* and knock back beer straight from the litre bottles.

'Eat,' says Gordito.

'I need to piss.'

'Flaco!' Flaco winces, puts his food down, picks up his gun and walks to me to the bathroom. He unties my wrists, keeps the door ajar; I piss with his barrel at my temple.

'Who are you...?' I try when I return.

'Your Mamacita... until Papi pays.'

'Does my father know where I am?'

'He knows where to deliver the money. Hope he loves you, kid?' They both laugh.

Must be thirty hours since I ate Mar's toast. I never touch plane food; Dar always takes me straight to Boicot for hotcakes. I eat a congealed *sopecito*. When I finish Flaco ties my hands again. They go into the tiled room and switch on the TV. After a few minutes I follow. From the doorway I ask for my phone.

'Go fuck yourself.'

'Shit, you...' I give Gordito the same look I give Mar about phone time but his eyes don't leave the TV screen. I go upstairs to think. I walk around. From there I look into the yard and its ten-foot-high locked gate with the small gap wreathed with razor wire. I go back to the room I slept in and push on the window bars, fixed into the cement frame. I could maybe smash the pane with my shoulder and try to attract someone's attention – Flaco and Gordito wouldn't hear me. I could let somebody know I was in trouble... I consider my options. I feel groggy. The last thing I remember was a car pulling up, the sound of doors closing, a hand on my face.

I fall asleep.

A pig nearby is having a fit, a heart-attack or... someone is killing it. The dogs in the yard go crazy. I get out of bed and go to the yard. Flaco is feeding the dogs biscuits; he calls the crazy little one Kiaris, the other Güero. I puke up in the broken toilet bowl. There's no water to flush and I don't have a free hand anyway. I sit on the steps. The pig's cries crescendo to fever pitch. It goes on and on… and suddenly falls quiet. Kiaris claps her paws like a praying mantis. She's so excited she pisses. Güero puts his head on my lap. The kidnappers' dogs nuzzle me.

Zeydeh has incredible stories of being a hidden child in the war and his escape to Israel. Pappou reminisces about the resistance in the Vitsi mountains during the Greek Civil War. Dar has a tale of bullets ricocheting off his Mustang's bonnet during a shoot-out in Harlem. Mar tells stories of when she covered Mexico City protests and Oaxaca's earthquake. I used to dream of something out of the ordinary happening to me. But now that I'm actually here, it doesn't feel glamorous. It's horribly serious. I should do something. But what?

Kidnapping was one of the reasons Mar moved to England. There's one every two hours here, she reckons. The drug traffickers need money to buy assault rifles. *Paseos millonarios* nab victims from taxis and do an 'ATM tour', pulling out all their money. They used to target the rich, but *secuestros exprés* pick on middle-class kids, held to ransom. It ends in one of two ways, freedom or death. Dar, a venture capitalist, says the odds are poor. If the ransom isn't paid, they terminate. Sometimes even if it is paid, they terminate. The cops only arrest one per cent of offenders. We had this conversation when we went rappelling in Querétaro. I figured that climbing the Peña de Bernal monolith was the riskiest thing I'd ever done but he said staying in DF was dodgier. Funny how my parents kind of talk the same; you can tell they've lived together. They have this way of hesitating before they explain something they're uncomfortable with. They loathe board games. Mar can't follow the rules and gets bored, but Dar gets stressed, furrows his brow and bites his lip.

Speakers mounted on a passing car announce the arrest of kidnappers and their three victims, kept for two months, here in Chalco. So this is where I am. I try to imagine two months of lying on this bed, staring at the meringue ceiling. Never heard of Chalco – sure doesn't look like Dar's neighbourhood. Roma has paved roads, wrought-iron gates, and pretty houses. And it's quiet. From the gap in the curtains I watch some fat guy with one eye park his moto-taxi in front of the house across the street. He pegs a piece of bright orange card on the side of it with 'SOLO HOY: VENDO CERDO' hand-written and brings out two speakers taller than himself. Then he cranks up the volume. Old-fashioned gangster *corridos*: 'They're running from the cops, they shoot their pistols in the air, the narcos are coming for them, they're making for the border... ai-ai-ai-aaaaaiiiiii!'

Perhaps I can just get away with it if I'm quick. Using the curtain as protection I ram my shoulder at the window; the glass cracks easily and I call for help. The music is so loud, One-Eye and his wife don't notice, but one of the kids building the fire for *churrasco* sees me. But just as our eyes meet, the bedroom door bursts open and Gordito pushes me on the floor, a blade pressed below my left ear. He turns my face to his smile, slides the blade under my collarbone and draws it from the shoulder to sternum. He leaves me bleeding. I pass out. When I wake my t-shirt is stiff with blood.

I'm homesick. For Dar's special Sunday waffles *con* Nutella. Or my favourite *lonchería* Café Tacuba, where Rivera had a wedding reception and some governor was assassinated, with its waitresses in starched white uniforms that pour hot soup into bowls of tacos, avocado, and chicken. For Dar especially, always talking with America or England. Investments aside, I feel like I'm his whole world. He explains seed markets, time diversity, cloud wars, and horizontal sectors. I think of our holidays... climbing, rafting, and snow-boarding; I remember getting woken in Colorado by horses eating hay outside our window. One day, he said, we're going to do one of those survival trips where they drop the two of us, father and son, in the middle of nowhere with nothing but a knife, a torch, and a bivvy bag and we just work it all out. Feels like I've been dropped in the outback already and I'm doing it solo. Dar always says, Niko, I'll leave you money, but you have to make it on your own, son.

I miss Mar, in her yoga gear, making me BLTs for lunch, guzzling a spirulina smoothie. Damn! I even miss her nagging. She worries too much about Boss Baby and simpers over her New Man, but she loves me lots. When I was ten she told me to expect a baby, but the IVF failed, so they used someone else's eggs. I even miss my English mates. They don't understand basketball and I don't get a word my maths teacher says. It's weird being in a boys' school. I like girls... but in real life they kind of annoy me. My cousins are moody and wear off-the-shoulder dresses that are too old for them.

I go next door. Flaco and Gordito are sitting on crates watching a narco-video of a guy in a baseball cap rapping. *I change my bitches every two weeks. When they are in love with me I dump them*; behind him nearly naked women writhe. One is bundled into the boot of a car by his henchmen. Two, wrists tied, flick their hair round and around. He keeps rapping, now with a helicopter parked behind him. Flaco and Gordito don't look up. Half a dozen empty litre-bottles lie on the floor. At the feet of the black-draped Santa Muerte, holding a globe and an hourglass, lie cigarettes, a black candle, and some twenty-peso notes. Mar told me some make human sacrifices to the Bony One. I sit on an upturned oil tin. Time passes so slowly I begin to nod.

After several hours Gordito's phone rings:

'*Si, Señor.*'

'*Si, Señor.*'

'*Si, Señor. Chido.*'

'*Ahorita. Si.*'

'*¡Vamos, güey!*' he elbows Flaco.

Flaco grabs me with one hand. In the other is his pistol.

'Follow him,' Gordito hisses.

'Don't fuck up,' adds Flaco.

Flaco pushes me into the back seat of the Chevy (seriously, it's so rusty I thought it was a museum piece). He opens the gate and Gordito drives out into thick night. Flaco locks up and sits next to me. From empty streets we pull onto a busier road. Pierced, tattooed boys, snack-sellers, a clown, beggars, fat old women. Burly drivers steer busses along the *avenidas*, agile bus boys banging on their sides with fists of fanned banknotes. There is music everywhere; louder in the fast busses, slower and quieter in traffic or from the shops or ghettoblasters on the street. I catch glimpses of beautiful faces with scars or acne, too much make-up, or tattoos. Denim and t-shirts, hoodies, and trainers. Faces aged by the city and poverty. A slack-throated girl covered in face-glitter hangs in the doorway of a bar. A couple devours each other with kisses. A kid holding her ma's hand waves at me. A prostitute in wedged espadrilles nursing a full-term belly leans up against the wall. Men fix a wheel on a *micro* beside a couple frying *tostadas*.

A plump dealer in a baseball cap passes a packet into a car window; the cops cruise past, lights flashing. A sign, 'Cárcel de Mujeres', stands over a mess of concrete overpass, the moving cars throwing zebra stripes of light across it. Two emaciated junkies cycle across our path into the speeding stream, without lights, reflectors, or jackets, chasing an ultimate high. A tall, busty woman with ginger curly hair, Botox lips, crammed into her jeans, swings her hips. At traffic lights, an almost corpse stumbles against my window, stinking of the glue he inhales from his soaked sleeve. The metro-buses are packed; mothers, grandmas, and kids in the pink seats at the front, men at the back in baseball caps, fleeces, backpacks, watching movies on their smartphones.

We park. Gordito tells Flaco we've twenty minutes to kill. Flaco undoes my wrists. We walk into a sticky-floored, dark, high-ceilinged bar. In the men's, an attendant with green hair sits on a toilet filled with green disinfectant, talking on her phone. An eleven-man band in rose-printed jackets, brass instruments, percussion, and vocals play at devil-speed. Several men and a few women stand at the table next to ours, drinking beers and shorts, laughing and dancing. Two girls with fixed smiles dance, press into each other. Another, in a skin of jeans and tank top, rubs herself like a cat against an old man. Gordito order beers. My elbows stick to the table. I drink, hands shaking.

I glance toward the entrance. And at the blacked-out windows.

'Make my day, kid,' says Gordito, his fingers grazing his hip where his handgun sits. We wait. And wait. As the band starts its fifth *corrido*, I say prayers, actual prayers to God, that it will happen like the movies. That Dar will come. He'll scan the gloom, find me, and walk over. He'll drop a backpack on the table and unzip it. Flaco and

Gordito will peer inside at the neat elastic-bound wads of freshly minted pesos. Gordito will pick up the bag and Flaco will follow him out. Dar's brawny arms will wrap around me. We'll hug, like we're the only two in the bar. In all of Mexico City. Robustly. With so much love. Pure love to shelter me from evil.

El Jebha

El Jebha is an hour from Ketama by coastal road – if there was one.
Perhaps we'll finish it in a year or two. Perhaps it'll take ten. In the
meantime, you have to take a bus from Al Hoceima and get off at the
crossroads at Tizzit-Echen. Which is ten houses, a fish café, a fish-
seller, and a gas station that collapsed in on itself. Then you wait for
the evening bus from Tetouan. Or does it go every other evening? No
one's sure. We'll send you in the opposite direction toward Tetouan
and you'll end up doubling back through the hamlet. At least you'll
find a bed there. In Tizzit-Echen you'll find nothing but grilled fish.
This makes you bad-tempered. Since not many of you come to El
Jebha, the problem doesn't crop up often.

So you arrive in Ketama, the centre of the hashish empire, a place
where every man, woman and child sells *kief.* And you ask:

Can I get a bus to El Jebha?

Want to buy hashish?

Not right now, thanks. Do buses stop here for El Jebha?

I have friend from Holland, from Ireland, and Allemande. You
know Allemande? He stay with me. We make good friends. *Ça fait.*
You want to stay at my place for free? Three kilometre away. *Muy
tranquilo.* You come, you eat, we smoke a little. *Vamos!*

No, thank you... I was just wondering about buses to El Jebha.

You have friends there or something? It's a nothing place, nothing there, nobody goes to this place. There's no bus. Come stay with me and we ask… maybe tomorrow.

You wonder if whoever it was that suggested you go to El Jebha made it up. Maybe you got the wrong name. You ask two policeman about the bus.

Oui, bien sûr. À huit heures. Là-bas… au carrefour.

The other says:

Peut-être… por cuarenta dirhams, vale?

We speak Arabic, Berber, Spanish, and French but you still don't understand us. If you accept the lift you get dropped at a crossroads, thirty kilometres still to go, no cars heading that way. After a few hours you despair, hitch a ride back, spend a night or two in Ketama where you give in to a spliff. Realising your time is up (your flight from Casablanca leaves tomorrow), you leave. El Jebha remains no more than a full stop on the map that you never visited.

But if you happen to be at the crossroads at the right time you might catch the bus. It's a long shot because no one knows if it comes every day, or every other. The sign on the front is in Arabic but you might just guess it's the one. You might find the broad-backed, short-necked driver stopping with his midget busboy for a midday meal at the shacks near the crossroads that serve tagine and chips in a swill of mud and refuse, swarming with flies. If you found that giant of a man with his small friend, filling up on lamb after midday, every day or on alternate days, he'd be the one to ask. He and his pocket-sized companion would grin broadly and agree they're headed to El Jebha, as if it were common knowledge. By then you might doubt a man's ability to tell a simple truth and, overcome with suspicion, walk away. But if you have faith in that bald, bulldog face, with its generous share of moles and creases, you might board his bus.

The modest fare of twenty dirhams indicates a journey of two hours. When you find yourself back at Tizzit-Echen, your suspicions of foul play might overwhelm you. But if you spot the sign at the crossroads of that god-forsaken hamlet claiming El Jebha is sixty kilometres away, you'll nurture some hope. The road starts innocently, curling its way around one mountain after the next. The tarmac dissolves to a thinning patchwork of asphalt on dirt. It narrows considerably the higher it rises, leaving behind groves of scalped cork trees and wending its way between nappy fields of marijuana. Looking down on the mud houses built around courtyards, you'll notice roofs strewn with plants drying in the sun, every shade between green and dark brown. Golden mushrooms of hay, secured with nets, rope, and rocks, cluster in the courtyards. Small boys herd sheep across parched soil and handsome women carry bundles of *kief* on their backs from the fields.

The road struggles higher still, till the bus parts clouds. After several stops you are the solitary passenger. The bus begins to descend. You catch sight of the sea and relax a little. Just then, the bus starts to swerve around the keenest of hairpin bends. At each hook you catch your breath, like a child stepping over cracks in the pavement. And then there's one, past believing. As you watch, your mind detaches from your body. It requires the driver, fubsy face scrunched in concentration, to overhang the precipice while pulling the gear-stick into reverse and bringing the clutch to biting point. If you were going to believe in God or miracles, this would be the moment. One tiny yaw and the bus will tumble like a Lego toy. The driver, though he masters this kink every day, or every other (even he's not sure), wipes his brow. And makes the turn. You spy a wishbone port. A tall-steepled lime and canary mosque dominates the handful of plain square buildings.

Stepping down from the bus you'll feel a pang of disappointment at my tumbledown village, strewn with crumpled black bags, Sidi water bottles, rotting vegetables, and fish bones. The driver will offer to show you to the best hotel. Pack on your shoulders, struggling to keep up, you'll be surprised by how much nicer the centre is than the outskirts. You're impressed, almost, by the fish restaurant, shaded garden with date palms, coffee bars, and the Hotel Al Hijra. Nestling over our café, every room has clean sheets and wires awaiting light fittings.

My brother Ahmet, one of eleven, owns the hotel and café. Another owns the fruit shop. Mo's a policeman. Aziz is in prison. The younger three live in Amsterdam. We were dirt-poor till we started to grow marijuana in the eighties; we built concrete houses, a restaurant, our café, and the school. In ninety-four my aunt left for Spain in a fishing boat. Then father went to Holland. Three from our village won the lottery to America. Others have gone to Al Hoceima or Tetouan.

Ahmet bought the café and I'm *el camarero*. Inside, it's dominated by the huge colour television tuned to Al Jazeera; outside, two dozen tables rotate around the building, chasing shade. In the early hours, men sit on all three sides. By nine or so, just at the side and front. At midday, a few remain inside. By late afternoon, the indoor tables are full. From five in the morning till seven at night, I serve fresh orange juice, avocado or banana shakes, mint tea or *café au lait*. While I wipe tables, my younger brothers forge new lives in Amsterdam. While I spin my silver tray, Ahmet lines his nest-egg and Mo rolls a fag out back of the station. While I wash empties, Nine Eleven scatters its debris, sealing shut boltholes to Europe. Aziz watches his back in the prison yard.

My sole pleasure is my black Mercedes. Dusty, old, stinking of exhaust, I cruise along the dock, watching fishermen emptying nets. Drive around the village, smoking. When there's a wedding, I stop outside the mosque and watch small boys go wild to tambourines. I married last year but nothing changed. Sometimes I drive out of the village till I get to a cliff that overhangs a long sliver of beach. I stop the car and stand at the edge and roll myself a joint. Above me, stars whisper of the lives of others. The portly moon swells or withers over the Amazigh sea. I let the hashish soak into my blood. The surf bubbles at the sand's edge. I peer into the dark; Spain is just across the strait, eight miles out of reach. My mobile rings. Ahmet tells me a foreigner has arrived.

The biggest scandal in El Jebha involved my brother, Aziz. When Mo got him a job in the police force we thought it would straighten him out. For three years things ticked over. Then this French guy shows up, a year back. He hangs out a few days, shoots the shit, drinks mint tea, smokes bhang, and asks questions. Nothing special. One night, he meets Aziz on the beat; stops to make conversation. The Frenchman asks him if he smokes. Of course he does. Wonders if he can get hold of some *kief* for him. Aziz reckons he can. A lot, he says. Probably, says Aziz. He wants a kilo, that same night. He can, but tomorrow, he says. They arrange a late-morning *rendez-vous*. The next day the Frenchman disappears on the early bus to Tetouan.

We've forgotten about him when, a few days later as I'm serving tea, Mo shouts from across the street to change channels. I flip to TV5; this presenter is describing our region as the largest in the world for marijuana, 'known locally as *kief*' over some footage of women picking. She says Ketama is the centre and the entire region depends on the crop.

'Even in the tiny, idyllic Mediterranean village of El Jebha...' and the screen fills up with a map that pinpoints us between Al Hoceima and Tetouan. The camera cuts to a close-up of Aziz, in uniform, telling us that yeah, he can get hold of a kilo, not tonight but tomorrow morning. The café falls silent; the liquidiser and espresso machine grind to a halt. Then all the men start talking at once. That same evening dozens of police arrive from Tetouan, filling all three hotels for the first time in living memory. They interrogate everyone, especially the local police. They hold Aziz under arrest, in his own station. Mo has no say. Aziz is put away for seven years. They discuss his fate in the café for months after, shaking their heads.

While Aziz languishes in his cell, I wait tables in mine.

Our fat friend, the bus driver, will bring you to the hotel. You'll quibble over the price of the room though you can't buy a sandwich back home for the cost of a night's stay. Stepping out later to explore, you'll be delighted by the quay. Sigh with pleasure at Marsdar's picturesque bay, a half hour's walk over the cliff past the mausoleum of a forgotten prophet. Perhaps you'll swim in the perfectly sheltered green-blue cove. And later, sit contentedly in our café enjoying a mint tea as dusk gathers and the breeze lifts.

I'll chat with you. *No pasa nada,* right? You'll tell me about your journey. About Tizzit-Echen and how there's nothing but fish there. About Ketama and the psycho druggies addicted to lying. About the snarled dirt road that leads down from the mountains and the turn where you said your prayers. And you'll probably complain the water isn't hot enough… or the signal is weak. After a couple of days in El Jebha you'll take the bus back to Tetouan, head off to the cobalt charms of Chaouen or the faïence sophistication of the Royal Cities. If you meet anyone who speaks your language in the next few days you'll most likely say of El Jebha, 'Such a charming spot… but I couldn't live there.'

MERCEDES AND THE
PIGEON MAN

'If the City is Guatemala's heart, Parque Central is its lungs and the Pigeon Man is its soul,' said Uncle Charles before he left us forever. He layered one metaphor over the next in a cartoon accent but what he said was worth hearing. He wasn't a real uncle, but he lived in our house for almost a year. Older than Uncle Edison, he was still a student. Of us. The only *Yanqui* I've ever met fluent in Kaqchikel, he was trying to work out why we didn't speak it any more.

He spent his mornings in Mamita's shop; recording interviews or filling in questionnaires with her customers. They spoke to Uncle Charles as if they'd been marking time their whole lives, waiting for him to ask. Impoverished childhoods, violent husbands, lost children, Civil War tragedies, local lore: they told him everything. Afternoons, he sat at his computer surrounded by books, tapping. He'd growl if I pushed his door open, even a fraction. But his work began in earnest when he abandoned the papers strewn across his desk.

He mined information over dinner. When answers eluded him, he returned to the same spot, days later, probing till he unearthed what he was looking for. Aunt Marta, Aunt Greysi, Uncle Edison, or Grandpa Edwin yielded treasures – even Mamita, when she let him. He burrowed till he struck cores of common truths. At his keyboard, he polished them into hypotheses. His devoted disciple, I copied his technique but, while the grown-ups never evaded his quarrying, they headed me off the moment I opened my mouth. Seven years old and piecing together my world; I never found a teacher of his calibre again.

One evening, while Mamita toasted *rellenitos* over the fire, he struck a lode I'd dug for in vain, resolving a burning mystery. Turns out my Papa was a cowboy, twelve years younger than Mamita, who'd run off to Jocotenango with a whore (her word) before Edwin was born. That same night, Uncle Charles told Mamá I was bright: if she did nothing else, she should send me to a proper *colegio*, not the village school where the teachers were still kids themselves. The silhouette of her pressed lips was her reply.

Uncle Charles told us of his orphan father adopted from Poland in the war. About his home town, New Orleans, destroyed by a hurricane and rebuilt by *Guatemaltecos*. He said we were kept poor so gringos could enjoy cheap coffee, bananas, sugar, and cardamom.

'If you don't understand where you come from, Mercedes, you'll never know where you're going.'

'Ask questions and know when to stay silent.'

'Learn English but don't lose your ancestral language: Kaqchikel may not get you a job, but it's your heritage.'

Now and again, Uncle Charles pulled on his leathers and disappeared in a plume of dust to the City, returning with fresh stories. Of Parisian-style boulevards and Ubico's miniature Eiffel Tower. Of the rubbish dump where families lived and toiled, sorting glass from cardboard. Or Cuatro Grados Norte's bars that spilled Ladinos onto its cobbled streets. Or Zona Uno's Perla and Lux: flaking Art Deco façades dredged with exhaust. Musicians plying the buses, thrashing bicycle-pedals fixed up with cans that made you tap your feet. Of limbless beggars on concrete overpasses and boys swallowing fire at traffic lights. Aurora Zoo's aged elephant, Snot, and the hippo that died swallowing a ball. But what I wanted to hear about most was the Pigeon Man in the Parque Central. Uncle Charles had a close-up of him on his phone, a glaze-eyed pigeon on his arm, feathers glinting. Seated in a weirdly fashioned booth, his flock smudged in flight.

'His perch is a director's chair with crossbars and a canvas canopy. Across it lies a pole hung with bags of *maicillo*. He told me they're God's birds and we're all in His hands. *El hombre de las palomas* has sat in front of the Cathedral for fourteen years. I told him you'd visit; he's going to look out for you, Mercedes, the wise one from San Antonio Aguas Calientes.'

I wanted to go at once. Uncle Charles said he'd take me to the plaza and buy a bag of *maicillo* to feed the birds. But a week later his father had died and he was gone.

I asked Mamita if we could visit the City. Little Edwin, for want of anything better to do, joined the chorus. She shook her head: 'One day, *mi amor*, one day.'

Months passed.

And years.

When I was in the last year of primary, Mamita said, 'Tomorrow we're going to the City.'

'Who?'

'Everyone: Greysi, Marta, Grandpa Edwin, Edison, Edwincito, you, me.'

She never explained why. My dreams reverberated with pigeon coos. Roused in the dark, Edwin and I dozed across laps and the hours of bus journey, waking at the Mercado Central. The grown-ups became awkward in the City's streets. Auntie Greysi teased Grandpa Edwin for bringing his *machete* and looking like a peasant.

'You didn't complain when I brought rabbit home,' he grumbled.

Uncle Edison sauntered at his side, hair gelled with Gorilla Snot. Mamita followed, the aunties falling behind, our hands tight in theirs. We stepped into shop doorways while the men waited outside. One store had reels of ribbon and lace hanging from the ceiling and glass counters filled with plastic eyes, sequins, and knots of colourful thread. In another, cubbyholes brimmed with sticks of cinnamon longer than my arm, green pods of cardamom, glistening *chile guaque* and rust-red *achiote*. At the *paca,* my aunts sifted through rainbow rails of hand-me-downs.

When we turned the corner into the plaza beneath the Cathedral there he was. A black lacquered straw hat with a cupola crown shaded a bulbous nose; his lips were framed by a bushy moustache and a grey wiry beard. Despite the heat, he wore a black vest over a thick cotton shirt tucked into heavy trousers above hobnail boots. He let out a low, strong whistle and the pigeons flew up, spanning an arc above us, filling our ears with the rhythm of their wings, fanning us with guano-scented air. He cradled his arm to create a roost, upturned palm filled with seed. A couple settled to feed.

I ran closer; Edwincito followed, clutching my blouse. Pigeons fluttered grey-purple wings to keep balance on his arm. They sidestepped, scaly talons gripping their fleshy perch, glass eyes staring vacantly. The fidgeting flock carpeted the plaza, twisting their oily necks and goose-stepping. Edwin jumped up and down and I rung my hands. We turned to Mamita, eyes pleading.

'Business first.' She flashed her gold tooth at us. We lingered, lost in the hovering and gliding, till we were dragged off, heads twisted over our shoulders. In the Portal de Comercio, the aunts peered into gloomy windows as we squinted back toward the sunlit square. Soon we turned through an arch to a passageway of high doors and balconies shut tight bar one, where a balding man sat at a sewing machine, the needle's rapid-fire rising and falling.

We turned one corner, then another, till we were inside a mall, paved with chequered red and white tiles. Out the other side were Sexta Avenida's turreted, port-holed concrete buildings. Above us, trapped between roofs, the smoggy City sky was cut into scraps by tangles of criss-crossed wires. Traffic lights flapped skimpy rags of torn posters. Women in make-up, jeans, and strappy high heels leant up against stalls selling CDs or shoes, and men in sweat-stained shirts shouted into mobiles.

We followed directions scribbled on a scrap of paper, folded in Mamá's palm, till we came to a brilliant orange house. A bronze plaque engraved with 'Abogado' hung on the door. Uncle Edison rang the bell. A woman, in a black uniform with a white apron, answered.

'Licenciado Hernández wrote us a letter on behalf of Charles Nowak,' Uncle Edison said. She didn't respond, so he added: 'Our appointment is for half past ten.' The maid threw a glance over her shoulder at the grandfather clock.

'Come in,' she relented and gestured at three high-back chairs. Edwincito and I rushed to sit on the first. The maid disappeared, returning a moment later.

'He'll see you now,' she sighed. We crowded into his office, around a large, shiny wooden desk. Mamá and Grandpa Edwin took the only two chairs. The rest of us stood.

'Aaaah,' said the lawyer, examining us, from Grandpa to Edwincito, through square frames: 'The beneficiaries. The Gómez family, every last one...'

We spent a long time in that airless dark room with its half-closed shutters. I longed to play in the yard that lay beyond the window but dared not ask. It seemed Uncle Charles was giving Mamá money to send me to school in Antigua and I wasn't sure what to make of this. But when at last I understood Uncle Charles was dead I started to wail. Aunt Marta hustled me out to the waiting room.

'Nobody tells me,' I repeated between sobs. 'Why doesn't anybody tell me anything?'

When I'd hushed, we returned to the dark room and stayed past midday. We made our way back through the City's muggy streets. A surly woman served us platters of noodles at a small *comedor*. I hardly touched the plate Edwincito and I shared. At Parque Central, Mamita noticed the clock. She said we hadn't time to feed pigeons; she didn't want to be riding home in the dark. Tears welled. With a sigh, Mamá slipped me a dull yellow *quetzal*. At the edge of the plaza, Edwincito and I broke into a run, pigeons fleeing the path we carved. I pressed the coin into the Pigeon Man's hand and he gave us two bags of *maicillo*. Unpicking the knots, I handed one to Edwincito. My fingers sifted through the silky pearls and I flung a handful. The pigeons flitted a few feet off the ground then settled back in a synchronised wave. They were free but grounded. This would become my story too, though I couldn't have known that then. Uncle Charles's legacy would let me take wing; the first in my family even to finish school, I'd go to university in the City, become a linguist and continue Charles' research to keep Kaqchikel and our culture alive.

The moment the last seed was gone, Mamita called. Edwincito

returned the empty bags to the Pigeon Man and galloped off. I went to follow him but, thinking better of it, skipped back.

'*Señor*...' I faltered, '*de las palomas*, my Uncle Charles, he's dead now, he knew you and promised to bring me to feed the pigeons. And now...'

'Mercedes!' Mamita's last call.

The Pigeon Man stretched out his huge paw, palm upturned. I put my hand in his. He smiled, lifting it slowly to his lips, and kissed the back of my wrist. I ran to the corner of the square. As I turned to wave, the Pigeon Man bowed his head.

A Note on Sources

'Writing the Vessels' and 'Whorls' include lines from the Dada and Spiralism manifestos respectively, drawn from *100 Artists' Manifestos: From the Futurists to the Stuckists,* ed. Alex Danchev (London: Penguin Modern Classics, 2011).

'Dorf and the Daisies' features ads adapted from the 1950s to 1970s.

'How to Preserve a Butterfly' includes extracts adapted from Bastiaan M. Drees, *A Guide for Collecting, Preserving and Displaying Insects and Other Arthropods* (College Station, TX: Texas A&M AgriLife Extension).

'Mu!' opens with the Mu koan, familiar to Zen practitioners, which can be found in the *Mumonkan,* or *The Gateless Gate,* a thirteenth-century collection of koans, compiled by Wumen Huikai.

'Mu' translates as 'no-self', 'has not', or simply 'not'. It is the answer to the question a monk put to Jôshû: "Does a dog have Buddha nature or not?"

Acknowledgments

With gratitude for the following imprints for publishing my stories: 'Empty Pockets' in *The Mechanics' Institute Review*, 'Tinderbox' and 'Family Trees' in *Exclamat!on*, 'Whorls' and 'Mercedes and the Pigeon Man' in *Chicago Quarterly Review*, 'Bone Metre' in *Ocean* and, later, as a stand-alone pamphlet of Paravion Press. 'Dorf and the Daisies' in *Consequence*, 'Writing the Vessels' in *Ambit*, 'The Upturned Bowl' in *Riptide*, 'Fifty-one Rolls' in *Algorithm*, 'Cane Stalks' in *The Cost of Paper*, 'Erosion' in Montag Press's anthology *Time and Propinquity*, previously in *Leaping Clear*, and 'How to Preserve a Butterfly' in *The Interpreter's House*. 'The Great Hush' was *Litro* editor's Sunday Story Pick in February 2023 and 'Sky-goer' appeared as 'Ready or Not' in *The Lakeshore Review*.

Deepest thanks go to my PhD supervisors at the University of Exeter, Andy Brown and John Danvers, the university's Buddhist chaplain, who kindly let me use his gorgeous *Leaf Study VII* as the collection's cover image. To my wise mother, Elaine, and my father, Alan. For my beautiful daughter, Danaë, on her path. To the inspirational monks and nuns at Northumberland's Throssel Hole Buddhist Abbey, Kathmandu's Kopan Monastery and the Shwe Oo Min Monastery, Kalaw. To my pragmatic teacher Ven. Robina Courtin at the FPMT, the erudite Desmond Biddulph of the Buddhist Society, and inspirational late Father Paolo Dall'Oglio at Deir Mar Musa. I owe a special debt of gratitude to my gifted editor, Sarah Ream, Sam Meekings for his thoughtful foreword, and my salutary publisher, Mary Petiet. And to my thoughtful readers, editors, and friends; Danai Daska, Craig Walzer, Sergio Sorcia-Reyes, Sam North, Stephen Clucas, Peter Mudford, Panagiotis Frangopoulos, Dafna Temkin, Viviana Miliaresi, Vipul Bhatti, Michael Lichtenstein, Yoonsil Oh, Vassilis Kavallierakis, Alex

Vasmoulakis, Maria Gandy, James Hewson, Laura Young, Adam Graff, Elizabeth McKenzie, Pippa Galvin, Ricky Romain, Jan Fortune, Cherry Potts, Maria Vogiatsi, Javier Molina, Lorraine Given, Kate Pemberton, Lane Ashfeldt, Daithidh MacEochaidh, Alex Graves, Robert Alan Jamieson, Mugambi Jouet, Christian van Gerbig, Valerie Gillies, Sandra Beltrao, Chris Seymour, Sally Murrani, Rinat Harel, Yangkyi Tenzin, Christopher Trevor, Clare Amsel, Krystyna Horko, Jo Cannon, Dimitris and Athena Koliousi, Flora Halaris, Naomi Fitzgibbons, Ocean Tawaih, Sue Learoyd Smith, Shiho Inoue, Henry Hocking, all the Pareskevopouli, Rosita, Derek, and Kyle Passarelli, and the late Chris Hegarty and Ted Gordon. And to the many dear ones who have contributed to my life and creative path. I bow to you all.

About the Author

Cassandra Passarelli has run a bakery, managed a charity, subedited for several magazines, set up a children's library in Guatemala, and taught yoga. She has a PhD in creative writing, from a Buddhist perspective, and held a short lectureship at Exeter University. She temporarily lives out of a backpack and eight banana boxes with prolonged stays in London and the Cyclades, and an eye on the Peloponnese. She has published stories with Paragon Press, Cinnamon Press, and Arachne Press as well as numerous US and UK literary journals including *Cold Mountain Review*, *The Mechanics' Institute Review*, *The Cost of Paper*, *Takahe*, *Adirondack Review*, *Ambit*, *Chicago Quarterly Review*, and *The Interpreter's House*.

About the Artist

John is an artist, poet and writer and has practiced Zen meditation since 1965. He retired in 2012 from an academic career teaching art and philosophy. He is the founder of Exeter Meditation Circle and runs the Dharma Roads podcast. John is the author of two books about Zen, Buddhism, philosophy and the natural world: *Agents of Uncertainty* and *Interwoven Nature*. He has published articles on mindful meditation, the arts, nature and ethics, and for many decades has given talks and workshops exploring meditation, creativity and the arts. Exhibitions of his artwork have been held in the UK, Australia and North America. John's collection of poems, *To see the light*, was published in 2020. Currently John is the Buddhist chaplain and an honorary associate professor at Exeter University.

Artist website: https://johndanversart.co.uk/
Exeter Meditation Circle: http://www.meditationcircle.org.uk/
Dharma Roads podcast: https://www.buzzsprout.com/1942523

About the Press

Sea Crow Press is an award-winning woman-run independent book publisher based on Cape Cod in Massachusetts committed to amplifying voices that might otherwise go unheard. We publish creative nonfiction, literary fiction, and poetry. Our books celebrate our connection to each other and to the natural world with a focus on positive change and great storytelling.

www.ingramcontent.com/pod-product-compliance
Lightning Source LLC
Chambersburg PA
CBHW010751310726
48974CB00004B/876